DEVIL TO PAY

VEGAS SLAYERS - BOOK 5

CHRISTINE POPE

This a work of fiction. Names, characters, places, and incidents are either the product of the author's imagination or are used fictitiously. Any resemblance to actual events, places, organizations, or persons, whether living or dead, is entirely coincidental.

DEVIL TO PAY

ISBN: 978-1-946435-93-4

Published by Dark Valentine Press

Cover design by Indie Author Services

Formatting by Indie Author Services

Chapter One

THE HOUSE ON WARM SPRINGS ROAD HAD good bones. Sure, the kitchen cabinets were from the Reagan administration, and whoever had chosen the barf-green tile backsplash should have been charged with a crime against the design gods, but Delia could see past all that. The layout worked and wouldn't need to be changed at all. Natural light flooded through the oversized windows, while the fireplace in the living room needed only a new insert to bring it up to date. The foundation was solid, the roof only five years old, and the previous owner—a snowbird who'd finally given up on the desert and decided to stay in Michigan year-round — had maintained the necessities even if she'd let the cosmetics slide.

"What do you think?" Caleb asked from across the kitchen, where he was measuring the space where the new cabinets would go. "Shaker style? Or are we going modern with this one?"

Delia held up two paint chips against the wall and squinted at them in the mid-morning light. Desert Sage versus Agreeable Gray. The sage had more personality, but personality was risky in a flip. Buyers in Henderson wanted neutral.

"White Shaker," she said. "We're not reinventing the wheel here."

He made a face. "Boring."

"Profitable."

Caleb grinned at her in response, and something in Delia's midsection seemed to turn warm and fluttery, the way it always did when he looked at her like that. Six months since they'd started this...whatever this was. "Dating" seemed way too casual a word for someone who'd helped you banish a demon lord, while "partners' felt downright clinical. "Lovers" was accurate but didn't begin to tell the whole story.

He came over to her so he could look at the paint chips up close, standing near enough that she could practically feel the heat radiating off him. Caleb always ran hot...literally. Delia supposed it was one of the perks—or side effects—of being a quarter demon.

"The gray," he said, then tapped the Agreeable Gray chip. "It's got some warmth to it. The sage reads cold."

She lifted an eyebrow. "Since when do you have opinions about paint colors?"

"Since I started dating a real estate agent who makes me look at paint chips every weekend." He plucked the sage chip from her hand and held it up to the light. "Also, this one's the same color as the pea soup my friends' moms used to make. Nobody wants to live inside pea soup."

That remark made her chuckle, and she took the chip back from him. "Gray it is. You're getting better at this."

A devilish glint flashed in his warm brown eyes. "I had a good teacher."

With the paint color settled, they worked through the rest of the morning, moving from room to room and discussing the other updates they needed to make, both of them seeming to understand what the other was thinking before they even spoke. Caleb handled the structural assessments, while she handled the design, the staging concepts, the calculations of what buyers in a particular neighborhood would pay for which upgrades.

In the master bathroom, she found him frowning at the shower enclosure. It was original to the house, a garish shade of salmon pink that builders had inexplicably loved in the eighties, especially for homes here in the Southwest.

"Rip it out?" she asked.

Caleb paused for a second, considering. "The tile's cracked behind the fixtures, and there's water damage in the subfloor." He tapped his knuckles against the wall, listening for something only he could hear. "We're looking at a full gut job. That'll be another eight to ten grand, minimum."

Something they hadn't really budgeted for, since Delia had thought this would be a cosmetic update and nothing more. She did the math in her head. They'd paid four-twenty for the property and budgeted sixty for renovations. If the bathroom pushed them over seventy, their margins got pretty damn tight. Unfortunately, a master bath with water damage was a dealbreaker for buyers.

"Full gut," she agreed. "Use the same tile we're putting in the guest bath. At least we can try to keep the costs down where we can."

Caleb nodded, then made a note in his phone. Putting together these puzzle pieces was the part of flipping she'd come to love. Every house was a problem to solve, a balance of investment and return, of what buyers wanted versus what they'd actually pay for. It was more satisfying than showing houses to clients who couldn't make up their minds, more tangible than the endless cycle of listings and open houses and negotiations that had defined her career at Dunne & Dunne.

The flip business had started almost by accident. After their confrontation with Vinea and the wedding chapel disaster in late May, they'd both needed something normal to focus on. Caleb had the capital from his gambling days, and Delia had the market knowledge from her years at Dunne & Dunne. The first house had been sort of a test run, a smallish three-bedroom, two-bath that they'd acquired after the demon-run Aegis Holdings had gone belly-up. The second had been bigger and more expensive, and they'd still cleared more than seventy thousand bucks from that one. Now they were on their eighth, and the money was good enough that Delia had started to wonder if she even needed to keep selling houses.

That thought felt disloyal, though. Dunne & Dunne was her mother's baby, a business she'd built from nothing after she decided to strike out on her own rather than just being a broker in someone else's agency. She'd scraped and networked and worked twelve-hour days and weekends until she'd become a household name in Las Vegas real estate. Delia had grown up in open houses, had learned what a mortgage was and what escrow meant before she even got to junior high. The business was supposed to be her inheritance, the whole point of all those sacrifices.

Except somewhere along the way, she'd discovered that she liked the building way more than the selling.

"We should wrap up," she said as she checked

her phone. Almost one o'clock. "I told the contractor we'd be out by noon. He's probably already circling the block, wondering why our cars are still here."

Caleb nodded and began packing up his measuring tape and the notebook where he'd been sketching cabinet configurations. They had a good crew for this flip, which was a minor miracle in itself. Finding reliable people had been half the battle in getting this business off the ground.

"Your place or mine tonight?" Caleb asked as they gathered their things and headed for the door.

The question had become a running joke between them, although lately it felt less funny and more like a problem they kept kicking down the road. Caleb's house on Pueblo Street was bigger and fully renovated. Delia's house was smaller but closer to her office, and it was the first real estate purchase she'd made on her own, without her mother's guidance or approval, and she loved being there.

"Mine," she said. "I need to grab some files for tomorrow."

Caleb didn't look bothered by her quick decision. "I'll get some takeout on the way over. That Thai place you like?"

"Perfect."

They walked out together, Delia locking the front door behind them while Caleb made a beeline for the big work truck he'd bought a few months ago after realizing that neither his Range Rover nor his Mercedes was really suited for hauling lumber or tile. The Henderson neighborhood was quiet, the kind of street where retirees weeded their gravel front yards and kept an eye on unfamiliar cars.

She was halfway to her little white Kona SUV when she noticed Caleb had stopped. He stood on the front walkway, head tilted slightly, his eyes scanning the street with an intensity that had nothing to do with admiring the neighbors' xeriscaping.

"What is it?" she asked.

"Nothing." But he didn't move. His nostrils flared slightly—another demon trait, that enhanced sense of smell—and his hands flexed at his sides. "Well, probably nothing."

Delia felt the familiar prickle at the base of her skull, her own senses trying to reach out and read whatever Caleb was feeling. Her psychic abilities had begun to strengthen after being exposed to an otherworldly portal in Laughlin, and the mess with Vinea and the would-be hellmouth in the heart of Las Vegas had made them even sharper. Caleb had been right when he'd said that her gifts would settle down if there was nothing to challenge them, and even the bond they shared was something that remained in the background, unobtrusive.

Still, she could feel emotions now if she

focused hard enough, could sense the residue of strong feelings in rooms and objects in addition to her sense for the energy patterns that surrounded her. Once, she'd walked into a house showing and known immediately that a violent argument had happened in the living room within the past twenty-four hours because she'd felt the echoes of it like heat rising from a burner that had just been shut off.

But the street here in Henderson felt blank to her, just asphalt and stucco and the distant hum of traffic from Boulder Highway. If something was watching them, it was either too far away or too well shielded for her to sense.

"Caleb?"

He shook his head, and the tension in his shoulders eased. "Sorry. I thought I felt something, but it must have been my imagination." A smile, but the expression didn't quite reach his eyes. "See you at your place in an hour?"

"An hour," she agreed.

She watched him climb into his truck and pull away, and told herself it was nothing. Caleb's demon senses picked up interference all the time—stray energies, old emotional residue, the occasional ghost too weak to manifest visibly. Las Vegas was a city built on human desperation and hope, and both left marks on the supernatural landscape even when a demon invasion wasn't involved.

Still, she found herself scanning the street one more time before she got into her car. The houses sat placid and unremarkable in the October sun. A woman walked a small dog on the corner, and a landscaping truck idled two doors down.

Across the street, a dark sedan with tinted windows sat parked against the curb. Delia couldn't see the driver, couldn't tell if anyone was even inside. She stared at it for a long moment, waiting for something—a flash of movement, a feeling, anything.

Nothing.

She got into her car and drove away, and if she checked her rearview mirror more often than usual on the drive home, she told herself she was just paying attention to the rush hour traffic...and not because every instinct was screaming at her that the black car had been up to no good.

Caleb stood at Delia's kitchen counter, dicing onions with a knife that was sharper than anything a home cook probably needed. He'd bought it for her last month, along with a proper cutting board and a set of cast-iron pans, and she'd raised an eyebrow at him but hadn't said no.

His things were everywhere in this house now. The knife, the pans, a spare jacket hanging in the coat closet. His phone charger permanently occupied the outlet next to her bed, and a toothbrush in the bathroom had migrated from the guest bath to her medicine cabinet without either of them acknowledging the relocation.

They were halfway to living together without ever having decided to live together. The ambiguity probably should have bothered him more than it did.

He finished the onions and scraped them into the hot pan, watching them sizzle and turn translucent. The Thai place had been packed, so he'd improvised by throwing together a stir-fry with whatever vegetables Delia had in the fridge, plus some chicken he'd picked up on the way over. Nothing fancy, but he figured one of them should probably learn to cook, and she was way too busy. Besides, he kind of liked the idea of being able to cook. It felt refreshingly normal.

Normal. There was a concept.

His reflection shimmered in the window above the sink—sandy hair, brown eyes, the kind of face that usually got described as "handsome" by women and "pretty" by guys who wanted to be insulting. Nothing in that reflection suggested the demon blood running through his veins. A quarter of his DNA came from something that had crawled out of Hell, but you couldn't see it at all... unless he let it show.

He flexed his hand, and for just a moment, he let the fire come. Orange flames licked across his knuckles, painless and controlled, as natural to him now as breathing. He watched them dance for a few seconds, then extinguished them with a thought.

The fire came more easily these days. So did the enhanced strength, the speed, the ability to sense demonic presences within a certain radius. Ever since Vinea, ever since the wedding chapel and the ritual that had nearly torn open a permanent gateway to Hell, everything had been...well, more.

He'd changed after that ritual, the residual power from all the energy he'd absorbed subsiding but never entirely going away. Or maybe the incident had simply unlocked power that had always been inside him, waiting for a crisis big enough to bring it out. Either way, the result was the same—he was more demon now than he'd ever been.

And that scared the shit out of him.

His father had been a cambion, a half demon. Daniel Lockwood, respectable bank president, pillar of the Greencastle community, cold and distant husband and father. Caleb had spent his childhood watching Daniel keep everyone at arm's length, watching him control every variable, manipulate every situation. Only later did Caleb understand that Daniel had been much more than cold; he'd been careful. He'd kept the demon contained and made sure no one ever saw what lurked beneath the banker's smile.

Daniel had never taught his son anything useful about being part demon. No guidance on controlling their powers, no explanation of what to expect as he grew older, no warning about the ways demon blood could twist your thinking if you let it. Just silence and distance and the unspoken message that this part of himself was something to be hidden and suppressed at all costs.

Now Daniel was gone, trapped in Hell forever after Belial fell. And Caleb was here in Delia's kitchen, cooking dinner and wondering how long before the demon in his blood would turn him into the same kind of man his father had been.

Or maybe something worse.

The door to the garage opened. "That smells amazing."

Delia dropped her bag by the door and kicked off her shoes, padding into the kitchen in her socks. She'd changed out of her work clothes into jeans and a soft gray sweater, her copper hair loose around her shoulders. She looked tired, but beautiful.

"The Thai place was mobbed," he said. "So you're getting the Caleb Lockwood special instead."

"Which is?"

"Whatever's in your fridge plus adequate seasoning."

She laughed and reached past him to steal a piece of bell pepper from the cutting board. "I can live with that."

They moved around each other in the kitchen, easy and casual. Delia set the table while Caleb finished the stir-fry, and by the time they sat down to eat, the tension from earlier today had faded enough that he could almost forget the prickle of wrongness he'd felt on that Henderson street.

Almost.

He'd circled the block twice on the way here, checking for the dark sedan he'd spotted as he was pulling away, looking for anyone who seemed too interested in his truck or his route, but he hadn't seen a damn thing. Either he'd imagined the surveillance, or whoever was watching them was better at staying hidden than he was at finding them.

Neither option made him feel much better.

"My mother called today," Delia said, and pushed some brown rice around on her plate. "She wanted to know if I'd looked at the numbers for the Paulson listing."

Vaguely, Caleb recalled that the property in question was a condo downtown, a place with a high price tag and some hefty HOA fees attached. "Had you?"

"Honestly, I'd forgotten it existed until she mentioned it." Delia stabbed a piece of chicken with more force than necessary. "She's been dropping hints about my 'commitment to the business.'"

Those words had some serious air quotes around them.

She went on, "And about how I've been distracted lately."

Caleb watched her carefully. "Are you? Distracted, I mean?"

For a beat or two, she didn't reply. Then she said, "Well, I'm building something with you. I'm learning new skills, and I'm making good money on these flips." She set down her fork and reached for her glass of wine. "I don't know if that counts as distracted or just...evolving, maybe."

"So what do you want to do?"

The question sort of hung there. Delia was quiet for a moment, her blue-gray eyes fixed on some point past his shoulder.

"I don't know," she said at last. "Every time I try to think about what I should do next, I feel guilty. My mom built that business from nothing, and she worked her ass off for it. And now I'm supposed to just walk away because I'd rather design a kitchen than show houses?"

"You should do whatever makes you happy," Caleb said at once. There was a whole lot about the world that he didn't know, but he knew what he'd just said was only the truth. "Your mother will understand."

Delia shook her head. "I'd like to think so. I mean, she's always encouraged me to chase my dreams, but was that partially because my dreams lined up with what she wanted?" A sigh, and then she continued, "And I know that's not fair. My mother never forced me to do anything I didn't want to do. But I still can't help feeling guilty about all this."

He supposed that was fair. Although it wasn't as if he was besties with Linda or anything, he'd bumped into her enough at the Dunne & Dunne offices that he could tell she was a kind woman, with a natural warmth and friendliness that had served her well over the years, had made her someone people went back to time after time, since they knew they could trust her with some of the most important transactions in their lives. She might be disappointed by her daughter's change of course, but he doubted she would give Delia too much grief for pursuing her dreams.

"She'll understand," he said.

Delia sent him a rueful smile. "I know. That's the problem."

He reached over to give her hand a reassuring squeeze, and they finished dinner in a sort of relaxed silence, then cleaned up together. She took care of rinsing the dishes and putting them in the dishwasher, while he busied himself with wiping down the countertops and making sure he didn't leave any trace behind of his meal prep. Delia's kitchen was like that, clean and neutral with its black granite countertops and white cabinets, and he wanted to make sure he couldn't be accused of making a mess.

"I've been thinking," he said, keeping his voice casual. "About the housing situation."

Delia went still, her fingers freezing mid-motion on the dish towel she'd picked up to dry off her hands. "What about it?"

Since he'd broached the subject, he knew he needed to plow ahead. "We've been doing this dance for months. Your place, my place, back and forth. Half my clothes are here. Half your books are at my house." He set down the sponge he'd been holding and turned to face her. "Maybe it's time we picked one. Or we could find something new together."

She didn't answer immediately. Her jaw tightened, and something flickered behind her eyes—not quite fear, but something close to it. The dish towel twisted between her fingers.

"That's a big step," she said.

"I know."

"And we've only been...I mean, it's only been...."

"Six months," he finished for her. "I know how long it's been. But we've also fought demons together. We've survived things that should have killed us. I feel like that might accelerate the timeline a little."

She didn't laugh at the joke, even though he'd hoped she would.

Instead, she turned away, focusing intently on drying a bowl that wouldn't fit in the dishwasher. "I'm not saying no. I'm just...I need to think about it. There's a lot going on right now. The flips, deciding what to do about Dunne & Dunne...everything."

"Sure." He kept his voice neutral, even as something cold seemed to settle in the pit of his stomach. "No pressure. Just wanted to put it out there."

"I appreciate that." She finally looked at him, and her smile was warm but didn't quite mask the tension in her shoulders. "I really do. I guess I just need some time."

"Take all the time you need."

They moved to the living room, put on a show neither of them really wanted to watch, and pretended the conversation in the kitchen hadn't happened. Delia curled against his side on the couch, her head on his shoulder, one hand resting on his chest. He wrapped an arm around her, and from the outside, it probably looked like everything was fine.

On the TV screen, detectives examined a crime scene filmed with the kind of dramatic lighting that would have made any real forensic tech laugh. Caleb watched without seeing, his mind circling back to that moment in the kitchen—the way Delia's face had closed off, the careful distance in her voice when she said she needed time.

He'd spent most of his life reading people, just because he knew he needed to watch everything he said and every reaction to his words so he wouldn't give anything away of who...of *what*...he was. He knew what avoidance looked like, and he knew what fear looked like when it wore the mask of reasonableness.

Delia was afraid of something. Not of him—he was almost sure of that. But of something. Commitment, maybe, of losing herself in a relationship the way she'd lost herself in what she thought her life should be. Of trusting someone else with her carefully constructed world.

He understood that fear. He had his own version of it, the voice that whispered to him in the dark hours in the middle of the night when he couldn't sleep.

What if you're too much demon to love? What if one day you wake up and the human part of you is gone?

He didn't have an answer to those questions.

Chapter Two

THE CAFÉ HER FRIEND PRU HAD CHOSEN sat tucked between a gelato shop and a store that sold high-end luggage, the kind of place where tourists wandered in expecting cheap coffee and walked out thirty dollars lighter. Delia had suggested somewhere less expensive, but Pru had waved her off with a reminder that her last case had paid out better than expected and she wanted to celebrate.

"Celebrate what?" Delia asked as they settled into a booth near the window. Outside, the mid-October sun blazed down on the tourists streaming past, a lot of them in shorts and tank tops despite the way the locals had already switched to jeans and shirts with sleeves. "You closed a case. That's just Tuesday for you."

Pru's dark eyes glinted with amusement. Her

hair had remained dark green, and it didn't seem as if she intended to cut it anytime soon, since it was now well past her collarbones, the longest it had been since the two of them had met back in ninth grade. She wore her usual fall uniform of black jeans and black boots, although today she had on a black T-shirt featuring some band Delia had never heard of. "It's not just any case. Remember that insurance fraud thing I was telling you about? The guy who claimed his Rolex got stolen?"

Oh, she remembered. Every time Delia heard about one of Pru's cases, she found herself a little amazed that so many people had the brass *cojones* to pull off those sorts of stunts. "The one who turned out to have three other Rolexes he'd reported stolen over the past five years?"

"That's the one." Pru grinned and picked up her menu. "Turns out he was selling them to a fence in Henderson and then filing claims. The insurance company was very happy with my work —happy enough to give me a bonus."

A nice surprise, since insurance companies didn't tend to be so gracious even when you were saving them money. "So lunch is on you."

"Lunch is absolutely on me. Get whatever you want."

The waiter appeared, a guy maybe five years younger than they were, with carefully styled hair and the kind of tan that suggested he spent his days off at the pool. They ordered—a chicken Caesar for Delia, some kind of elaborate avocado toast thing for Pru—and settled back with their drinks. Iced tea for Delia, because it still felt a little too warm for coffee despite the calendar insisting it was fall, and a lavender latte for Pru, who had always been willing to try whatever weird concoction was trendy at the moment.

"So," she said as she wrapped her hands around her cup and leaned forward slightly. "How are things with Mr. Tall, Dark, and Demonic?"

Delia couldn't quite hold back a smile. "Things are good. We're working on the Warm Springs house—the one in Henderson I told you about. It should be ready to list in about six weeks if we don't hit any more surprises."

"Surprises?"

"Water damage in the master bath. We had to gut the whole thing."

Pru blinked in sympathy. "That's going to eat into your margins."

"A little. We'll still come out ahead, though." Delia took a sip of her tea and watched the ice cubes clink against the glass. "Caleb's been great about the whole thing. He's got a good eye for this stuff now, better than some of the inspectors I've worked with."

That comment made Pru tilt her head in question. "Demon senses?"

"That's my guess," Delia replied. The tables next to them were unoccupied, so it was probably safe to talk about this kind of stuff. "He won't admit it, but I'm pretty sure he can hear things in the walls that normal people can't."

Their food arrived, and for a few minutes, they focused on eating. The café hummed with conversation around them—a mix of tourists comparing notes on which shows to see and locals grabbing a quick lunch between meetings. It was the kind of background noise Delia found comforting and anonymous, completely unremarkable.

"So things are good," Pru said after a while as she speared a piece of avocado with her fork. "Business is good. Caleb is good. What's the 'but'?"

Delia looked up. "What makes you think there's a 'but'?"

"Because I've known you for almost fifteen years, and I can tell when you're chewing on something." She pointed her fork at Delia. "Spill."

For a moment, she considered deflecting. She was good at that kind of thing; years of practice in real estate had taught her how to redirect conversations, how to answer questions without really answering them. But this was Pru, who had seen her through bad haircuts and worse boyfriends, who had let Delia cry on her shoulder when Bill told her the wedding was off and walked out.

Her friend had never once judged her for any of it, because that was just Pru.

"Caleb brought up the living situation a couple of days ago," Delia said at last. "He wants us to pick a place or maybe find something new together."

A dark eyebrow lifted. "And that's a problem because...?"

"It's not a problem. It's just...." She pushed a crouton around her plate. "It's a big step."

"You've been together for six months. You've fought demons together. You literally helped him close a portal to Hell twice." Pru leaned against the back of her chair, arms now crossed. "I think picking a house is kind of small potatoes compared to all that."

"This is different."

"How?"

Delia didn't answer right away. Instead, she stared out the window at the tourists passing by, at a woman pushing a stroller and a guy in a Hawaiian shirt taking photos of absolutely nothing interesting. The words felt stuck somewhere in her throat, tangled up with feelings she couldn't quite name.

"When we're fighting demons," she said slowly, "everything is clear. There's a threat, we deal with it, we survive. It's scary, but it's simple." She looked back at Pru and forced herself to add, "This stuff—the relationship stuff, the future stuff—it's not simple. There are so many ways it could go wrong."

Her friend appeared unmoved by this argument. "There are so many ways it could go right, too."

"I know. I know that. But...." Delia let the words trail off, frustrated with her own inability to articulate what she was feeling.

Pru uncrossed her arms and leaned forward, her expression softening. "Del, what are you *actually* afraid of here?"

The question felt much more difficult than Delia had expected. She opened her mouth to give some easy answer—that it was too soon, that she wasn't ready, that there was too much going on—but none of those excuses felt true. Or rather, they felt true on the surface but hollow underneath.

"I don't know," she confessed. "I just...every time I try to think about it, I freeze up. Like if I make a decision, I'm locking myself into something I can't get out of."

"You mean like a commitment?"

The words came out before Delia could stop them. "I mean like losing control...of my life, of my choices. Maybe everything I've worked for."

Pru was quiet for a moment, studying her with sharp dark eyes. Then she said, "You know what I think?"

Delia's mouth twitched. "I have a feeling you're going to tell me whether or not I want you to."

Her friend's expression remained uncharacteristically serious. "I think you've spent the past few years trying to control every variable. Ever since Bill left, you've had this tight grip on your career, your finances, your relationships...or lack thereof. It's like you try to plan everything down to the last detail because you think if you control everything possible, nothing bad will happen." Pru paused there, and Delia wondered what she was thinking. Maybe of all the ways her own life had been out of control, through no fault of her own. "But sometimes you have to let yourself trust that things will work out."

Trust wasn't something Delia had wanted to allow in her life lately. Except...she trusted Caleb, didn't she? He'd always been there for her, ever since that first moment when he'd walked into her office all those months ago. But she heard herself reply, "That's easy for you to say."

Pru shrugged. "Actually, it isn't. But here's what you need to remember about building a life with someone—you can't do it alone. That's kind of the whole point. You have to let them carry some of the weight." She reached across the table and squeezed Delia's hand. "Caleb's not asking you to give up control. He's asking you to *share* it. There's a difference."

She knew Pru was right—she usually was, annoyingly enough—but knowing something and feeling it were two very different things.

"When did you get so wise?" she asked, trying to lighten the mood.

Pru grinned. "I've always been wise. You just don't always listen."

They finished their lunch, the conversation drifting to lighter topics—Pru's latest cases, the current drama with her next-door neighbors in her condo building, who fought almost constantly but didn't seem to want to break up, the band she was thinking about going to see next month. But underneath it all, Delia couldn't stop thinking about what her friend had said.

You have to let them carry some of the weight.

She wasn't sure she knew how.

The house on Desert Inn Road was a complete disaster.

Caleb stood in what had once been a living room, surrounded by the wreckage of walls he'd spent the last three hours tearing down. Drywall dust coated every surface, including him, and the October heat had turned the interior into something approaching a sauna even though he'd propped open every window and door he could find.

The place had been a foreclosure, picked up at auction for well under market value because no one else had wanted to deal with the nightmare of deferred maintenance and questionable renovation choices the previous owners had made. Someone had tried to turn the single-story ranch into a two-story by adding a second floor that wasn't properly supported, and the electrical panel looked like it had been wired by a drunk electrician in the dark.

It was exactly the kind of project Caleb loved.

He grabbed a sledgehammer and swung it into what remained of the wall that separated the kitchen from the dining room. The impact reverberated up his arms, satisfying in a way that was hard to explain. Out here, alone, with no one to see him, he didn't have to hold back.

Another swing. The wall crumbled.

He let the fire come, just a little, not enough to be dangerous, just enough to heat his hands, to add an edge to his strength. The sledgehammer moved faster, hit harder. Drywall and studs came apart like they were made of cardboard.

For a few minutes, he lost himself in the rhythm of destruction. Swing, impact, debris. Swing, impact, debris. His muscles burned in the good way that meant he was pushing himself, and beneath it, something darker hummed—the demon in his blood, relishing the release of power, the freedom to be what he was without pretending otherwise.

It felt good. Too good.

He stopped, chest heaving, and looked down at his hands. The fire had crept up past his wrists, orange flames licking at his forearms like eager pets. He hadn't even noticed.

With a sharp exhalation, he extinguished them. The flames vanished, leaving only the faint smell of sulfur and the uncomfortable awareness of how close he'd come to losing himself in the sensation.

This is how it starts, he thought. *This is how you become something you can't come back from.*

He set down the sledgehammer and walked outside, needing air that wasn't thick with dust and the memory of fire. The backyard was a wasteland of dead grass and a swimming pool that had been drained and left to crack in the sun, but at least the sky was open and blue above him.

His phone vibrated in his pocket. He pulled it out and saw Delia's name on the screen.

"Hey," he said.

"Hey, yourself." Her voice was warm, and some of the tension in his shoulders eased just from hearing it. "How's the demo going?"

"Messy. I've got about three more walls to take down, and then I need to figure out what the hell the previous owners did to the plumbing."

"That bad?"

"Let's just say I'm pretty sure some of the pipes are held together with duct tape and prayer."

She laughed, and he smiled despite himself.

"Dinner tonight? I was thinking we could try that new Italian place on Flamingo."

"Sounds good. Seven?"

"Seven works. I'll make a reservation." A pause, and then she asked, "Is everything okay? You sound tired."

He glanced back at the house, at the dust still settling in the doorway. "Just a long day. Nothing a shower and some pasta won't fix."

"Okay. See you tonight."

"See you."

He ended the call and stood there for a moment, phone in hand, staring at nothing. The fire was gone, but he could still feel it under his skin, waiting.

Always waiting.

His father had never talked about this. Daniel Lockwood had taught his son exactly two things about being part demon: hide it, and control it. No explanation of what the fire felt like when it wanted to be let out, no guidance on how to walk the line between using his abilities and being consumed by them. Just cold silence and the unspoken message that this part of himself was something to be ignored, something to be suppressed at all costs.

And maybe Daniel had been right. Maybe the suppression was the point, the only way to stay human when part of you wasn't.

But Daniel was gone now, stuck in Hell with

the rest of the cambions and their quarter-demon sons, and Caleb was here with more power than he'd ever had and no roadmap for how to handle it. Every time he used his abilities, he felt the demon side of himself growing stronger, more confident, more willing to push boundaries. And every time he pulled back, he wondered if he was just delaying the inevitable.

He didn't want to become his father…but he was starting to wonder if he had any other choice.

The afternoon sun beat down on his shoulders as he walked back inside to finish the demolition. This time, he kept his hands cold.

The offices of Dunne & Dunne occupied a corner suite in a professional building just off Sahara, close enough to the Strip to be convenient but far enough away to avoid the chaos. Delia had spent countless hours in those rooms over the years, first as a student doing homework at her mother's desk on those days when her dad got stuck at work late and Linda couldn't get away from the office, then as a licensed agent building her own client list, and now as a partner whose name was technically on the door, even if it still felt like her mother's business.

This morning, although the place was just the

same as it had always been, the walls felt as if they were closing in.

"The Henderson market is softening," her mother was saying as she scrolled through listings on her laptop. "We should probably adjust our pricing strategy for the Mitchell property. Maybe come down five percent and see if that generates more interest."

Delia nodded, trying to focus on the numbers on the screen in front of her. The Mitchell property was a four-bedroom colonial that had been sitting for sixty days, which was far too long in this market. Her mother was right—they needed to adjust. Nothing crazy, of course, but wary buyers often responded to even small price drops. However, her mind kept drifting to the Warm Springs house, to the tile samples she wanted to look at this afternoon and the cabinet hardware she'd bookmarked on her phone.

"Delia?"

She blinked. "Sorry. What?"

Linda's expression was patient enough, but there was the slightest edge to her voice as she said, "I asked if you'd reviewed the comps for the Mitchell listing."

"I looked at them yesterday." That was technically true. She had looked at them briefly before getting distracted by a wholesale tile supplier's website. "The pricing adjustment makes sense."

"Mm-hmm." Linda set down her tablet and leaned back in her chair. She was dressed impeccably as always, in a cream-colored blouse and tailored slacks, her highlighted light brown hair pulled back into an expensive tortoiseshell clip. At fifty-five, she looked barely forty, a combination of good genes and careful grooming, along with the ever-present understanding that she worked in an industry where appearance mattered. "Can I ask you something?"

In Delia's experience, that particular question rarely led to a good outcome. But she made herself reply, "Sure."

"Are you happy here?"

It wasn't the question she'd been expecting. She'd braced herself for a gentle nag about the Mitchell listing, or the Paulson condo she'd been neglecting, or even her general lack of focus. Not this.

"Of course I'm happy here," she said, and heard how hollow that sounded even as the words left her mouth.

Her mother's gaze was steady. "You can tell me the truth. It's pretty obvious to me when you're somewhere else."

Of course it would be obvious. She was Linda's only child, and they knew each other about as well as two women could. Even so, Delia found herself saying, "I'm just tired. Caleb and I are working on a new flip, and it's been taking up a lot of time and energy."

"I know. That's what I wanted to talk about." Her mother's voice softened as she asked, "The flipping business is going well?"

At least Delia knew she didn't have to hedge when she answered that question. "Really well, actually. We've made good money on the last few houses, and we're learning a lot."

"And you enjoy it."

It wasn't a question. She hesitated, then nodded. "I do. I know that's probably not what you want to hear—"

Linda looked genuinely surprised by that response. "Why wouldn't I want to hear that? Honey, I was happy when you got your license and came to work with me full time, but I never wanted you to feel trapped here."

Trapped. She'd never let that word enter her mind as she was mulling over her situation, but now she couldn't avoid it any longer. Was that how she felt?

"I'm not trapped," she said quickly. "I love this business. I love working with you."

"But?"

There it was again. The question everyone kept asking, the one she kept dancing around.

"There's no 'but,'" she said. "I'm committed to

Dunne & Dunne. But I also like the flipping. That's all."

Linda was quiet for a moment, her expression thoughtful. Then she said, "If you want to focus on the flipping, we should probably talk about what that might look like for the business. I'd rather have that conversation now than have you burn out trying to do both."

Guilt bubbled up from somewhere deep within. Her mother had done so much to help her get started in this business, and now Delia couldn't even be honest with her.

"I don't want to leave," she said, and hated how much those words sounded like a lie. "I just need to figure out how to balance everything. That's all."

Her mother studied her for a second or two longer, then gave a small nod, one that seemed more like an acknowledgment than an acceptance. "Okay. But the offer stands. Whenever you're ready to have that conversation, I'm here."

"Thanks, Mom."

Her mother smiled, although something in her expression seemed very tired. However, she only closed up her laptop and left, saying she needed to meet a client for a house showing.

After Linda was gone, Delia sat alone in the conference room, staring at the listing printouts spread across the table—the Mitchell property, the Paulson condo, and a dozen other files that needed her attention, all of them representing people who were trusting her with some of the biggest financial decisions of their lives.

She should have been energized by that responsibility. Instead, she was just exhausted.

Pru's words echoed in her head.

You can't do it alone. You have to let them carry some of the weight.

But how was she supposed to let anyone carry anything when she couldn't even admit what she was feeling, when every difficult conversation felt like a trap she was too afraid to spring?

She gathered up the files, shoved them into her bag, and headed for the door. She had tile samples to look at and a flip house that needed her attention.

The real conversations could wait another day.

Chapter Three

THE GRAY HALF-LIGHT OF EARLY MORNING slipped through the blinds, creating soft shadows in the bedroom. Next to Caleb, Delia slept on her side, one hand tucked under the pillow, her copper hair spread across the pillowcase in a tangle she'd complain about later.

He didn't move. Instead, he only lay there, watching her breathe, letting himself have this quiet moment before the day started and everything got complicated again. These were the times he liked best, the in-between hours when the world felt still and safe, when he could almost forget what he was.

Almost.

Something was different this morning, though. He couldn't pinpoint it at first; it was just a vague sense of wrongness, like a note played slightly out of tune. His demon senses had been prickling at him for days now, picking up interference he couldn't identify, and he'd written it off as stress or paranoia or the lingering unease from that black sedan he'd spotted in Henderson, the one that had looked so out of place in the quiet suburban neighborhood.

But this was something else, something that seemed much closer.

He inhaled slowly, letting his enhanced senses reach out the way he usually tried not to, opening himself up to the information his demon blood could provide. Delia's scent was familiar—that unique combination of her shampoo and her skin and something underneath that was just *her*, a fragrance he'd know anywhere.

Except now there seemed to be something layered over it.

Something new.

It was faint, barely there, like a whisper underneath a conversation. A second heartbeat, too fast and too small to be hers, and an energy signature he'd never encountered before, something that felt like Delia but also like...him.

His breath caught.

No. That wasn't possible.

He pushed himself up on one elbow, staring down at her as if he could see through her skin to whatever was happening inside. His heart was pounding now, loud enough that he was surprised it didn't wake her. He forced himself to focus, to reach out with his senses again and make sure he wasn't imagining things.

The second heartbeat was still there. It was faster than an adult's would be, fluttering like a bird's wings. And that energy signature—it was demon, unmistakably demon, but mixed with something else, something that felt like the particular flavor of Delia's psychic abilities.

It couldn't be what he was thinking, though. They'd been careful. She was on the Pill, had been for years. He'd been with her long enough to know that she took her pill every morning before brushing her teeth, and she had the prescription delivered from an online pharmacy because she didn't want to waste time picking it up in person. Anyway, they'd never had any scares before, and they'd been intimate for months. This was just his demon senses going haywire, picking up some stray energy or residue from one of their recent encounters with the supernatural. Las Vegas was full of weird energy. That had to be it.

Except the energy wasn't coming from outside. It was coming from her. From *inside* her.

Delia stirred, her eyelids fluttering. "Mmm," she murmured, "what time is it?"

"Early." His voice sounded rough, a hoarseness he supposed he could have blamed on the early hour, even though he knew that wasn't the problem. "Go back to sleep."

But she was already stretching, wincing as she did so. "God, I'm exhausted. I feel like I could sleep another twelve hours." She blinked up at him, and even in the dim light, he could see shadows under her eyes, darker than they should have been. "Did you sleep okay?"

The lie came automatically.

"Fine."

He watched her sit up, pushing her hair back from her face with one hand, and that second heartbeat thrummed in his awareness like a drumbeat he couldn't ignore. Now that he'd noticed it, he couldn't stop sensing it. It was there with every breath she took, every movement she made.

"I'm going to make coffee," she said, then swung her legs over the side of the bed. She paused there for a moment, one hand pressed to her stomach, her face tightening briefly. "Ugh. I think I ate something weird yesterday. My stomach's been off all week."

Caleb's mouth went dry. "Yeah?"

"Probably just stress," she replied, expression unconcerned. She stood, wobbling slightly, and reached for the nightstand to steady herself. "Too much going on. I'll be fine once I get some caffeine in me."

She padded out of the bedroom in her worn T-shirt and sleep shorts, and Caleb sat there for a long moment, trying to convince himself he was wrong. He *had* to be wrong. There was no way his demon blood could override modern contraception. That wasn't how biology worked.

Except he didn't actually know how his biology worked. His father had never explained any of this, had never explained anything, really, beyond the basic imperative to hide what they were. Caleb had no idea what his blood was capable of, what unexpected complications might arise from mixing demon with human. Hell, his parents had never even said whether they'd been trying for a child or whether he'd been an unhappy accident. He'd been fumbling in the dark his whole life, guessing at the rules, hoping he didn't break anything important.

And now—

He got up and pulled on a pair of jeans, then followed her to the kitchen.

Delia was standing at the counter, watching the coffee drip into the pot in an unfocused way that suggested she wasn't really seeing it. She looked tired—more tired than he'd noticed lately, now that he was paying attention. The past few weeks, she'd been going to bed earlier and sleeping later, and if she'd mentioned her exhaustion at all, it was only in the context of having way too much on her plate.

But he'd seen her push away her breakfast more than once, claiming she wasn't hungry, which wasn't like her. She was slender, but she always had a good appetite. And he'd also noticed her wincing when she moved certain ways, rubbing at her lower back when she thought he wasn't looking.

He'd assumed it was just stress. Overwork. The normal toll of trying to balance too many things at once.

Now he wasn't sure.

"Delia."

She turned toward him, russet eyebrows raised. "Yes?"

The question sat on his tongue, heavy and impossible. He didn't know how to ask it without sounding insane. But he couldn't *not* ask, couldn't spend another minute with this uncertainty clawing at him.

"When was your last period?"

For a long moment, she only stared at him. Then her expression shifted to something between confusion and irritation. "What? I don't know. I've been busy." She turned back to the coffee pot, at the same time reaching up to grab a mug from the cabinet. "Why would you ask that?"

"Just humor me. When was it?"

"I don't keep track down to the day, Caleb. It's not like I circle it on a calendar or—" She stopped there, and her hand froze on the cabinet door, mug apparently forgotten. He watched her shoulders go rigid, watched the subtle shift in her posture as the question actually seemed to register in her mind.

The kitchen went very quiet. Even the coffee maker seemed to hold its breath.

"Oh, my God," she said.

"Delia—"

"No. No, that's not—" She turned away from the cupboard, face now so pale that her eyes seemed to glitter like sapphires in contrast. "I'm on the Pill, Caleb. I take it at the same time every day. I haven't missed a pill in the past five years."

"I know," he said quietly. The last thing he wanted was for her to think he was accusing her of orchestrating all this.

"So it's not possible." But her voice now sounded uncertain. He could hear her heartbeat accelerating, could sense the wave of fear and confusion radiating from her. And underneath it, steady and oblivious, that second heartbeat continued its rapid flutter. "It's not possible. Right?"

He didn't answer.

He didn't have to.

She pressed a hand to her stomach...to her flat, unchanged stomach, which showed no sign of what might be happening inside. "How long? When did I—" She shook her head, obviously trying to focus. "Five weeks? Maybe six? I thought

I was just stressed. I thought the nausea was because of something I ate. I thought—"

The tumble of words stopped, and he could see her running back through the past several weeks, reexamining every symptom she'd dismissed. The exhaustion. The nausea. The mood swings she'd blamed on the situation at Dunne & Dunne and her worry about not knowing what she should do. All of it was now adding up to something she hadn't let herself consider.

"We need to get a test," Caleb told her.

Delia stared at him without speaking. Her hand was still pressed to her stomach, fingers splayed as if she could feel something there. Then she nodded, a sharp jerky motion, and walked past him toward the bedroom without saying another word.

The coffee maker beeped, announcing that the pot was ready. Neither of them touched it.

They didn't talk on the drive over to the drugstore.

Delia sat in the passenger seat of her Kona, since they'd decided it would be less conspicuous than Caleb's truck, and she didn't trust herself to drive. Her hands were clasped in her lap, fingers twisting around each other, and she stared straight ahead at the road, even though she wasn't the one behind the wheel.

Her mind wouldn't stop racing, running calculations she didn't want to make. Five weeks. Maybe six. She tried to remember the last time she'd had her period, but the days blurred together in a haze of flip houses and tile samples and appointments with clients. Late September, maybe? She'd been so busy with the Henderson house that she hadn't been paying attention to her own body.

Which was stupid. She was usually so careful about these things, so aware of her own rhythms and cycles. But the past month had been chaos—the water damage discovery, working up the nerve to finally talk to her mother, Caleb's question about moving in together. She'd been so focused on trying to manage everything around her that she'd lost track of what was happening inside.

The irony wasn't lost on her. Pru had just told her she couldn't control everything, and now here was proof of that very concept, undeniable and growing.

If it was growing. If there was actually something there.

She was on the Pill. She might have made a mistake or two when she was younger, but it had been at least five years since she'd missed a dose. She'd never had a scare, never had any reason to think it wasn't working perfectly. The Pill was ninety-nine percent effective when taken correctly, and she took it correctly. She was meticulous about it, just like she was meticulous about pretty much everything else in her life.

But Caleb wasn't entirely human. And if something was growing inside her, then it wouldn't be entirely human, either.

She'd seen enough over the past few months to know that demon blood came with unexpected complications. Caleb could heal faster than normal humans, could sense things ordinary people couldn't, could summon fire from nothing and teleport himself from place to place. His biology didn't follow normal rules.

Why had she assumed his reproductive biology would be any different?

"Pull over here," she said as they approached a strip mall with a CVS. "I'll go in. You can wait in the car."

Caleb glanced at her, his fingers tight on the steering wheel. "I'll come with you."

"No." The word was sharp, and she wanted to shake her head at herself. Getting angry with him was stupid. This wasn't his fault. Voice softening, she added, "I just...I need to do this part alone. Okay?"

He looked like he wanted to argue, but then he

nodded and pulled into a parking space near the entrance. Delia got out before she could change her mind, before the trembling in her legs could convince her to stay in the car where it was safe.

The automatic doors slid open with a cheerful chime, and cold, air-conditioned air hit her face, sort of unnecessary when the temperature outside was in the upper fifties. The store was mostly empty at this hour; she saw a few early-morning shoppers grabbing coffee and newspapers, an employee stocking shelves in the back. Nobody paid any attention to her as she walked toward the family planning aisle.

It was near the back, tucked between the vitamins and the feminine hygiene products. She stood in front of the pregnancy tests for what felt like an eternity, staring at the rows of boxes with their promises of early detection and easy-to-read results. First Response. Clearblue. The CVS store brand. Digital tests and line tests and tests that claimed to work five days before your missed period.

Her hands shook as she reached for the closest one. Then she grabbed two more, different brands with different detection methods. Three tests, because she needed to be sure. A single positive could be a false positive, could be a faulty test or a chemical pregnancy or a mistake.

But three positives—

Three positives would mean something she couldn't explain away.

She paid at the self-checkout, fumbling with her credit card twice before she got the tap reader to scan the chip correctly. The machine seemed unbearably loud, beeping and whirring as it processed her purchase. The bag it dispensed was plain white plastic, anonymous, giving no hint of what was inside.

The walk back to the car felt endless. She was hyperaware of every step, every breath, every stir of uncertainty within her. Caleb was watching through the windshield, his face pale and tense, and she wondered what he was sensing. Could he feel her fear? Could he hear that second heartbeat from this distance?

Could he already tell what the tests were going to say?

She got into the car without speaking, clutching the bag in her lap like it might explode if she held it wrong. Caleb didn't ask any questions, thank God. He just started the engine and drove them home, the silence between them thick enough to choke on.

Back at her house, she went straight to the bathroom without stopping to take off her jacket or put down her purse. The tests came out of the bag one by one—First Response, Clearblue Digital, CVS Early Result. She lined them up on the counter, read the instructions even though she knew how they worked—everyone knew how they worked—and then she did what she needed to do.

Three tests. Three sticks lined up on the counter like soldiers awaiting orders.

And three minutes. That's what the boxes said. Three minutes to know if her entire life was about to change.

She sat on the edge of the tub, arms wrapped around herself, and stared at the tile floor. The pattern was familiar; she'd picked it out herself when she bought the house, had spent hours agonizing over the shade of gray and the size of the squares. Such a stupid thing to think about right then, but her mind kept latching onto irrelevant details as if they could anchor her to reality.

Outside the door, she could hear Caleb pacing —four steps in one direction, turn, then four steps back. The rhythm was almost soothing, a reminder that she wasn't alone in this, that whatever happened next, he was there.

Except she didn't know what she wanted to happen next. She couldn't even begin to process the possibilities. A baby. Caleb's baby. A child that would be part demon, part human, part something neither of them understood. Was that even viable? Could her body handle a pregnancy like that? What would it do to her, carrying something that wasn't entirely human? What would happen when it was born?

Part of her mind knew those were silly questions, that Caleb and six other men just like him had been born in Greencastle, Indiana, had grown up to be healthy and whole, giving no sign of the demon blood that flowed in their veins. And the child she carried would have even less demon in them, would only be an eighth demon. Sure, her psychic abilities might throw a bit of uncertainty into the mix, but she was purely human, no matter what strange gifts she possessed.

To be honest, she didn't even know if she wanted children. The question had always been something to think about later when she had her life figured out. She was twenty-eight, focused on her career—careers, plural, now that flipping had become more than a side project. She wasn't ready to be a mother. She hadn't planned for this.

But when had anything in the past year gone according to plan?

The timer on her phone went off. She'd set it without remembering, her hands moving on autopilot while her brain refused to engage.

For what felt like an eternity, she couldn't move. The tests sat there on the counter, their little windows full of answers she wasn't ready to see. She could hear her own heartbeat pounding in her ears, could feel her hands trembling as she gripped the edge of the tub.

Just look, she told herself. *Whatever it says, you need to know.*

She rose to her feet on legs that felt like they belonged to someone else. The counter was only three steps away, but crossing those three steps felt like walking through water.

The first test—First Response—showed two pink lines. One dark, one fainter but unmistakable. Positive.

The second test—CVS Early Result—showed a plus sign, clear and definitive. Positive.

The third test—the digital one, the one that left no room for interpretation—displayed the word in stark black letters.

PREGNANT.

All three positive. That meant there was no room for doubt, no possibility of error, no comfort of *maybe* or *wait and see* or *it might be wrong.*

She was pregnant.

The bathroom seemed to tilt around her. She grabbed the counter to steady herself, knocking one of the tests onto the floor, and for a moment, she thought she might throw up. Not from morning sickness, but just from the sheer overwhelming weight of what those three little sticks were telling her.

She bent to pick up the test she'd just knocked over, then opened the bathroom door.

Caleb stood in the hallway, handsome features taut, his dark eyes fixed on her with an intensity that would have been unnerving if she'd had any emotional bandwidth left to feel unnerved. He'd stopped pacing the moment the door handle turned, and now he stood frozen, waiting, barely breathing.

She held up the tests, all three of them clutched in one shaking hand. Her mouth opened, but no words came out. What was there to say?

Caleb's expression went through a series of emotions. She watched it happen in real time—the flash of hope, quickly followed by terror, and then something raw and vulnerable she'd never seen on his face before. He stepped toward her and stopped, as if he wasn't sure he was allowed to touch her.

"I don't understand," she heard herself say. Her voice sounded strange, disconnected from her body, like someone else was speaking through her mouth. "I'm on the Pill. I take it every day at the same time. I never miss. This shouldn't be possible."

"Demon blood." Caleb's voice didn't sound like his, either, almost detached, as if some part of his brain had decided the best way to handle this was to look at the situation clinically. "It must have overridden the hormones. My metabolism burns through medication faster than normal—I should have thought about whether that could affect—" He stopped there, his jaw tight. "I didn't know. I swear to God, Delia, I didn't know that could happen. I would have told you. I would have—"

"It's not your fault." The words came automatically, even though she wasn't sure she believed them yet. "You didn't know. Neither of us knew."

But someone should have known. Someone should have warned them that demon biology didn't play by human rules. Except there was no one to warn them—no guidebook for dating someone who was a quarter demon, no FAQ section for what to expect when you're expecting the supernatural.

They were on their own. They'd always been on their own.

"What do we do now?" she asked.

Caleb shook his head slowly. "I don't know." He moved closer, carefully, giving her space to pull away if she wanted to. When she didn't, he took her hand—the one not holding the tests—and laced his fingers through hers. His skin was warm, almost hot, the way it always was. "But whatever we decide, we'll do it together. Okay? This isn't just on you. This is both of us."

Together. The word echoed in her mind, overlapping with Pru's voice at the café. *You can't do it alone. You have to let them carry some of the weight.*

She'd been so afraid of losing control, of being locked into something she couldn't escape. But standing here in this hallway, holding Caleb's hand while their whole world rearranged itself around them, she realized that control had always been an illusion. Life happened whether you planned for it or not. The only choice was whether you faced it alone or with someone beside you.

"Together," she repeated.

It wasn't a decision about the pregnancy. It wasn't a plan or a commitment or an answer to any of the thousand questions swirling in her head. But it was a start, she supposed.

She let him pull her into his arms, let herself lean against his chest and feel the steady beat of his heart beneath her cheek. The tests fell from her hand onto the hallway runner—three little pieces of plastic that had just upended everything they thought they knew about their future.

"We should probably talk about this," she said, her voice muffled against his shirt.

"Probably." His arms tightened around her. "But maybe not right this second. Maybe right this second, we should just breathe."

So they breathed in and out, while the morning light grew stronger through the windows and the rest of the world went on without them. There would be time for conversations later, for questions about what this meant and what they were going to do and how they were going to handle a pregnancy neither of them had planned for. There would be time for fear and hope and everything in between.

But for now, she'd take comfort from what she had and the sensation of Caleb's arms around her as they stood in the hallway, trying to find their balance in a world that had shifted under their feet.

Chapter Four

Delia was pretty sure the house had never been this clean. She stood in her living room, microfiber cloth in one hand, as she surveyed the results of three hours of frantic activity. The baseboards gleamed, and the windows sparkled. She'd reorganized her bookshelf twice—first alphabetically, then by color, then back to alphabetically because the color thing was ridiculous, even if it looked kind of pretty. The kitchen counters were bare except for the coffee maker and a bowl of lemons she'd arranged like she was staging the place for a showing.

Stupid, really. She had someone come in twice a month to clean, so the house was pretty much always presentable.

This was different, though. Stress-cleaning. That's what Pru called it, anyway, a compulsive need to impose order on her physical environment when Delia felt as if her life was spinning out of control.

Caleb sat on the couch, watching her stare at the newly rearranged bookshelves as if they held the secrets of the universe. He'd arrived twenty minutes ago, after they'd spent the morning apart —him at his house, her here, both of them supposedly "processing." Problem was, she hadn't processed anything. No, she'd just scrubbed grout until her fingers cramped and tried not to think about the three positive pregnancy tests currently sitting in her bathroom trash can like unexploded ordnance.

"Do you want to sit down?" he asked at last.

"I'm fine," she said shortly.

A frown pulled at his brows, which were much darker than his sandy blond hair. "You've been standing in the same spot for two minutes."

Delia looked down at her feet, planted on the freshly vacuumed rug, and forced herself to move to the armchair across from him. Sitting down felt wrong, though. If she stopped moving, everything would become real in a way she wasn't sure she was ready to face.

"So," Caleb said.

"So."

Silence descended, uncomfortable in a way their silences had never been before. Usually, they could sit together without talking and it felt easy, natural. Now the quiet pressed against her eardrums, thrumming with everything she knew she should be saying but somehow couldn't.

Caleb leaned forward and reached for her hand. She let him take it, felt the familiar warmth of his skin against hers. It should have been reassuring, right?

Except she wasn't sure if anything could reassure her right now.

"We should get married."

The words fell into the silence like a grenade. Delia's first instinct was to pull her hand back, and she had to consciously stop herself from doing so.

"Caleb—"

"I'm serious." His dark eyes were intent on her face. "We should make it official. Make sure you and the baby are—"

"What?" she cut in. "Protected? Is that what this is about?"

Another frown. "What's wrong with wanting to protect you?"

"Nothing...or maybe everything." She finally pulled her hand back, then tucked both hands in her lap, where they couldn't betray her by trembling. "I just found out I'm pregnant three hours ago, Caleb. And now you've decided to propose?"

His dark gaze didn't flicker. "Is the timing the problem, or is it me?"

A very good question. Too bad she didn't have a real answer. She settled for saying, "That's not fair."

"Neither is you acting like I'm attacking you when I'm trying to—"

"To what?" she cut in. "Fix things? Make decisions so I don't have to?"

At once, his jaw tightened. "Someone has to make decisions, Delia. We can't just ignore this and hope it goes away."

"I'm not trying to ignore it. I'm just...I guess I'm just trying to breathe." She got up from the chair, unable to sit still any longer, and walked to the window. The afternoon light was flat and gray, the sky the color of old dishwater. "You don't understand. I thought I had everything worked out. My career was going great, I was getting some money saved up, I—"

"I'm really sorry I disturbed your perfect world," Caleb retorted. "But maybe it's time to talk about the way you don't seem to want anything that might tie you down."

She planted her hands on her hips. "That's not what this is about."

"Isn't it?" Now he was on his feet, too, the couch between them like a barrier. "Because from where I'm standing, it looks like you've been avoiding any decision that might affect your future.

Where we live. Whether we're actually building something together or just—"

"Just what?" she demanded.

"I don't know," he said. Anger had begun to flare in his expression, but she didn't see any sign of the reddish flames that made an appearance when his demonic blood started to act up. Was he holding back, doing what he could to keep that side of his nature in check? He added, "Maybe you're just playing house until something better comes along."

The accusation might as well have been a slap in the face. She could feel the blood draining from her cheeks as she stared at him, thunderstruck. "Is *that* what you think? That I'm waiting for something better?"

"I think you don't want to commit to anything you can't walk away from." His voice was quieter now, but no less intense. "And a baby is pretty goddamn hard to walk away from."

"So is marriage," she returned. "Maybe that's why I'm not jumping at the chance to add another permanent decision to the pile."

"Or maybe you just don't want to marry me."

The words hung there, raw and wounded. Delia could see the hurt beneath his anger, the fear he was trying to cover by making it seem as if he had a plan already worked out. Part of her wanted to close the distance between them and tell him that wasn't it at all, but another part, the part that felt cornered and overwhelmed and completely out of control, dug in its heels.

"Maybe I don't want to be railroaded into a decision because you've decided it's the right thing to do."

Caleb flinched. Actually flinched like she'd hit him, and remorse immediately flooded through her. "Railroaded? Is that what you think I'm doing?"

She knew she should have just shut up, but she still found herself replying, "Well, what would you call it?"

"Trying to take care of you. Trying to make sure our kid has—" He paused there and dragged a hand through his hair, leaving it even messier than before. His last haircut had been weeks ago, but he'd been too busy to get another one. "Forget it. You're right. I'm trying to control everything. That's what I do, apparently."

Something in his voice made her pause. The anger was draining out of it, replaced by something that sounded almost like resignation.

"Caleb—" she began.

"Maybe I should go." He was already moving toward the door, jaw tense and his shoulders rigid. "Give you space. That's what you need, right? Space to think without me pushing you into a corner."

Knowing how desperate she sounded, she began, "No, that's not—"

But he was already reaching for the doorknob, and the words dried up in her throat. She wanted to call him back and tell him that she did want to marry him someday, once she'd had a chance to catch her breath and figure out which way was up. Why couldn't she explain that it wasn't about him, not really—it was about her, about the way something in her seized up every time she felt the ground shifting under her feet.

Instead, she just stood there while he opened the door and walked through it.

The click of the latch engaging sounded very loud in the empty room.

She sank onto the couch, one hand unconsciously drifting to her stomach. There was nothing to feel there, of course—she was barely six weeks along, if the math was right, and there wouldn't be any physical sign for weeks yet. But she pressed her palm flat against her abdomen anyway, as if she could somehow communicate with whatever was growing inside her.

I'm sorry, she thought. *I don't know what I'm doing. I don't know how to do any of this.*

The tears came then, hot and unexpected, spilling down her cheeks faster than she could wipe them away. She curled forward, arms wrapped around her middle, and let herself cry.

The sledgehammer slammed into the wall, and a section of drywall crumbled in a satisfying cascade of dust and debris.

Caleb pulled back and swung again, putting his shoulder into it, feeling the impact travel up his arms and into his spine. The wall was already half-demolished because he'd been at this for an hour, ever since he'd arrived at the flip property on Desert Inn Road and decided that manual labor was preferable to thinking.

It wasn't working, though. The thoughts kept coming anyway, crowding in between each swing.

Railroaded. That's what you think I'm doing.

Another swing, and more drywall crumbled. His demon strength made the work easy—too easy, maybe. He could have had this wall down in five minutes if he'd really let loose. Instead, he was pacing himself, dragging out the destruction, because he needed the physical outlet and didn't have anywhere else to put all this anger.

Was he angry with Delia? Not really. Angry with himself, mostly. At the way he'd handled that discussion, charging in with a proposal like he was solving a problem instead of talking to the woman he loved about something that scared them both.

She's right, he thought as the sledgehammer bit

into a stud. *You were trying to control everything. Just like—*

He didn't finish the thought because he didn't need to. The comparison was already there, lurking at the edges of his consciousness like a shadow he couldn't ignore.

Daniel Lockwood had been a lot of things—cold, distant, manipulative—but above all, he'd been controlling. Every interaction carefully managed, every social situation calculated like a chess move. Even teaching Caleb to hide his demon nature had been about control, about making sure their secret stayed safely buried.

And now here he was, proposing marriage like it was a strategic move rather than a declaration of love. Trying to lock things down and make them official so he could get everything organized and planned before the chaos could spiral any further out of control.

The apple doesn't fall far from the tree, whispered a cool voice in his head, one that sounded uncomfortably like his mother's.

He swung the hammer again, harder than necessary, and a chunk of drywall flew across the room.

"Remind me never to get on your bad side."

Caleb spun, hammer raised, before his brain caught up with his reflexes and identified the voice. Ty Carter stood in the doorway of what had once been a bedroom, arms crossed, watching him with those unnervingly bright blue eyes.

"Jesus." Caleb lowered the hammer, his heart still racing. "How long have you been standing there?"

"Long enough to see you commit assault and battery on that innocent wall." Ty stepped into the room, picking his way through the debris with the easy grace that seemed to characterize everything he did. His dark hair was pulled back in its usual ponytail, and he was dressed casually...jeans, a Henley shirt, his ubiquitous motorcycle boots... but he somehow still managed to look like he'd stepped out of a Renaissance painting. The hazards of having angelic blood, Caleb supposed.

"I'm renovating."

"You're destroying. There's a difference." Ty surveyed the damage, one eyebrow raised. "Want to tell me what that wall did to deserve this?"

Caleb set the sledgehammer down and leaned on its handle, suddenly exhausted. The adrenaline was draining out of him, leaving behind a hollow ache that had nothing to do with the way he'd been punishing his body for the past hour.

"Delia's pregnant."

Ty's customary mild expression didn't change —he had an unnerving ability to absorb information without showing any visible reaction—but something shifted in his eyes.

"I see."

"And I proposed this morning, about three hours after she found out."

The half angel still appeared preternaturally calm. "Ah."

"And she said no. Or she didn't say yes, which I suppose amounts to about the same thing." Caleb set down the sledgehammer and picked up a chunk of drywall and turned it over in his hands, not really seeing it. "She accused me of trying to railroad her into a decision."

Ty was quiet for a moment, then went over to sit down on an overturned bucket, apparently unconcerned about getting dust on his jeans. Well, it wasn't as if he was wearing an Armani suit or something. "Was she wrong?"

The question stung, mostly because Caleb had been asking himself the same thing for the past hour. "I don't know. Maybe not."

"What were you trying to accomplish with the proposal?"

"I wanted—" He stopped himself there so he could ponder that question. What *had* he wanted? "I wanted to make sure she was protected. Her and the baby. I wanted to make it official, so there wouldn't be any question about—"

"About what?"

"About us," Caleb replied. "About what we are to each other." The words came slowly, dragged from somewhere deep inside that he wasn't sure he wanted to acknowledge. "About whether I'm going to stick around or disappear like—"

He stopped himself, but it was too late. The comparison was already hanging in the air, obvious to both of them.

"Like your father?" Ty said quietly.

Caleb threw the chunk of drywall across the room. It hit the far wall and exploded into powder. "Maybe she's right. Maybe I am just like him. Maybe this is all I know how to do—push and control and try to manage everything because I don't want to know what might happen if I don't."

The half angel sent him a considering look. "Do you really believe that?"

"I don't know what I believe anymore."

Ty was silent for a long moment, his bright blue eyes fixed on Caleb's face with an intensity that felt almost physical. Then he said, "You're not Daniel Lockwood."

Caleb shrugged. "You never met him."

"I've heard enough. From you, from what the people I've been working with have pieced together over the years. And I know this—" He leaned forward, expression now almost earnest. "You're here, tearing yourself apart over a fight with the woman you love. Daniel Lockwood never cared enough about anyone to be afraid of hurting them."

Those words made him pause. God, he wanted to believe them. He wanted to believe that the fear gnawing at him—fear that he was becoming his father, fear that he was going to ruin everything good in his life—was irrational and unfounded, a ghost story he'd told himself for so long, he'd started to believe it.

But wanting to believe something and actually believing it were two different things.

"She needs time," he said at length. "That's what she said. Everything's happening too fast."

Ty was quiet for a moment. Then he asked, "Is she wrong about that?"

"No. But—" It was harder than he'd thought to articulate the fear that had been driving him all morning, but he knew he needed to face it now, get that black beast out of the darkness. "What if time makes everything worse? What if the longer we wait, the more she convinces herself that this was a mistake? That *we* were a mistake?"

"Is that what you think?"

"I think I'm scared of losing her." He hated to make such a raw admission—the Caleb Lockwood he'd once been would never have allowed himself to show that kind of weakness—but he knew Ty Carter would never betray his secrets. "I think I've spent my whole life trying not to need anyone, and now I need her so much it scares the crap out of me. And I don't know how to handle that except by trying to—"

"Lock things down," Ty said. "Make it official."

"Yeah."

The half angel nodded slowly, like Caleb had just confirmed something he'd already suspected. "I don't think that's control. It's fear. And there's a difference."

"Is there?"

Maybe a very slight smile. "Your father controlled people because he wanted power over them. You're trying to secure commitments because you're afraid of being abandoned." Ty's voice was gentle but matter-of-fact, the way he always sounded when he was saying something that cut a little too close to the bone. "The behavior might look similar from the outside, but the motivation is completely different. And motivation matters."

Caleb turned that explanation over in his mind, examining it from different angles. It made a certain kind of sense. Daniel had never seemed afraid of anything, had never seemed to *feel* much of anything, really, except cold calculation. He'd kept everyone at arm's length, not because he was afraid of losing them, but because they simply didn't matter enough to him to warrant any other approach.

Whereas Caleb was afraid of losing Delia. Terrified of it, really. He'd been scared ever since Laughlin, when he'd thought he'd lost her...when he'd finally acknowledged to himself that what he felt for her had moved well beyond casual attraction into territory that made him vulnerable in ways he'd sworn he would never allow himself to be.

"So what do I do?" he asked, knowing how plaintive he sounded.

"Give her time. You need to trust her to figure out what she wants." Ty paused there, that small smile returning to the corners of his mouth. "And maybe try proposing again when you're not both in crisis mode."

"Sound advice."

"I have my moments." Ty paused there, and his eyes narrowed ever so slightly. "But you do need to talk to Delia. This baby...it could be powerful. I know it will be special. And that means you have to get your life straightened out so you can deal with that."

Before Caleb could reply, the half angel vanished, as he often did at inopportune moments.

Powerful.

Just great.

Caleb looked around at the demolished room, at the dust settling on every surface, at the chunks of drywall scattered across the floor. He'd made a hell of a mess in here.

But messes could be cleaned up. The real question was whether Delia would want to clean up their particular mess.

The Dunne & Dunne office was quiet that afternoon. Linda was out showing a property in Summerlin, and Delia didn't have any client meetings scheduled. She sat at her desk, staring at a spreadsheet she hadn't updated in over an hour, and tried to pretend she was functioning like a normal human being.

There was a joke.

The knock at her office door made her jump, even though she'd been half-expecting it ever since she'd texted Pru half an hour ago with,

Can you come by? I need to talk.

"It's open."

Pru came through the door, a cup of iced tea in either hand and a look of concern on her face that suggested she'd already guessed this wasn't a routine social call. As usual, she was in black from head to toe, although today she'd switched out one of her band T-shirts for a black top with the sleeves rolled up.

"Okay, spill," Pru said as she set one of the cups

on Delia's desk. "Your text sounded like you were either dying or getting married, and since you're clearly still breathing, I'm assuming it's the second option."

The laugh that escaped Delia's throat sounded more like a sob. "Not exactly. Or—maybe? I don't know. It's complicated."

Pru settled into the chair across from the desk and tilted her head to one side, gamine features sharp with interest. "Complicated how? Did Caleb finally pop the question?"

"He proposed this morning."

Big brown eyes widened. "And?"

Delia released a breath, then replied, "And I basically told him no. Or I didn't say yes, which I suppose amounts to about the same thing, and then we had a huge fight and he left, and I've been sitting here for three hours trying to figure out if I just ruined everything."

Pru's eyes widened even further, but she didn't interrupt. She just waited, the way she always did when Delia needed space to get the whole story out.

So Delia told her. All of it—the pregnancy tests, Caleb sensing something was different before she'd even suspected. The way he'd proposed, as if he felt he had to rather than wanting to.

The fight that had followed.

By the time she was done, half the ice in her tea

had melted and her voice had begun to go hoarse, but she still felt somehow lighter.

"Holy shit," Pru said at last, after Delia finally had stopped talking. "I mean, I knew you two were getting serious, but pregnant? That's—"

"A disaster?"

"I was going to say 'unexpected,' but sure, I suppose 'disaster' works, too." Pru took a long sip of her own iced tea, dark eyes now thoughtful. "So let me make sure I'm tracking here. Caleb proposed because you're pregnant. You said no—or didn't say yes—because it felt like he was trying to manage the situation rather than actually asking you to marry him. And now you're sitting here wondering if you made the right call."

Delia gave a weary nod. "That about covers it."

"Okay. So here's the question." Pru set down her tea and sent Delia a very direct look. "*Do* you want to marry him?"

The question she'd been trying to avoid all morning. She opened her mouth to answer, then closed it again.

Damn it.

"I don't know," she finally managed.

Not even a second of hesitation. "Bullshit."

"Excuse me?"

"I said bullshit." The word hadn't been uttered harshly, but something firm in Pru's tone told Delia that she wasn't going to put up with any stupid excuses. "You *do* know. You've known for months. I've watched you with him. I've seen the way you look at each other, the way you've built this whole life together without ever actually committing to it. You know exactly what you want. You're just too scared to admit it."

Delia's eyes burned, and she blinked. She'd already cried enough, and she had a feeling Pru wouldn't have a lot of patience for that kind of breakdown, not when it seemed clear that she thought Delia had caused most of her own problems. "It's not that simple."

Maybe a very small frown. "Isn't it?"

"No," Delia said at once. "Because wanting something and being ready for it are two very different things. I love him, Pru. If you'd asked me six months from now whether I wanted to marry him, the answer would have been yes. But this—" She made a vague gesture, one that took in the office, her belly and the secret it was hiding, the entire mess her life had become. "I didn't plan for any of this. And now I have no idea what to do."

"Okay." Pru gave a slow nod, like she was filing that information away. "So the issue isn't Caleb. The issue is that you're losing control of the situation, and it's freaking you out."

"That makes me sound pathetic," Delia remarked.

"No, just human." Pru reached for her iced tea

and took a sip before setting it back down again. "Come on—we've known each other since we were fourteen years old. I know how much you need to feel like you've got everything under control. And I know why—your whole life, you've been the responsible one, even when you were the lead singer in a punk band. You were the one who made sure people had designated drivers or a place to crash. You were always able to handle everything."

Delia wasn't sure she'd been such a paragon, but she didn't feel like arguing ancient history right then. "And now I'm pregnant with a quarter demon's baby, and I can't even pick which house I want to live in."

"Exactly. Everything's spinning out of control, so your instinct is to slam on the brakes." Pru reached across the table and squeezed Delia's hand, surprising her a little. Usually, Pru wasn't the demonstrative type. "But here's what you have to understand. You can't control a pregnancy, and you can't control how Caleb responds to fear—and yeah, that proposal was definitely a fear response. He's not trying to railroad you. He's scared, and his instinct when he's scared is to protect the people he cares about. There's a difference."

Delia thought about the way he'd flinched when she'd accused him of trying to railroad her.

He'd been scared, too. She'd been so focused on her own panic that she hadn't really seen it, but it was obvious in hindsight. He'd been just as frightened as she was—maybe more so, given everything he knew about his father, about what his demon blood might mean for their child.

And instead of recognizing that fear, she'd attacked him for it.

"I think I really screwed up," she said.

Pru shrugged. "Possibly. Or maybe you both messed up, which kind of tends to happen when two scared people try to have an important conversation without telling each other that they're scared." She released Delia's hand and leaned back in her chair. "The real question is what you do next."

"What do you mean?"

"I mean this isn't over unless you want it to be," Pru said simply. "Caleb's not going anywhere—I'd bet my brand-new MacBook Pro on that. The man is stupid in love with you. So the real question is, what do *you* want?"

Delia had to sit with that for a moment, letting the question settle into her bones. What did she want? Beneath the fear and the panic and the desperate need to get her footing back—what did she actually want?

The answer was simpler than she'd expected.

"I want him," she said after a moment. "I want to build a life with him...a family. I'm just—" She swallowed hard. "I'm scared of screwing up...and of becoming dependent on someone and having them disappear."

That comment got her a frown. "Has Caleb ever given you any reason to think he'd disappear?"

"No. But—" She stopped herself there, a little surprised by where that sentence was headed.

"But?"

Delia thought about her parents—her solid, dependable parents who'd been married for thirty-two years and still held hands at dinner and leaned in for kisses when they didn't think anyone else was watching. They'd never disappeared, never even threatened to. But she'd watched friends' families fall apart, had seen what happened when people built lives together, only to have them collapse.

Maybe that was the real fear. Not that Caleb would leave, but that anything could happen. Life didn't come with guarantees. You could plan and prepare and try to control every variable, and still end up blindsided by something you never saw coming.

Like having your fiancé walk out in the middle of your wedding planning...like getting pregnant despite taking the Pill religiously.

Like realizing that control had always been an illusion, and the only real choice was whether to face the uncertainty alone or with someone beside you.

"I need to talk to him," she said.

Pru smiled—a real smile this time, not the worried half-grimace she'd been wearing since she walked in. "Yeah, you do."

"But not yet. I need—" Delia took a breath and tried to organize her thoughts. "I need to figure out what I actually want to say first. I don't want to just apologize and have us end up in the same place. I want to actually fix this."

"That sounds more like the Delia I know." Pru rose from her chair and picked up her iced tea. "Take your time, think it through. But don't wait too long, okay? The man demolished half a house today—Ty texted me about it. He's not exactly processing in healthy ways, either."

"He did what?"

"Sledgehammered an entire wall into oblivion, apparently. Ty had to have a whole heart-to-heart with him in the rubble." Pru shook her head, but she was still smiling. "You two are a disaster. A perfect, well-matched disaster."

Delia laughed despite herself—a real laugh, the first one all day. "I'll call him tonight."

"Good." Pru paused at the door. "And for what it's worth, I think you're going to be okay. Sure, this is scary and unexpected, but you're won't be doing it alone. That counts for something."

"Thanks, Pru."

Her friend smiled, then headed out.

After she was gone, Delia sat in the quiet office

for a long time. Her hand drifted to her stomach again, pressing flat against the place where something impossible was growing.

She still didn't know what the hell she was doing, but maybe that was okay. Maybe the point wasn't to have all the answers in advance. Maybe the point was to figure them out together, one day at a time, with someone willing to demolish walls when he got scared and come back anyway.

She picked up her phone and started typing.

Can you come over tonight? I think we need to talk.

The response came almost immediately.

I'll be there at 7.

Delia set down the phone and let out a breath. Whatever happened next, at least they'd face it together.

That had to count for something.

Chapter Five

THE DOORBELL RANG AT SEVEN ON THE dot. Caleb had been roaming around his living room for the past twenty minutes, unable to sit still, unable to focus on anything except the clock on the wall and the slow crawl of its hands toward the appointed hour. He'd changed clothes twice—first into something too casual, then into something that felt too formal—before settling on jeans and a plain gray Henley that split the difference.

Stupid. He was acting like this was a first date instead of a conversation with the woman he'd been sleeping next to for months.

But it felt like a first date, in a way. Or maybe more like a job interview, one where the stakes were higher than any he'd ever faced. The next few hours would determine whether they had a future together...or whether everything they'd built was about to come crashing down.

He opened the door.

Delia stood on his porch, her copper hair loose around her shoulders, wearing a pair of dark jeans and the blue-gray sweater he loved her in because it was almost the same color as her eyes. Her face was pale, and there were shadows under those striking eyes that she hadn't been able to completely hide with concealer.

"Hi," she said.

"Hi."

They stood there for a moment, neither of them moving, the cool evening air wafting past them. Then Caleb stepped back and held the door open wider.

"Come in."

She walked past him into the living room, every line of her slender body tight with tension. He watched her take in the space—the leather couches, the floor-to-ceiling fireplace with its dramatic black soapstone slabs, the large windows that looked out onto the backyard, dimly lit by the moody landscape lighting he'd had installed during the renovation process. She'd been here dozens of times, but tonight she was looking at it like she was seeing it for the first time.

Or maybe she was just trying to decide whether it would be a suitable place to raise a child.

"Can I get you something?" he asked. "Water? Tea?"

"I'm fine." She turned to face him, blue-gray eyes intent on his face. "Can we sit down?"

They settled on opposite ends of the couch, a careful distance between them. The last time they'd sat here, they'd been tangled up in each other, laughing about something one of them had said. Now the space felt as wide as the Grand Canyon.

"I'm sorry," they both said at the same time.

A startled laugh escaped Delia's throat. "You go first."

Caleb shook his head. "No, you. Please."

She was quiet for a moment, her hands clasped in her lap. Then she said, "I shouldn't have accused you of trying to railroad me. That wasn't fair. You were scared and trying to help, and I threw it back in your face."

"You weren't wrong, though." The admission cost him something, but he forced the words out anyway. "I was trying to control the situation. I saw a problem and tried to fix it, and I didn't stop to think about what you actually needed."

"That's not—" she began, but he shook his head.

"It is, though." He shifted on the couch, hearing the leather creak slightly under his weight, and made himself meet her eyes. "I've been thinking about it all day. About why I proposed the way I did, why my first instinct was to lock everything down and make it official." He paused, knowing he needed to use exactly the right words or risk screwing up things even further. "I think I was scared that if I didn't act fast, I'd lose you. That you'd realize this was all too complicated and walk away."

Her expression softened at once. "I'm not going to walk away, Caleb."

"I know," he replied. Well, he could tell her that he knew, but something in him relaxed to hear her say so without a second of hesitation. "Or at least, I know that now." He shifted again, now letting his back touch the cushions. "But this morning, all I could think about was my father and the way he controlled everyone around him to make sure they did as he said and followed all the rules. His rules, I mean."

Delia's head tilted slightly, and a strand of coppery hair slipped over her shoulder. "You're not your father."

A bitter smile caught a corner of his mouth. "That's what Ty said."

"Well, he's right." She shifted closer on the couch, close enough that now he could feel the warmth of her body. "Your father controlled people because he didn't care about them. From the way you've talked about the man, they didn't seem to be much more than pieces on a chessboard to him. But you proposed because you care too much. Those aren't the same thing at all."

Caleb shrugged. "Maybe not. But the result looked pretty similar from where you were standing."

She didn't bother to deny it, which he appreciated. One of the things he loved about Delia was her honesty, her refusal to sugarcoat things just to make him feel better.

"I have my own stuff to work through," she said after a moment. "I've been so focused on trying to control what I could that I forgot relationships don't work like that. They're supposed to be...." She trailed off there, clearly searching for the right word.

"Messy?"

A small smile tugged at her lips. "I was going to say 'collaborative,' but sure, messy works, too."

They sat in silence for a moment, but it was a different kind of silence from before. This time, it felt more like two people catching their breath after a long climb.

"I'm scared," Caleb said at last, knowing he couldn't be anything less than utterly truthful if he wanted this to work. "Not just about us, but about the baby. About being a father." He forced himself to keep going, to say the thing he'd been avoiding all day. "What if I screw this kid up the way Daniel screwed me up? What if I don't know how to be a good parent because I never had one?"

Delia reached over and took his hand. Her fingers were cool against his perpetually warm skin. "I'm scared, too. Not about the same things, but —" She paused for a moment, seeming to gather her thoughts. "I keep thinking about all the supernatural stuff we've dealt with. Calach and Vinea and whoever's behind the Styx Group. What happens when we have a baby to protect? What if my abilities aren't enough to keep our child safe?"

He tightened his fingers on hers. "Then we'll figure it out. That's kind of the point, right? Neither of us has to do this alone."

She was quiet for a moment, her thumb idly moving across the back of his hand. Then she said, "I've always had a plan, you know? College, career, the general shape of how my life was supposed to go. And I've been lucky—I had my parents, Pru, a support system that most people would kill for. But this…." She shook her head. "This wasn't part of any plan. I'm pregnant with a baby that's part demon, my psychic abilities are getting stronger, and I don't even know what questions to ask, let alone where to find the answers. For the first time in my life, I can't just research my way through a problem or ask my mom for advice."

He sent her a very direct look. "Is that a bad thing?"

"I don't know. Maybe not. Maybe it's just different."

Caleb moved on the couch, closing the distance between them until their shoulders touched. "So... what do we do now?"

"I think we need to make some decisions," Delia replied. "Real ones, not panic decisions." She straightened slightly, and he could see her mind starting to work, organizing and categorizing the way it always did when she was trying to solve a problem. "We need to figure out where we're going to live, and we'll need to tell our families. We'll also need to figure out what a demon pregnancy even looks like, because I'm pretty sure my regular OB/GYN isn't going to be much help, even though she was nice enough to squeeze me in yesterday for a real blood test."

Which he assumed had proven what they already knew, that Delia was definitely pregnant.

Caleb wasn't even sure who to ask about carrying a part-demon's child. His mother? There was a joke. Even if he hadn't been trying to keep his whereabouts from her, he doubted she'd be able to provide any motherly pearls of wisdom about managing a pregnancy with a child that was part demon.

True, there were other women in Greencastle

who'd also had children with their half-demon partners, but they weren't really an option, either.

Not when they all thought he was dead.

Instead, he thought he should focus on the here and now. "That's a lot of 'we.'"

"Yeah, well." Delia squeezed his hand. "I'm trying out this whole partnership thing and seeing how it feels."

Partnership. Not him trying to protect her, not her trying to maintain control. Instead, it would be both of them working on things side by side.

Something inside him seemed to relax, and he pulled in a relieved breath.

"Okay," he said. "Where do you want to start?"

Obviously, she'd been thinking about that, because she replied right away. "The house thing seems most urgent. We can't keep bouncing back and forth between two places, especially once there's a baby involved."

He'd been thinking about this all afternoon, in between destroying that wall and talking to Ty. "What if we just pick one of our places for now? Yours makes more sense—it's closer to your office, and your house definitely feels more baby-friendly. We can look for something new once things settle down a little."

Delia's eyes widened slightly. "You'd move into my house?"

"Why not?" he asked. "It's a good house. And

you'd be more comfortable there, right? It's your space."

"I just—" She broke off there, and he could see how she was processing the offer, weighing it against whatever assumptions she'd been harboring. "I mean, this is your space, too, and I suppose I thought after you spent so much on the reno...."

He shrugged. "It's just a house. And while it looks impressive, I don't think all this black and white is going to be complemented too well by having baby barf stains everywhere."

Now Delia actually laughed. "Baby barf doesn't fly that far, you know."

He grinned. "I'll take your word for it."

Her expression sobered almost at once, though. "I guess I just figured you'd want us to find somewhere neutral so we can start fresh."

"Eventually, sure. But right now, with everything else going on...." His shoulders lifted again. "It makes sense to keep things simple. Besides, it would be better to wait until after the first of the year to put this place on the market. You know how people hate to move before the holidays."

Of course she did, because she'd been in the real estate business for years.

However, she didn't say anything in reply. Instead, she was quiet for a moment, and he could almost see the wheels turning in her head. Then she nodded. “Okay. My place for now. Until we find something that’s ours.”

“Sounds like a plan.”

They looked at each other, and he could almost feel the way something in the air seemed to change. The tension that had been coiled between them all day was already beginning to ease, replaced by something that felt almost like relief.

“What about....” Delia hesitated, then seemed to steel herself for what she meant to say next. “What about getting married?”

Caleb’s heart wanted to skip a beat, but he forced himself to stay calm. “What about it?”

“I know I didn’t exactly give you an answer this morning. And I’m not—I don’t want to just pretend you didn’t ask.”

He gazed directly at her and took both her hands in his. “I meant what I said. I want to marry you. But not because we’re panicking, and not because it feels like the responsible thing to do.” He paused, then went on, “I want to marry you because I love you. Because I can’t imagine my life without you in it. And I want you to say yes because you feel the same way, not because you feel pressured.”

Her eyes were bright with unshed tears, although she blinked them back. “I want you to ask me again when we’re not both freaking out. When we've had time to breathe and figure out what we're doing."

That was an easy enough request. "I will."

"Promise?"

He lifted her hand to his lips and pressed a kiss to her knuckles. "Promise."

They sat in the quiet living room as the evening deepened outside the windows. There was still so much to figure out—Delia's family to tell, for one thing, and some logistics to work through—but for now, he was content with the way matters stood between them.

"We should probably eat something," she said eventually. "I haven't had anything since breakfast."

It cheered him to hear that she wanted to eat. "I can make pasta. Or we could order in."

"Pasta sounds good." She leaned her head against his shoulder. "Can we just sit here for another minute first?"

"Yeah." He wrapped an arm around her and pulled her closer. "We can do that."

Three days later, Delia found herself sitting in Pru's living room, trying to figure out how to broach the subject of what came next.

The apartment was quintessentially Pru—a big

black leather sectional, vintage concert posters on the walls, a state-of-the-art computer setup in one corner that she used for her private investigator work. The only real splashes of color came from her collection of succulents, which lined the windowsills in an impressive array of greens and purples.

Caleb sat beside her on the couch, his thigh pressed against hers in silent support. Across from them, Ty Carter had claimed the armchair and somehow managed to look elegant despite his faded jeans and motorcycle boots. Pru was perched on one arm of the sectional, a bottle of sparkling water in hand.

"So," she said, glancing between Delia and Caleb, "you said you wanted to talk about next steps. I'm assuming that means you two have worked things out?"

"We have." Delia reached for Caleb's hand and laced her fingers through his. "We're keeping the baby. We're moving in together—at my place for now. And we're going to figure out the rest as we go."

Pru nodded, something like satisfaction flickering in her dark eyes. "Good. That's what I was hoping you'd say." She took a sip of her water. "So what do you need from us?"

"Honestly? We're not entirely sure yet." Delia looked over at Ty, who had been watching the exchange with his usual unreadable expression. "But Ty, you mentioned something when you talked to Caleb the other day. About the baby being powerful. I was hoping you could tell us more about what that means."

Ty straightened slightly in his chair. "May I?" He gestured toward Delia, and she realized he was asking permission to approach.

"Sure."

He rose from the armchair and came over so he could kneel in front of her, his bright blue eyes intent. "May I?" he asked again, holding out one hand, palm up.

Delia glanced at Caleb, who nodded slightly. "Okay."

Ty placed his hand on her abdomen, just above her navel. His palm was warm, and she felt a faint tingling sensation where his skin touched hers through the fabric of her shirt. He closed his eyes, and she could have sworn she saw a faint glow emanating from his hand, although it might have only been a trick of the light.

Then again, she'd seen him blast in the front door at Angel's Dream Wedding Chapel with something that looked like a miniature supernova, so she supposed a pale white glow wasn't too big a deal for him.

After a moment, he opened his eyes and sat back on his heels. His expression remained neutral, but there was something in his gaze that made her stomach tighten.

"Well?" Caleb asked.

Ty rose to his feet and returned to his chair before speaking. "The child is healthy and strong." He paused, seeming to weigh his next words. "And powerful. More than I initially suspected."

Delia's hand went instinctively to her stomach. "What does that mean?"

"The combination of bloodlines is unusual." Ty's gaze moved between her and Caleb as he continued. "Caleb's demon heritage is significant, but your psychic abilities add another layer. The child will inherit traits from both of you, and those traits will interact in ways that are difficult to predict."

"Will that be dangerous for Delia?" Caleb asked, his jaw tightening slightly.

"Not inherently. But you should be prepared for complications. The child's abilities may manifest earlier than expected. Delia's own powers may fluctuate during the pregnancy as the baby's energy interacts with hers." The half angel looked deadly serious. "If you need anything—protection, knowledge, resources—call me immediately. Don't try to handle everything on your own."

Pru had been quiet during this exchange, but now she spoke up. "What kind of complications are we talking about here?"

"Psychic surges, most likely," Ty replied. "Delia may find her abilities amplified or harder to control as the pregnancy progresses. She may pick up emotions or thoughts she wouldn't normally be able to sense. There could also be physical symptoms that don't align with a typical human pregnancy." His tone was matter-of-fact, but not unkind. "I can provide guidance as issues arise, but much of it will be new territory."

Delia absorbed all this, already noting the potential problems. Amplified abilities. Unpredictable powers. A baby that might start manifesting supernatural traits before it was even born.

And all that on top of morning sickness and mood swings and swollen ankles.

"There's something else," Ty went on, and something in his voice made everyone go still. "Given the child's potential power and the recent increase in supernatural activity in the city, I'd recommend increasing your security. Wards on your home, regular check-ins, perhaps some basic protection training for Delia."

"You think someone might come after us?" Caleb asked, his voice sharpening.

"I think it's wise to be prepared. A child with your combined bloodlines would be valuable to certain parties. Better to take precautions now than be caught off guard later."

The room fell silent as the weight of his words

settled over them. Delia found Caleb's hand and held on, so glad to have him there next to her, solid and comforting and real.

"We'll be careful," she said. "And we'll call you if anything seems off."

Ty nodded. "That's all I ask."

Pru, apparently deciding the serious portion of the conversation had gone on long enough, set down her water bottle and sent Delia a sharp look. "All right, doom and gloom aside—have you told your mother yet?"

Delia winced. There was a conversation she really wasn't looking forward to. "Not yet. We're kind of working up to it."

Her friend crossed her arms. "You're going to have to do it eventually. The longer you wait, the more hurt she'll be that you didn't tell her sooner."

"I know." Delia allowed herself a sigh. "I'm just trying to figure out how to explain the whole 'my boyfriend is part demon and our baby might have supernatural powers' thing without giving her a heart attack."

"Maybe lead with the pregnancy and work up to the rest," Pru suggested. "Baby steps. Pun intended."

Caleb groaned. "That was terrible."

"I know... and I'm not sorry." Pru grinned, and some of the tension in the room seemed to dissipate. "Seriously, though. You two have people in your corner. Use us. That's what we're here for."

Delia couldn't help smiling in reply. Pru was right, of course. There was no reason to act as if she had to do everything on her own. Maybe it was time to accept that she didn't have to.

"Thank you," she said, and meant it.

Pru waved a dismissive hand. "Don't thank me yet. Wait until I start sending you unsolicited opinions about nursery colors. Then you can decide if you're grateful."

The conversation turned to lighter topics—the logistics of hers and Caleb's current flips, how long she could reasonably continue working before she had to pull back and concentrate on the baby... Pru's strongly held views on the proper way to decorate a baby's room, which seemed to revolve around everything being black and white because apparently infants liked high contrast.

By the time she and Caleb left an hour later, Delia couldn't help feeling hopeful. Maybe a fragile and tentative kind of hope, but no less real for all that.

Plenty of hard conversations still lay ahead. They'd have to talk to her parents first, but she supposed Caleb's mother would need to know at some point, too.

Or maybe not. He seemed pretty set on not having any contact with her, and Delia knew she'd have to respect his wishes if he decided he didn't want Brooke Lockwood to know anything about her impending grandchild.

They could figure that out later, though. Nothing had to be decided today.

Well, except the big decision that she and Caleb had already made, which was that they were going to do this together, and that one day, he'd ask her to marry him again.

She knew that time she'd say yes.

Chapter Six

Moving in with Delia didn't take very long. Caleb had accumulated some stuff over the past year, but not that much of it, and he figured that most of the furniture in his house would stay behind when he put the place on the market. What he actually needed fit into his truck and required only a couple of trips to take over to her place—some books, his laptop and various electronics, a few kitchen items he'd grown attached to. By the end of the first day, his things were scattered throughout her house, mingling with her stuff like they belonged there.

Which, he supposed, they did now.

In fact, the adjustment turned out to be easier than he'd expected. Delia's place was smaller than his, but it was a lot cozier. She had family photographs displayed in the living room and family room, and throw blankets draped over the couches, and it felt like a real home instead of a showpiece. Sure, he was proud of the remodel they'd done on the Pueblo Street house, but now he realized he'd been so bound up in how it looked that he hadn't stopped to think whether he truly felt comfortable there. At any rate, he found himself relaxing into her home in a way he hadn't anticipated, settling into her routines like slipping into a well-worn pair of jeans.

They spent the first few days establishing new patterns, deciding whose side of the bed was whose, and how to navigate a single bathroom in the morning without tripping over each other. These were all small negotiations, the kind that felt more like play than conflict.

But before that first week was even over, they'd started talking about the future. Not just the immediate future—appointments with Delia's OB/GYN and family conversations and all the logistics of combining two lives—but the longer term. They needed to figure out where they'd want to raise a child, and what kind of space they'd need.

"We should at least look," Delia said one evening, curled up on the couch with her laptop open to the MLS website, where they'd be able to find homes that had been newly listed. It was a good way to catch things before they hit Zillow or

Redfin. "Even if we don't buy anything right away, it couldn't hurt to see what's out there."

Caleb peered over her shoulder at the screen and watched her scroll through listings. "What are you thinking? Stay in the valley, or head out toward Summerlin?"

"Summerlin, maybe," she replied. "It's a really nice area with good schools. And it's not too far from my parents' house."

He raised an eyebrow. "Is that a selling point, or a warning?"

She elbowed him, even as she grinned. "Selling point...mostly."

So they started looking in earnest, taking some time out from their two current flips to view the homes in person.

The first house they went to was in a new development off the 215, with modern architecture, clean lines, and walls of glass that flooded the space with desert light. Caleb loved it immediately—the open floor plan, the sleek finishes, the way the whole place felt like it belonged in an architectural magazine.

Delia appeared less convinced.

"It's very...." She paused in the middle of the living room and turned in a slow circle so she could take in the space. "White."

He'd had a feeling she'd say something like that. "It's minimalist."

She made a face. "It would be like living inside an Apple store." She ran a hand along the kitchen island, all white quartz and brushed nickel fixtures. "Where would we put the baby's stuff? The high chair and the toys and all the mess that comes with having kids?"

Since the house was nearly four thousand square feet, he guessed there must be someplace to store that kind of crud. "We'd figure it out."

For a second or two, she didn't reply. Then she shook her head. "I really don't want to spend the next eighteen years worrying about fingerprints on the cabinets."

He thought that was a fair point, so they moved on.

The second house was more to Delia's taste—a bungalow in an older neighborhood, all warm wood and built-in shelving and a wraparound porch that looked like something out of a magazine spread about cozy living.

Caleb liked it less.

"It's small," he said as he stood in the master bedroom, which was really more of a master closet with delusions of grandeur.

"It's cozy," she replied, undaunted.

No, cozy was sitting with your feet up and a blanket over your lap while you sipped brandy and had a fire going in the fireplace. This was just...

cramped. "It's barely twelve hundred square feet. Where would we put an office? Or a nursery?"

"There's a second bedroom," she replied calmly.

"That *is* the second bedroom." He gestured at the space around them. "This is the master. And I can touch both walls without fully extending my arms."

Delia looked like she wanted to argue, but she couldn't quite manage it. The house was charming, but it was also clearly designed for a couple without children, or possibly for very small elves.

So they headed over to the third house.

It was a mid-century ranch that had potential—good bones, decent yard, the kind of place that would clean up nicely with a little work. But as they walked through the rooms, Caleb could feel his enthusiasm waning. It was fine, the kind of house you bought because it checked enough boxes, not because it made you feel anything. Really, the house they were in right now was worlds better, even if it wasn't located in Summerlin. He didn't see the point in moving if it was a downgrade from what they already had.

"It's okay," Delia said, echoing his thoughts.

"Yeah."

They looked at each other, and he could see the same disappointment in her eyes. After three days of this, they still hadn't found anything that felt right.

"Maybe we're being too picky," she said as they drove away.

"Or maybe we just haven't found the right place yet," he told her, wanting to offer her what encouragement he could.

The right place, as it turned out, was waiting for them in the Vineyards.

They almost hadn't gone to see it. The listing had popped up that morning, and when Delia had first pulled it up on her phone, she'd been skeptical, mainly because of the price. The home was located in a guard-gated community in Summerlin and had four bedrooms and four baths, with over four thousand square feet. The pictures showed a graceful, Mediterranean-style two-story home with a courtyard entry, all warm stucco and clay tile roofing.

"It might be kind of much," she told him. "Even if it's gorgeous."

The house was listed for over two million dollars. "It's in our price range," he said, and she lifted an eyebrow.

"Two million dollars is our price range?"

They hadn't talked much about finances yet. Delia knew he had a bunch of money squirrelled away, but she'd never asked exactly how much. And while paying cash for their new home might put a dent in his savings, he knew they'd recoup most of it—maybe even all—once he sold his house. Renovated mid-century homes were very hot right now.

"It's not a problem," he told her. "In fact, the last time I was getting stuff out of my old place, one of the neighbors across the street came up and asked if I was going to sell the house. I told him I was, but hadn't gotten around to putting it on the market yet. He offered me 1.5 right then and there. Cash."

Delia's eyebrows lifted. "And when were you going to tell me about this?"

"When I had the chance," he said easily. "Which is now. So the Pueblo Street house will cover most of the cost of this one...if we decide to buy it, of course."

For a moment, she didn't reply. Then she said, "We might as well look. What's the worst that could happen?"

The worst that could happen, as it turned out, was falling in love.

They pulled through the guard gate mid-afternoon that same day, following the winding streets past manicured lawns and impressively large homes until they reached a cul-de-sac at the end of Mersault Court. The house sat at the curve of the circle, its courtyard entrance partially hidden by a low wall topped with wrought iron.

The listing agent met them at the door, a

polished blonde in her fifties who clearly recognized Delia from the business and spent the first five minutes making small talk about the market. Caleb tuned most of it out, his attention caught by the entry courtyard with its fountain and mature plantings, the kind of space that felt private and welcoming at the same time.

Inside, the house was even better than the online photos had suggested. The foyer opened into a proper living room, two stories high, with a curved staircase rising along one wall and a second staircase on the opposite side. Dark wood floors stretched throughout the main level, warm and rich without being oppressive. The kitchen was a cook's dream—Sub-Zero refrigerator, Wolf range, quartzite counters that caught the light from the windows overlooking the backyard. An island big enough to actually work at, with seating for casual meals.

"The previous owners did a full renovation about two years ago," the agent was saying. "New appliances, updated bathrooms, refinished floors throughout."

Caleb followed Delia through the family room, where a stone fireplace dominated one wall, and into a study with built-in bookshelves that made his fingers itch to start organizing. Four bedrooms total—the primary suite downstairs, with a bathroom that featured both a rain shower and a free-standing soaking tub, plus three bedrooms upstairs, one of which was currently configured as a loft library with views over the backyard.

"This could be the nursery," Delia said quietly as she stood in one of the upstairs bedrooms. The windows faced east, catching the morning light, and the room was large enough for a crib, a changing table, and a reading chair. All the things they'd need.

"Yes," Caleb replied. "It could."

They ended up in the backyard, standing by the pool while the agent gave them space to talk. The late afternoon sun slanted through the landscaping, dappling the water with shifting patterns of light and shadow. Beyond the fence, the Spring Mountains rose in the distance, their peaks pale in spots with traces of early-season snow.

"So," Delia said.

"So," he repeated, then waited. He already knew what she was about to say.

"This is the one, isn't it?"

Caleb looked around the yard—at the courtyard they'd entered through, at the house rising behind them with its warm stucco and arched windows, at the pool where their child might learn to swim someday, and finally at the mountains standing watch in the distance.

"Yeah," he said. "I think it is."

They made an offer that evening. Over asking,

because this was Vegas and the market was competitive, and because some things were worth every penny.

Making space for the necessary conversation with her mother turned out to be a lot harder than finding a house. Delia had been putting off that talk for days, finding excuse after excuse to delay the inevitable. She needed to wait until she had more information, until she and Caleb had figured out their living situation. Mercury needed to be out of retrograde, and the stars had to align.

Or something like that, anyway.

But the house situation was handled—their offer had been accepted the day before, and they were scheduled to close in mid-November if all went well—and she was running out of excuses. So on a Thursday afternoon, she found herself sitting in her mother's office at Dunne & Dunne, her hands clasped in her lap and her heart beating somewhere in the vicinity of her throat.

"This is a nice surprise," Linda said as she looked up from her computer and gave her daughter a warm smile. Since the weather had finally started to cool down, she wore a blazer—deep coral today, paired with cream slacks and tasteful gold jewelry—and her hair was still perfectly styled even though they were getting toward the end of their work day. "I thought you were showing that condo in Henderson this afternoon."

"I rescheduled." Delia pulled in a breath and made herself add, "I needed to talk to you about something."

Something in her tone must have registered, because Linda's expression shifted from friendly interest to concern. She closed her laptop and gave her daughter a very direct look.

"What's wrong? Is it Caleb? Are you two—"

"We're fine. Better than fine, actually." Another breath. "Mom, I'm pregnant."

The silence that followed lasted approximately half a second before Linda was out of her chair and around the desk, pulling Delia into a hug that was equal parts fierce and gentle.

"Oh, sweetheart. Oh, my goodness." She pulled back, her eyes already bright with tears, and brushed a stray strand of hair away from her daughter's face. "How far along? When did you find out? How are you feeling?"

Well, at least those were all questions that were easy enough to answer. "About seven weeks. We found out last week, and I saw my doctor the other day to confirm everything. And I'm fine—tired, a little nauseous sometimes, but mostly fine."

Something about her mother seemed to relax

after hearing this news. "And Caleb? Is he happy? Is he being supportive?"

Delia couldn't help smiling as she replied, "Very. We're actually buying a house in Summerlin, in the Vineyards. It has four bedrooms and a big backyard. Definitely room for a family."

Linda's face lit up. "That's wonderful. That's —oh, I'm going to be a grandmother." She laughed, a watery sound that matched the tears now shining in her eyes. "I can't believe it. I'm going to spoil that child rotten, you know. It's a grandmother's prerogative."

"I know." Delia hugged her mother again, feeling some of the tension she'd been holding inside start to relax. This part, at least, had been easier than expected. But there was still more to say.

"Mom, there's something else I need to tell you."

Linda pulled back, her expression now shifting to something more guarded than the obvious joy she'd displayed a moment earlier. "What is it?"

"It's about work." Delia made herself continue to hold her mother's gaze. "I've been doing a lot of thinking lately. About what I want, about where I see myself in five or ten years. And I...." She paused, trying to decide on the best way to phrase what she needed to say next. "I don't think residential sales is where my heart is anymore."

A long moment passed. Delia watched her

mother's expression go through several stages—confusion, realization, and finally something that looked a lot like pain.

"The house flipping," Linda said quietly. "That's what you want to do."

"Yes."

"I see." Linda stepped back, her hands dropping to her sides. She moved to the window and looked out at the parking lot below, her back very straight. "How long have you been feeling this way?"

"A while," Delia replied. "Months, probably. I didn't want to say anything because I didn't want to hurt you, and I kept thinking maybe I was wrong, maybe I just needed to give it more time. But the pregnancy made me realize—" She paused there, then made herself go on. "I don't want to spend the next twenty years doing something that doesn't make me happy. I want to be excited about my work, not just going through the motions."

Still staring out at the parking lot, her mother said, "And flipping houses makes you happy."

"It does. Working with Caleb, seeing a property transform, solving the puzzles of renovation and design—that's when I feel most alive, most myself." She went over to the window so she could stand next to her mother. "I'm sorry. I know this isn't what you wanted to hear."

Linda was quiet for a moment or two. When

she finally turned to face Delia, her eyes were wet again, but her expression had softened.

"Do you know what I wanted when I started this business?" She didn't wait for an answer and instead went on, "I wanted to build something I could be proud of. Something that would last. And part of that—" Her voice caught, but she didn't stop. "Part of that was imagining you here eventually. Carrying on what I'd built."

Even though she'd known her mother would probably say something like this, Delia found herself tensing. "Mom—"

"Let me finish." Linda took her daughter's hands in hers. "I wanted that, yes. But more than that, I wanted you to be happy. To find work that fulfills you, that makes you excited to get out of bed in the morning. And if that's flipping houses instead of selling them...." She managed a shaky smile. "Then that's what you should do."

"You're not angry?" Delia asked. Her entire body still felt tight, waiting for the explosion, even though she realized now it would never come.

She should have understood that. Linda Dunne was not the explosive type.

"I'm disappointed...and I'm allowed to be disappointed." Linda squeezed her hands. "But I'm not angry. You're my daughter, and I love you, and I want you to build the life that's right for you. Even if it's not the life I imagined."

The tears came then for both of them. They stood there in Linda's office, holding each other and crying and laughing at themselves for crying, until they finally pulled apart and her mother started talking about bringing in a new broker to handle Delia's clients and whether they could still do lunch once a week, even if they weren't working together anymore.

"Of course we can," Delia said. "And you can come see the new house as soon as we close. And be there for every ultrasound appointment, if you want."

"Try and stop me." Linda hugged her one more time, fierce and brief. "Now go home to that man of yours and get some rest. You're growing a grandchild in there."

Another hug, and then Delia left the office feeling like a thousand-pound weight had been lifted from her shoulders. One difficult conversation down. Several more to go—her father, eventually Caleb's mother if she could convince him that he needed to reach out to her, all the other people who would need to know—but this had been the most important one.

She was halfway to her car when her phone pinged inside her purse.

A text from Caleb.

Call me when you can.
Something weird at the Catalina
flip. Might be nothing, but I want
your take.

The brightness within her dimmed slightly. She'd learned to trust Caleb's instincts about weird things. In their world, "weird" usually meant trouble.

She touched the button for his number as she got in the car.

The Catalina property was a ranch house in the east valley that they'd been working on for six weeks now. New roof, updated plumbing, complete kitchen renovation. It was supposed to be ready for listing by the end of the month, and Caleb had stopped by for a final walkthrough to make sure everything was on track.

That was when he'd noticed the scratches.

They were small, barely visible unless you were looking for them, clustered around the back door and one of the side windows, the kind of marks that might have come from an animal trying to get in...except no animal Caleb knew of would leave scratches like these. They were too regular, too deliberate.

And the window latch had been tampered

with. He could see the faint marks where someone had worked it open from the outside, then closed it again carefully, trying to leave no trace.

"Nothing's missing," Delia said as she stood beside him in the kitchen. She'd driven straight here after leaving Dunne & Dunne, and now they were both staring at the back door, hoping it might provide some answers. "You're sure?"

"I checked everything," he told her. "The tools are all accounted for, and the materials are where we left them. Even the copper pipes are still here, and that's usually the first thing to go if someone breaks into an unoccupied house."

An unwelcome but generally acknowledged fact. Materials thieves were one of the more unpleasant aspects of flipping houses. "So someone broke in, looked around, and left without taking anything."

"That's what it looks like."

Delia frowned at the scratches on the door frame. "Surveillance?"

It was the same conclusion he'd reached. Someone had broken in not to steal, but to gather information. About the property, about them, about...something.

"I already called Pru," he said. "She's going to check the security systems at our other properties and see if anything else has been compromised."

"Good." Delia was still studying the door, her

expression thoughtful rather than troubled. "This could be nothing, right? Some random break-in where the burglar got spooked before they could take anything?"

"Could be," he allowed.

"But you don't think so."

Caleb shook his head. His demon senses had been prickling ever since he'd walked through the door, that familiar tingle at the back of his skull that usually meant something supernatural was afoot. The scratches themselves didn't feel demonic, but there was still a residue here, a faint wrongness that put him immediately on edge.

"I think we should be careful," he said at last. "Both of us. No more going to properties alone until we figure out what's going on."

Delia nodded slowly. "You think this is connected to...?" She touched her stomach, a gesture he'd noticed her making more often lately. "To what Ty said? About the baby being valuable?"

"I don't know. Maybe, maybe not." He came over so he could wrap an arm around her shoulders. She felt so slender, too delicate to be carrying another life inside her. However, he knew hers was the slender strength of tensile steel, something that would bend but never break. "All the same, I'd rather be paranoid and wrong than careless and right."

"Agreed."

They locked up the property and drove home separately, Caleb in his truck and Delia in her Kona. The whole way back to her house—their house now, he reminded himself—he kept checking his mirrors, watching for anything out of the ordinary.

The streets were clear, and the evening traffic was its normal cloggy mess. Nothing seemed off.

But that prickling sensation at the back of his skull didn't fade, and when he pulled into the driveway and saw Delia's car already there, the relief he felt was sharper than it should have been.

Something was coming. He could feel it.

He just had no idea what it was.

Chapter Seven

PRU'S PHONE CALL CAME JUST AFTER EIGHT the next morning, interrupting the scrambled eggs Caleb was making for breakfast...and letting Delia know something was up, because her friend rarely stirred before eleven unless the apocalypse was happening.

"You need to come over," Pru said. "Both of you. I found some things you're going to want to see."

Delia exchanged a look with Caleb, who had paused with the spatula in midair. Whatever Pru had found, it clearly couldn't wait.

"Give us twenty minutes," Delia told her.

They made it in fifteen.

Pru's condo was in a complex off Las Vegas Boulevard, a tall, ten-story building in a neighborhood of other condos and lofts. After the incident with Vinea in May, she'd converted her second bedroom from storage space into an office that looked like something out of a spy movie, with multiple monitors, server racks humming quietly in the corner, and cables snaking across the floor in organized bundles. A whiteboard covered one wall and was currently filled with what looked like a network diagram connected by arrows and question marks.

"Coffee's in the kitchen," she said as she let them in. Because this morning was chillier than it had been for a while, she wore an oversized black sweater and leggings and Uggs, the ensemble somehow making her look even more petite than usual. A mug sat next to her keyboard. "And there's hot water and herbal tea for you, Delia. Help yourselves. This is going to take a while."

Giving up her morning coffee was not something Delia was particularly enjoying. However, she murmured a thank-you to Pru and got herself some peppermint tea, while Caleb leaned against the doorframe, arms crossed. He'd already had coffee this morning and clearly just wanted to get down to business. "What did you find?"

Pru dropped into her desk chair and pulled up something on her center monitor. "I've been running security audits on all your properties since the Catalina break-in. Two more were accessed."

The peppermint tea was almost sweet, but it

tasted bitter right then. “Which ones?” Delia asked, cradling the mug in both hands.

“Someone disabled the security system at the Henderson flip for about thirty minutes three days ago. No sign of forced entry, but the logs show the alarm was offline between two and two-thirty in the morning.” Pru clicked to another screen and pulled up a timeline of system events highlighted in red. “And the Eastgate property. Same deal as Catalina—scratches on a window, latch manipulated. Nothing taken, nothing damaged.”

“They’re casing all our properties,” Caleb said, eyes narrowing.

“That’s what I thought, too. But it might be worse than that.” Pru swiveled her chair so she faced them, her expression now grim. “I did some digging into other potential breach points. Financial records, business filings, the usual stuff someone might want if they were building a profile on you two. The bank accounts look clean, and the business records haven’t been accessed. But then I started thinking about what else someone might want to know, especially given....” She gestured vaguely at Delia’s midsection.

Delia’s stomach tightened, and she was sort of glad she hadn’t eaten anything that morning. “And?”

“Your medical records were accessed four days

ago. Someone downloaded them from your OB/GYN's patient portal."

What the hell? She set down her cup of tea because her hands had started to shake. "How is that even possible? Those systems are supposed to be secure, right?"

"They are...for normal hackers." Pru's dark gaze was steady. "Whoever did this was good." She pulled up another screen, this one showing lines of code that meant nothing to Delia. "They used a zero-day exploit to get into the portal's backend, grabbed everything in your file, and wiped the access logs. If I hadn't been checking the server's shadow copies, I never would have found it."

Clearly, Pru had been doing a lot more over the past five months than just getting her home office in order. She'd always sworn up and down that she wasn't a hacker, but she'd always been brilliant with computers, and it seemed obvious that someone must have taught her a few new tricks.

Caleb had gone very still. "What records were accessed?"

"Everything in her file," Pru replied. "Medical history, insurance information, appointment schedules." She paused there before adding, "Including the bloodwork that confirmed the pregnancy."

A heavy silence followed that revelation. Delia

found herself pressing a hand to her abdomen, a gesture she now did almost without thought.

"Someone knows," she said.

"Sure looks like it," Pru replied. "And they've been systematically gathering information about both of you—your properties, your routines, your medical status. I can't believe any of this is random. It's targeted surveillance by someone with serious resources and serious skills."

Caleb's jaw, dusted in dark stubble because he hadn't bothered shaving the past couple of days, had tightened. "Can you trace who?"

"I've tried. Believe me, I've spent the last eighteen hours trying." Pru gestured at the whiteboard with its maze of connections. "Whoever's running this operation knows what they're doing, and they've got infrastructure in place to stay hidden."

Delia stared at the whiteboard, at all those arrows leading nowhere. "So we have no idea who's watching us."

"Not yet. But I'm not giving up." Pru reached for her mug and took a sip of what Delia guessed was probably stone-cold coffee. "In the meantime, I've already beefed up security on all your systems. Changed your passwords, added two-factor authentication everywhere I could, and set up alerts for any unusual access attempts. But that's just digital. You need to think about physical security, too."

What, she and Caleb were supposed to go around with bodyguards all the time or something?

She didn't like the idea of that at all.

Maybe it was time to get some additional advice.

"Ty," she said. "We need to talk to Ty."

They met him at a coffee shop in Henderson, a quiet place with booths in the back where they could talk without being overheard. The shop was mostly empty at this hour—a few remote workers with laptops, a mother with a sleeping toddler in a stroller—and the ambient noise from the espresso machine provided enough cover for their conversation.

Ty arrived looking tired, his dark hair pulled back in its usual ponytail, his sky-blue eyes shadowed with something that might have been worry. He slid into the booth across from them and listened without interrupting as Pru walked him through everything she'd found.

"I've been sensing it, too," he said when she was done talking. "Demonic energy, scattered around the valley. But it's strange—I can feel that something's there, but I can't pinpoint any locations. It's like trying to see through fog or hear a conversation through a thick wall. I know there's something on the other side, but I can't make out any details."

"Shielded?" Caleb asked, as if such a possibility wasn't all that strange.

"Has to be. And shielding that effective takes power...serious power." Ty wrapped his hands around his coffee cup, although Delia doubted he actually needed the warmth. "The kind of power that most demons don't have access to. We're talking about someone—or multiple someones—who can mask their presence from angelic senses. That's not a common ability." Another pause, and then he added, "To be honest, I don't think even Vinea could have pulled this off. His power was brute force—overwhelming, yes, but not subtle. Whoever is behind this shielding is operating on a different level entirely. It feels more refined, and a lot more patient."

"The Styx Group?" Delia asked. "I mean, they've been pretty quiet lately, but what if they're not as gone as we thought?"

"Could be them...or it could be something else entirely." Ty's expression was troubled. "The people I work with have been monitoring supernatural activity in the region for months. There's been an uptick since the incident with Vinea, although it's mostly base-level stuff...more possessed individuals, residual dark energy hanging around, which makes sense, considering what Vine and his minions tried to unleash. But this feels deliberate...and focused specifically on the two of you."

"Because of the baby," Caleb said, his voice flat and not sounding very much like his usual insouciant self.

"That's my assumption. A child with your bloodline, Caleb, combined with Delia's psychic abilities...." The words trailed off, and Ty shook his head. "That's going to attract attention from certain quarters, the kind of attention you definitely don't want."

Delia thought about what Ty had said when they'd first told him about the pregnancy. *This child will be powerful. Very powerful.* At the time, it had sounded almost abstract, a problem for the future. Now that future felt uncomfortably close.

"What do we do?" Caleb asked. He didn't look overly troubled, but an edge to his voice told her that he was more tense than he appeared.

"Increase security. You need some wards on your home. I can help with that, and also show you some techniques that should make it harder for anything demonic to approach without triggering an alarm." Ty set down his coffee cup. "And you need to check in with me at least twice a day. If I don't hear from you, I'll assume something's wrong and come looking. And I'll stay on alert and keep monitoring for any changes in those energy signatures."

"And if you find whoever's watching us?" Delia asked.

"Then we'll deal with them." Ty met her gaze squarely, and for a moment, she saw something old and fierce behind the calm expression. "Whatever that takes."

They spent another hour going over logistics—ward placements, emergency plans, backup meeting locations if their primary channels were compromised. Ty drew diagrams on napkins, explaining the theory behind demonic wards and how to strengthen them with the right materials and intentions. By the time they left the coffee shop, Delia's head was spinning.

Caleb took her hand as they walked to the car. His fingers were warm and should have been reassuring. Right then, though, she didn't know whether anything could have given her much comfort.

"We'll figure this out," he told her.

She wanted to believe him.

A week passed. Seven days of heightened awareness, of checking over her shoulder, of jumping at unexpected sounds. Ty's new wards hummed quietly around their house, and they fell into a routine of twice-daily check-ins as they continued to watch for any sign of surveillance.

And absolutely nothing happened.

The silence should have been reassuring. Instead, it felt like the held breath before a scream.

On the eighth day, Delia drove to Spring Valley for a client consultation. The call had come through her old channels at Dunne & Dunne; Linda was still fielding requests for her ghost-clearing services, even though Delia had officially stepped back from residential sales. This one seemed straightforward enough, a family who'd bought a 1960s ranch house six months ago and had been experiencing what they described as "strange feelings" ever since. Cold spots in the hallway, the sensation of being watched...their dog refusing to enter the master bedroom.

Strange feelings usually meant a residual haunting, the psychic equivalent of a water stain on the ceiling. Nothing dangerous, just uncomfortable. She'd done dozens of these consultations during her career, and they rarely took more than an hour.

The house was on a quiet street lined with mature trees, their leaves just starting to turn with the first hints of autumn, which came late in this part of the world. Desert landscaping dominated most of the front yards in the neighborhood, but this house had grass—real grass, brown at the edges from the heat but stubbornly green in the center. Someone must be paying a fortune in water bills to maintain it.

Delia parked at the curb and sat for a moment, centering herself the way she always did before these visits. She visualized her awareness as a door, currently closed, that she could open when she was ready to communicate with whatever might linger in the house.

Then she got out of the car and made her way up the path to the front door.

The moment she crossed the threshold, grief slammed into her. It came without warning, a wave of sorrow so intense that her knees buckled. She caught herself on the doorframe, gasping, while the homeowner, a woman named Becky Ferrera, in her forties with worried eyes and silver threads in her dark hair, rushed forward, asking if she was all right.

Delia couldn't answer. The grief wasn't hers, but it felt like hers, pressing down on her chest, filling her throat with a sob she had to fight to contain. Underneath it came confusion, disorientation, a desperate longing for something lost and irretrievable. The ghost's emotions, but amplified a hundredfold, broadcasting directly into her mind with no filter, no buffer, no control.

Too much. Too loud.

She forced herself to breathe, to find the

boundary between herself and the presence flooding through her. It was like trying to separate two colors of paint that had already been mixed—she could see where her feelings ended and the ghost's began, but pulling them apart took effort, requiring every mental technique she'd ever developed.

Slowly, painfully, she managed to find her footing.

"I'm fine," she told Becky, although she could hear how breathless she sounded. "Just—the energy here is stronger than I expected. Give me a moment."

The consultation took almost two hours instead of the usual half hour or so. The ghost was an elderly man who'd died in the house fifteen years earlier, and he was still confused about his passing, still mourning the wife who'd preceded him by six months. His name had been Harold, and he'd lived in this house for forty-three years, raised three children here, celebrated anniversaries and birthdays and ordinary Tuesday dinners with the woman he'd loved since high school.

Normally, Delia would have sensed his presence as a gentle pressure, maybe caught flickers of his emotional state if she reached for them deliberately. Today, she felt everything—his decades of contentment in this house, his quiet pride in the family he'd built, his bewilderment at finding himself alone, his desperate hope that somehow, somewhere, Margaret might still be waiting for him.

She helped him move on. This wasn't the first time she'd had to talk a spirit through this kind of letting go, so she gently guided him toward whatever came next. She didn't know exactly what that was—she'd never been able to see that far—but she knew the peace that came over spirits when they finally released their grip on the physical world. She felt it wash through Harold, felt his gratitude and his relief and his lingering love for the wife he would finally join, and by the time his presence faded, she was shaking from the effort.

Becky thanked her profusely, pressed a check into her hand, and asked if there was anything else she needed to do. Delia managed to tell her that the house should be fine now, but to reach out if anything continued to feel strange. Afterward, she walked to her car on legs that felt like they might give out at any moment.

The drive home seemed endless. Her head throbbed, and the emotion of every person she passed seemed to press against her awareness...the frustration of a driver stuck in traffic beside her, the joy of a child in a minivan who'd just been promised ice cream, the deep-seated weariness of a construction worker waiting at a bus stop. The couple in the car behind her was arguing about a late electric bill, their anger spiking like static, and a teenager whizzed past on a bike, radiating an anxiety that told her he was late for something important.

Delia knew she'd never felt any of this before. Her ability to speak with ghosts had always been safely contained, and it never followed her after she was done sending a spirit on to the next world. She opened the door when she wanted to, and she shut it when she was done.

Now the door was stuck open, and she had no idea how to close it.

By the time she pulled into the driveway at her house, her fingers were trembling on the steering wheel. She sat there for a moment, trying to gather herself, trying to rebuild some kind of barrier between her mind and the world outside, except the effort only made her head pound that much harder.

Caleb was waiting for her when she got inside. He'd been at the Henderson flip all day, but he must have come back early, because his truck was already in the garage—they were storing the Range Rover and the Mercedes at the Pueblo Street house for now—and he was in the kitchen, pulling ingredients for dinner out of the refrigerator.

"Hey," he said as soon as she came through the door. "How'd the consultation—" He stopped there and looked more closely at her face. "What's wrong?"

"Nothing," she said. "I'm fine. Just tired."

She tried to walk past him toward the bedroom, wanting nothing more than to lie down in a dark room with a cold cloth over her eyes. But he caught her arm. His hand was warm through her sleeve, and the moment he touched her —

Love. Deep, fierce, terrifying love. Fear underneath it—fear about the break-ins, fear about the pregnancy, fear about her safety and the baby's safety, and whether he was strong enough to protect them. Worry, sharp-edged, about the dark circles under her eyes and the pallor of her skin. Determination to keep her safe no matter what, to stand between her and anything that might threaten her. And beneath all of it, a desperate, aching tenderness that made her ache in return.

She gasped and pulled away.

Caleb stared at her. "What just happened?"

"I—" She pressed her hands to her temples. Her head wouldn't stop pounding. "I felt you... everything you were feeling when you touched me."

His eyes narrowed. "That's new."

"That's a massive understatement." She sank onto the couch, suddenly too tired to stand. "It started at the consultation. The ghost's emotions hit me the moment I walked in the door, before I even tried to reach for him. Usually, I have to open myself up deliberately, but this time they just—flooded me. No warning, no way to shut it out. And then on the drive home, I was picking up everyone. Random strangers in other cars, people on the sidewalk. Their feelings were just *there*, pushing into my head whether I wanted them or not."

Caleb sat down as well, although she noticed he was careful not to touch her. "Your abilities are getting stronger."

"They're getting out of control." The words were sharp, her frustration lending an edge to her voice. "I've always been able to manage them. But now...." She shook her head. "It's like someone turned the volume all the way up and smashed the dial."

He was quiet for a moment. Then he said in a murmur, "The pregnancy."

"That's what I'm afraid of." She looked down at her hands as they lay clasped in her lap. Seven weeks along now, barely anything, and yet everything was already changing. "Whatever's happening, it has to be connected to the baby."

Caleb's dark eyes were shadowed with worry. "We need to call Ty."

An hour later, the half angel sat in their living room, his expression thoughtful as Delia described what had happened that afternoon. He listened without interrupting, those clear, sky-colored eyes focused on her with an intensity that might have been uncomfortable if she hadn't grown mostly used to it over the past few months.

"I suspected this might happen," he said when she was done with her story. "The baby's demon blood is interacting with your natural psychic gifts. It sounds like they're amplifying each other. Feeding off each other, in a sense."

"'Amplifying' is one word for it," Delia muttered. She hadn't asked for any of this. How in the world was she supposed to function if she got blasted by everyone in a mile radius the second she stepped out the door?

"It's going to get more intense." Ty's voice was gentle but matter-of-fact. "As the pregnancy progresses, your abilities will continue to expand. The demon blood has its own kind of power, and that power is resonating with what you already have. By the third trimester...." His shoulders lifted, although Delia wasn't sure that he'd shrugged because he also didn't know what was going to happen...or because he did and wanted to shield her from that information for as long as possible. "We'll need to prepare."

"Prepare how?" she asked. "What happens in the third trimester?"

"I don't know exactly. A psychic carrying a part-demon child isn't the sort of thing any of us has encountered before." Ty spread his hands. "But I know it won't be subtle. You'll need to learn to shield yourself, or you'll be overwhelmed every time you're around other people."

"How?" Delia heard the edge of desperation in her own voice. "I've never needed to shield before." Even as she spoke, she knew that wasn't precisely true. During Vinea's assault on the city, she'd learned to build a wall around her mind to keep out the worst of the ley line energy that had flooded through Las Vegas. But that had been different. She'd never needed to use that sort of wall to protect herself from the day-to-day energies around her.

Things were different now, unfortunately.

Very different.

She went on, "When I was working with ghosts, my ability was small enough that it didn't really interfere with my day-to-day life."

"Well, it's not small anymore," Ty replied. "But that doesn't mean you can't learn to manage your talent the way it's manifesting now. The techniques are different, that's all. Instead of controlling a trickle, you'll be learning to control a river."

"That's reassuring," she said dryly.

Maybe a flicker of a smile touched his mouth. "I can teach you. You already know the basics, so I just have to give you more techniques to build walls around your consciousness." His expression turned serious. "It will take practice, and it won't be easy. But you're not helpless here, Delia. You have more power than you realize. The challenge is learning to use it, rather than letting it use you."

She knew she never wanted to experience again the grief that had crushed her in that Spring Valley house.

"When can we start?" she asked.

Three days later, Caleb was back at the Henderson flip. The demolition was supposed to be straightforward—he and his crew were opening up the wall between the kitchen and the family room, removing a non-load-bearing section to create the open floor plan that buyers expected these days. Tony Marchetti was his lead guy, a solid contractor in his fifties who knew his way around a sledgehammer, showed up on time, did quality work, and didn't ask questions when Caleb occasionally displayed more strength than a normal guy his size should have.

The problem was the support beam.

It shouldn't have been there. The blueprints

showed the wall as non-structural, and Tony had checked twice before they started swinging. But somewhere in the sixty years since the house was built, someone had done unpermitted work, adding support where the original plans hadn't called for it. What looked like a simple partition wall was actually helping to hold up a section of ceiling joists.

Tony's sledgehammer connected with the wrong spot.

Caleb heard the *crack* as soon as the sledgehammer made contact, a deep, structural groan that resonated through the house like a wounded animal. He looked up and saw the ceiling sagging, a support beam dropping free of its housing, four hundred pounds of lumber and drywall and roofing material starting to fall directly toward Tony's head.

He didn't think. No, he just moved.

Enhanced strength flooded through him, his demon blood answering his desperate need without hesitation. He closed the six feet between them in a heartbeat, his hands coming up, his body positioning itself between Tony and the falling debris. He caught the beam before it could crush Tony, his arms taking the full weight, his legs bracing against the floor as the impact drove through him.

The force pushed him to one knee. His muscles

screamed with the strain, even with the boost from his enhanced strength; four hundred pounds was four hundred pounds, no matter what kind of blood ran through your veins.

"Tony—*move*—"

Tony scrambled backward, eyes wide, his sledgehammer clattering to the floor as he put some distance between himself and the sagging ceiling. Caleb held the beam, arms trembling, until Tony was clear. Then, slowly, carefully, he lowered it to the floor. The wood groaned as it settled, and a cloud of dust rose from the impact.

In the silence that followed, Tony stared at him. "How the hell did you do that?"

Caleb's mind raced, trying to find a plausible explanation and knowing there really wasn't one. "Adrenaline," he said, doing his best to keep his voice steady. "You hear about mothers lifting cars off their kids, right? Same principle. Emergency strength."

Tony didn't look convinced. His weathered face was pale, and his gaze kept moving between Caleb and the beam on the floor. "That thing weighs four hundred pounds easy. Maybe more with the drywall attached."

"Adrenaline's a powerful thing." Caleb stood from his crouch and brushed the dust off his jeans. "You okay? That was close."

"I'm...yeah. Yeah, I'm okay." Tony ran a hand

over his face, and Caleb saw how his fingers were trembling. "Jesus. If you hadn't been there...."

"But I was. That's what matters." Caleb gestured at the sagging ceiling. "We're going to need to shore this up before we do anything else, and probably get a structural engineer in here to assess the damage."

The shift to practical concerns seemed to help distract Tony from what had just happened. He nodded, his contractor's instincts taking over. They spent the next two hours working on getting some temporary supports in place, then made some calls to the insurance company and the structural engineer Caleb kept on retainer. By the time they had the situation stabilized, the near-disaster had faded into just another construction story, the kind Tony would tell over beers for years to come.

But Caleb couldn't shake it so easily.

He drove home as the sun was setting, his shoulders aching with a kind of fatigue that had nothing to do with physical exertion. His enhanced strength always seemed to take something out of him afterward, a kind of payment for the power he'd borrowed from his demon blood.

Delia found him sitting on the back patio an hour later, staring at the sky as it shifted from orange to purple to the deep blue of early evening.

"Tony called," she said, and settled into the

chair beside him. "He wanted to make sure you were okay. He said you saved his life today."

Caleb shrugged. "He's exaggerating."

She didn't blink. "He told me you caught a four-hundred-pound beam with your bare hands."

Caleb said nothing.

"That's not something a normal person can do," Delia continued. Her tone was quiet, almost contemplative. "Not even with adrenaline. I've seen you do things before—the strength, the speed —but this is the first time someone else has seen it, too."

"I know." He looked at his hands and spread them open in front of him. They looked normal enough, human. But he knew what they were capable of now, the strength that lived in his bones and his blood, waiting to be called upon. "I didn't think. Tony was in danger, and I just—reacted. I let the demon side take over without fighting it."

"And it worked. It saved his life."

"Yes." He closed his hands into fists, then opened them again. "But where does it end? If I start leaning into this, start accepting what I can do, how do I know when to stop? How do I know I won't become...." He couldn't finish the sentence, but he didn't have to.

Like my father.

Delia didn't say anything right away. When she

spoke, her voice was thoughtful rather than worried.

"You saved a man's life today by being yourself, by using the abilities you were born with." She reached over and took his hand, and he braced himself for the flood of emotions she'd described—but either she was getting better at shielding, or he was learning to read her expressions instead, because all he felt was the warmth of her palm against his. "You're part demon, Caleb. That's not going to change. Maybe instead of being afraid of it, you should accept it."

The words echoed what Ty had told him weeks ago, what he'd been telling himself in his weaker moments. *Accept it. Stop fighting.*

"And if accepting it means losing control?"

"You didn't lose control today. You *used* your control. You made a choice in a split second to save someone's life." She squeezed his hand. "That's not the same as letting the demon take over. That's being who you are—all of who you are—and using it for something good."

He wanted to believe her. He wanted to believe that the line between using his powers and being consumed by them was something he could walk without falling.

"You're not your father," Delia continued. "Daniel hid what he was and never let anyone get close enough to see the real him. He was cold and distant and absent even when he was present. You're the opposite of that, Caleb. You're here with me, building a life." Her grip on his hand tightened. "The demon blood is part of who you are... but so is everything else. Your generosity, your warmth. The way you make me laugh when I'm taking myself too seriously." A small smile curved her lips. "The fact that you make really excellent scrambled eggs."

He huffed a laugh despite himself. "That's what defines me? My scrambled eggs?"

"Among other things." She rose from her chair, tugging his hand so he'd stand with her. "Come inside. I'll make dinner for once, and you can tell me about the Henderson property and whether we need to bring in a structural engineer or just burn the place down and start over."

"That's not how house flipping works," he told her, but she only grinned.

"It's how *some* house flipping works. I've seen the shows."

He let her pull him to his feet, let her lead him inside, her hand warm in his. The fear was still there, coiled at the base of his spine, but alongside it was something that might have been hope.

Maybe she was right. Maybe acceptance didn't have to mean losing control.

Maybe it could mean finding it.

Chapter Eight

THE WAREHOUSE SAT AT THE END OF A dead-end road near the airport, in the kind of industrial area that tourists never saw and locals generally forgot existed. Chain-link fencing topped with razor wire surrounded a parking lot full of potholes, and the building itself was a squat concrete rectangle with no windows and a single rusted loading dock. The only indication that anyone had been here recently was the fresh tire tracks cutting through the dirt near the entrance.

Caleb studied the structure from behind a dumpster fifty yards away, his demon senses reaching out to probe the space ahead. Three presences inside, maybe four. Demonic, definitely, but lesser demons rather than anything with real power, the kind of foot soldiers that got assigned to guard duty because they weren't good for much else.

"You're sure this is the place?" he asked.

Pru was crouched beside him, her dark green hair tucked under a black cap and her elfin features tight with focus. She wore all black as usual, but tonight the outfit served a practical purpose rather than an aesthetic one. The Glock holstered at her hip was loaded with blessed ammunition, and she carried two bottles of holy water in her jacket pockets.

"A shell company called Meridian Holdings owns this property," she said, pitching her voice low so they couldn't be overheard. "Meridian is a subsidiary of a subsidiary of a company that traces back to Styx Group through about six layers of corporate fiction. So yeah, I'm sure."

Two weeks of intense investigation had led them here—two weeks of Pru digging through financial records and corporate filings, while Caleb and Ty canvassed the city, looking for any trace of the demonic energy that had been shielding their watchers. The break had come three days ago when Pru had found an anomaly in a utility payment, a single data point that didn't fit the pattern of a defunct company. From there, she'd managed to unravel the whole thing.

"Delia's in position?" Caleb asked.

Pru checked her phone. "Ty has her in the car two blocks east of here. He'll keep her safe."

Caleb really hated the idea of leaving Delia behind, even with Ty watching over her. Her psychic abilities had been growing more unpredictable by the day, and he worried about what might happen if something triggered them while she was alone. But bringing her into a demon stronghold was out of the question. Whatever was waiting inside that warehouse, it wasn't something he wanted her anywhere near.

"All right." He rose from his crouch and rolled his shoulders to loosen the tension that had settled there. "Let's go."

They moved along the fence line, staying low and using the shadows for cover. The night air was cool, the kind of desert evening that made the summer's heat feel like a distant memory. Above them, the sky was clear and dark, the stars washed out by the glow of the city to the west.

The loading dock door was locked, but that didn't matter. Caleb let the fire come to his hands, a controlled burn that heated the metal of the lock until it softened and gave way. The door groaned as he pushed it open, and he felt rather than heard the shift in the air inside, the sudden alertness of the demons who'd detected the noise.

So much for stealth.

The warehouse interior was a single large space divided by makeshift partitions into a series of smaller rooms. Emergency lighting cast everything in a dim red glow, and the concrete floor was stained from decades of industrial use. He moved forward, his senses stretched to their limits, tracking the demonic presences as they converged on his position.

The first demon came around a partition at a dead run, all claws and fangs and mottled gray skin. It was roughly humanoid, maybe seven feet tall, with too many joints in its limbs and eyes that burned like hot coals. A lesser demon, the kind that existed to serve more powerful beings and didn't have much in the way of independent thought.

Flames erupted from Caleb's hands, a concentrated blast that caught the demon full in the chest. It screamed, a high-pitched sound that seemed to come from somewhere other than its throat, and staggered backward. But Caleb wouldn't give it time to recover. He closed the distance in two steps, and drove one fist into its burned chest with enough force to crack bone.

The demon went down. It wasn't dead, but it sure wasn't getting up anytime soon.

Behind him, Pru's gun went off twice. He turned to see her standing over a second demon, this one smaller and faster than the first, with sleek black skin and needle-sharp teeth. The blessed bullets had torn through its shoulder and hip, and it writhed on the concrete, hissing in pain.

Pru didn't hesitate. She pulled one of the holy water bottles from her pocket and poured it directly onto the creature's face. The demon's screams cut off abruptly as the blessed liquid ate through its flesh like acid, and within seconds, it had dissolved into a puddle of smoking goo.

"One more," Caleb said. He could feel it somewhere deeper in the warehouse, circling around to flank them. "Moving to our left."

They pushed forward, past the fallen demon and into the maze of partitions. The third demon was waiting for them behind a stack of crates, and it definitely seemed smarter than the others. Instead of charging, it threw something, a chunk of concrete that caught Pru in the shoulder and sent her sprawling with a muffled curse.

Caleb moved without thinking. Fire bloomed around his fists as he vaulted over the crates and landed on top of the demon, driving it to the ground. It clawed at him, raking furrows through his jacket and into the skin beneath, but he barely felt it. The demon blood in his veins was singing now, demanding release, and he let it have what it wanted.

The fire consumed the demon in seconds. When it was over, nothing remained but ash and the stink of brimstone.

Caleb stood there for a moment, breathing hard, his hands still wreathed in flame. The power felt good, felt *right,* in a way that should have worried him more than it currently did. This was the most he'd used his abilities since Vinea, since the Earl of Hell's ritual had nearly torn open a permanent gateway to the underworld. He'd been holding back ever since, afraid of what might happen if he let the demon side of himself off its leash...if he let all the unholy energies he'd absorbed twine with his demon blood and turn him into something other than Caleb Lockwood.

But holding back meant people would get hurt.

He extinguished the flames with a thought and turned to check on Pru.

She was already on her feet, rubbing her shoulder but otherwise unhurt. "I'm fine," she said before he could ask. "Just going to have a hell of a bruise tomorrow." Her dark gaze swept the warehouse, taking in the aftermath of the skirmish. "Are we clear?"

Caleb reached out with his senses again. The three demons were dealt with, and he couldn't feel any other presences nearby. "Clear."

"Then let's see what they were guarding."

The answer lay behind the final partition, in what had once been an office space. Someone had converted it into a surveillance center, and the sight of it made Caleb's blood burn all over again.

Photographs covered one entire wall. Delia at the Dunne & Dunne office. Caleb working on the Henderson flip. Both of them at the Vineyards house they'd put an offer on. The images were time-stamped and annotated, a meticulous record of their movements over the past several weeks.

But the photographs were only the beginning. A large table dominated the center of the room, and spread across its surface were maps, documents, financial records, bank statements. The floor plans of every property they owned or were renovating. And there were medical records, with Delia's OB/GYN file sitting right there in plain sight.

"Jesus," Pru breathed. "They've been tracking everything."

Caleb moved to the table, his eyes scanning the documents. Purchase histories. Tax records. A timeline of their relationship, starting from the day he'd first walked into Dunne & Dunne to hire Delia as his real estate agent. Someone had been studying them with obsessive thoroughness, building a complete picture of their lives.

And in the center of it all sat a folder marked with Delia's name. Inside were printouts of her bloodwork, the results that had confirmed the pregnancy. Notes filled the margins, written in a language Caleb didn't recognize but suspected was demonic. The word "viable," that one written in

English, appeared multiple times, circled in red ink.

They knew about the baby. They'd known from almost the beginning.

"Grab everything you can," Caleb said. He knew they didn't have time to stand there and be shocked. "We need to know what else they have on us."

Pru was already moving, shoving documents into a duffel bag she'd brought for exactly this purpose. Caleb helped, working quickly and methodically, trying not to think too hard about what all of this meant.

Someone powerful was watching them, someone with resources and patience and a specific interest in Delia's pregnancy. The Styx Group was supposed to be defunct, its leadership scattered after Vinea's defeat, but clearly someone had picked up the pieces and continued the work.

The question was who.

Two blocks away, Delia sat in the passenger seat of Ty's pickup truck and tried not to crawl out of her skin.

She could feel Caleb. Not just the vague sense of his presence that she'd grown accustomed to over the past few months, but something much sharper and more immediate. His adrenaline was a buzz in her chest, his focus a tightening at her temples. When the fight started, she'd felt that, too, and the surge of power when he'd let the fire loose had hit her like a wave of heat despite the cool night air drifting in through the half-open windows of the truck.

Her hands had started to shake. She pressed them flat against her thighs and took a slow breath.

"He's fine," Ty said from the driver's seat. His voice was calm, almost preternaturally so. "I can sense them both. The fight's over."

"I know." She *did* know, could feel Caleb's pulse gradually slowing as the danger passed. But knowing and believing were two different things, and her body hadn't yet gotten the message that it was okay to relax.

Their psychic connection had been growing stronger by the day. They'd always shared a bond—or at least, ever since Laughlin and she'd been exposed to energies that had awoken hidden gifts inside her. But what had started as occasional flashes of emotion had now become a constant low-level awareness, a sense of Caleb's presence that hummed at the edge of her consciousness like a radio playing in another room. She couldn't shut it off. She'd tried, using the shielding techniques Ty had taught her, but where Caleb was concerned, her defenses seemed to have as many holes as Swiss cheese.

Maybe it was the baby. Maybe the demon blood growing inside her was creating some kind of bridge between them that bypassed her normal controls. Or maybe she just loved him too much to keep him out.

Either way, it was getting harder to tell where she ended and he began.

"Something's wrong," she said suddenly.

Ty went still. "What do you mean?"

She didn't have words to explain the dread that had suddenly gripped her. There was a new presence, something she hadn't sensed before, moving through the darkness toward the warehouse. It didn't feel like the demons Caleb had been fighting. Those had registered as hot spots of malevolent energy, angry and simple. This was colder, more calculating, and it was approaching from a direction Caleb and Pru hadn't covered.

"There's another one," she said. "Coming from the side. They don't see it."

Ty reached for the door handle, but Delia was already out of the truck, even though she didn't remember making the decision to move. One moment she was sitting in the passenger seat, and the next she was running, her sneakers pounding against the cracked asphalt of the empty street.

She shouldn't have been able to feel it so clearly,

shouldn't have been able to pinpoint its location with such accuracy. But the baby's power was flooding through her, amplifying everything, and she could see the demon in her mind's eye as if she was standing right next to it. A fourth demon, bigger than the others, smarter. It had waited outside during the fight, letting its lesser brethren serve as a distraction, and now it was circling around to catch Caleb from behind while his guard was down.

She couldn't let that happen.

The warehouse loomed ahead, and she could see the loading dock door standing open, a rectangle of dim red light against the darkness. The demon was approaching from the west side, where a small door led into what had once been an employee entrance. Caleb was inside, his back to that door, and he had no idea what was coming.

Delia reached.

She'd done this once before, during the Vinea ritual, when she'd tapped into the psychic lattice that connected all the sensitive points throughout Las Vegas. That had been different, though. That had been a desperate gamble, a last-ditch effort to stop a demon lord from tearing open a permanent gateway to Hell. This was instinct, pure and raw, her mind stretching out toward the demon with a force she hadn't known she possessed.

Stop.

The word wasn't spoken aloud. It didn't need to be. It was a command, a will made manifest, and it hit the demon like a ton of bricks. A barrier erupted between them, a shimmering wall of psychic energy that materialized in the air directly in the demon's path.

The creature slammed into it and screamed.

Delia felt the impact reverberate through her, felt the demon's rage and pain as the barrier burned against its skin. It staggered backward, clawing at the air, and she pushed harder, forcing the barrier forward, driving the demon away from the door, away from Caleb.

She felt him spin toward the commotion, could feel his shock as he registered the demon's presence and then the barrier, that wall of visible energy holding it at bay. He moved fast, faster than any human could, and a moment later, fire erupted from his hands and engulfed the demon.

The creature's death hit her like a punch to the gut. She gasped, her knees buckling, and then Ty was there, catching her before she could fall.

"I've got you," he said. "Easy. You're all right."

No, she wasn't all right. She was shaking so hard that her teeth were chattering, and there was a ringing in her ears that wouldn't stop. But Caleb was alive, was safe, and the demon that had been about to ambush him was nothing but ash on the concrete.

She'd done that. Somehow, impossibly, she'd done that.

Caleb emerged from the loading dock at a run, Pru right behind him. His worried gaze found Delia immediately, and within seconds, he'd closed the distance between them and pulled her into his arms.

"What the hell was that?" His voice was hoarse, caught somewhere between fear and awe. "Delia, what did you just do?"

"I don't know." The words were shaky, breathless. "I felt it coming, and I just...I reached, and...."

She couldn't finish the sentence. The adrenaline was fading, and in its wake came exhaustion, a sort of aching weariness that made it hard to keep her eyes open. She sagged against Caleb's chest, and he held her tighter, one hand cradling the back of her head.

Ty approached them, his expression thoughtful rather than alarmed. "That was significant power," he said. "Psychic energy strong enough to physically manifest as a barrier and harm a demon. I've seen something similar before, but only from those with angel blood."

"Are you saying Delia is part angel?" Caleb demanded, and Ty immediately shook his head.

"No," he replied, and despite her current weariness and confusion, she couldn't help being a bit relieved. She honestly didn't think she could handle having angel blood on top of everything else. "I'm only saying that Delia's abilities are transforming into something that has similar qualities."

"Because of the baby," she said.

"Almost certainly." Ty's gaze dropped briefly to her midsection. "The demon blood is acting as a catalyst, accelerating the development of your natural gifts. The question is whether you can learn to control it before it becomes dangerous."

"Dangerous how?" Caleb asked. His hands were clenched at his sides, and she guessed he was trying very hard to keep his worry and fear in check.

"Psychic abilities at this level are unpredictable. Without proper training and control, they can overwhelm the user. Burn out the mind." Ty's voice was gentle but matter-of-fact as he continued. "Delia's going to need to work harder than she has been. We need to find time to train every day, not just when we can squeeze it in."

She wanted to argue, wanted to say that she was fine, that she could handle whatever was happening to her. But she was still trembling in Caleb's arms, still feeling the echo of that barrier in her mind like a bruise on her consciousness, and she knew Ty was right.

"Okay," she said. "Every day."

Caleb's arms tightened around her. "We should get out of here. The fire's going to draw attention."

She blinked, then looked past him toward the warehouse. Sure enough, smoke was rising from the loading dock, and she could see a flicker of flames through the open door. Pru must have set a fire to destroy the surveillance center, to eliminate whatever evidence they couldn't carry out.

"There's more," Pru said. Her voice sounded bleak. She was standing a few feet away, the duffel bag slung over her shoulder, and her dark eyes were fixed on Caleb. "Something Ty needs to see."

They moved quickly after that, Caleb half-carrying Delia to Ty's truck while Pru jogged ahead to retrieve her little green Mini Cooper. Within minutes they were pulling away, leaving the burning warehouse behind them. In the distance, Delia could hear sirens beginning to wail, emergency responders drawn by the smoke and flames.

No one spoke during the drive. Delia dozed against Caleb's shoulder, too exhausted to stay fully conscious, her mind drifting in and out of awareness. She caught fragments of conversation, and then they were parking in front of a small house she didn't recognize.

"Where are we?" she asked groggily.

"Ty's place," Caleb said. "We need to go through what Pru found."

They piled out of the cars and followed Ty into the house, a mid-century bungalow that looked as if it had been updated during the past couple of years, with white oak floors and plain white walls. The place was sparse and minimalist, with clean lines and neutral colors and very little in the way of personal effects.

Somehow, it looked like exactly the sort of place where Ty Carter would be living.

Pru emptied the duffel bag onto the small, round dining table and spread out the documents they'd salvaged from the surveillance center. Delia watched as Caleb sorted through them, his jaw tightening with each new discovery.

"They knew everything," he said. "Our properties, our finances, our schedules. They've been tracking us for months."

Ty picked up one of the documents, a printout of what looked like a calendar with various dates marked in red. His expression shifted as he studied it, the color draining from his face.

"What is it?" Delia asked.

"Moon phases," Ty said. "Supernatural significances. Ritual timings." He set the calendar down on the table and pointed to one date that was circled multiple times in red ink with notes scrawled in the margins. "October thirty-first. Halloween."

Delia looked at the notes. She couldn't read the language, but she could make out a few words that had been written in English. *Optimal convergence. Veil thinnest. Maximum power available.*

"Whatever they're planning," Ty said, "it's timed for Halloween." He looked up, meeting each of their eyes in turn. "That's less than two weeks away."

The room fell silent. Delia reached for Caleb's hand and felt his fingers close around hers, warm and steady despite everything.

They'd destroyed the surveillance hub, and they'd taken out the demons guarding it. But they still didn't know who was behind all of this, or what they were planning to do.

And now they had a deadline.

Less than two weeks to figure out what was coming...and find a way to stop it.

"We need a plan," Delia said. Her voice sounded steadier than she felt, and she supposed she should be grateful for that. "We need to figure out who's running this operation and what they want."

"Agreed." Caleb squeezed her hand. "But first, we need to get you home and have you get some rest. You're running on empty."

She wanted to argue, wanted to insist that she could push through, but her body was already betraying her. The exhaustion from the psychic barrier was dragging at her, making it hard to keep her eyes open. And Ty was right. She needed to be stronger, needed to learn to control whatever her abilities were becoming before the next crisis hit.

"Fine," she said. "But we have to start planning tomorrow."

Caleb nodded. "Sure."

They gathered up the documents and headed for the door. Behind them, the calendar lay on the table, that red-circled date staring up at the ceiling like an accusation.

Halloween. Less than two weeks.

And they still had no idea what they were up against.

Chapter Nine

THE DAYS AFTER THE WAREHOUSE RAID had all blurred together in a haze of tension and exhaustion.

Delia stood at the kitchen counter, staring at the coffeemaker as it burbled its way through its cycle, and tried to remember if she'd already eaten breakfast. The morning light streaming through the window seemed too bright, and there was a persistent ache behind her eyes that no amount of sleep seemed to touch.

Not that she was getting much sleep anyway.

Her abilities had been growing stronger every day, and not in ways she could control. Yesterday, she'd walked into the grocery store to pick up a few odds and ends, and had been hit with a wave of emotions so intense that she'd had to abandon her cart and flee to the parking lot. The cashier's anxiety about an upcoming surgery. A toddler's tantrum-fueled rage. The quiet grief of an elderly man buying flowers for his wife's grave. All of it had crashed into her without warning, a cacophony of feelings that weren't hers but felt like they were.

And the ghosts were worse.

She'd always been able to sense spirits when she tried, when she opened herself up deliberately to whatever lingered in a space. Now they came to her unbidden, flickering at the edges of her vision, their emotions pressing against her consciousness like hands against glass. Three days ago, she'd seen a woman in a flowered, big-skirted 1950s dress standing in the corner of their bedroom, and the spirit's confusion and longing had been so overwhelming that Delia had burst into tears before she could get her shields up. She had no idea who the woman could have been, since the house had been built around 2010, long after anyone would have worn a dress like that, but she guessed the ghost must have once lived in the home that had been torn down to make way for the new development.

Caleb had held her while she cried, his arms warm and solid around her, and he hadn't asked questions she couldn't answer. But she'd felt his fear through their bond, the terror he was trying so hard to hide.

The coffeemaker beeped. She poured herself a cup out of habit, then remembered she wasn't supposed to have caffeine and dumped it down the sink.

"You okay?"

She turned to find Caleb in the doorway, already dressed for the day in jeans and a Henley, his sandy hair still damp from the shower. He looked tired, with bruised smudges under his warm brown eyes that matched the ones she saw in her own mirror every morning.

"Fine," she said automatically. "Just forgot I can't have coffee."

He came over to her and pressed a kiss against her forehead. "I can make you some of that herbal stuff Ty recommended. The one that's supposed to help with the nausea."

The nausea. Right. That was the other thing, the constant low-grade queasiness that surged without warning and sent her running for the bathroom at odd hours. The pregnancy books said it was normal, that it should pass by the second trimester, but the books didn't account for carrying a baby that was part demon. She had no idea what was normal for her situation.

"Maybe later." She leaned into Caleb, letting herself draw comfort from his presence. Their connection was as strong as ever, and she could feel his worry, his love, his desperate need to fix things he couldn't fix. "Have you heard from Pru?"

"She texted this morning. Her flight landed at

John Wayne International, and she's heading to the hospital now."

Pru's mother had overdosed three days ago. Katie Nelson had been in and out of rehab for years, had been doing well in California by all accounts, but something had triggered a relapse. The hospital had called Pru as next of kin, and she'd been on a plane within hours.

Delia had insisted that she go. Pru had wanted to stay, had argued that they needed her here with Halloween creeping closer and closer, but Delia had pointed out that Ty was still in town and that family came first. Besides, what could Pru do that the rest of them couldn't? She wasn't psychic or some kind of otherworldly being, wasn't anything but a human with a talent for digging up information.

Now, with Pru gone and the house too quiet, Delia was starting to regret that decision.

"She said she'll try to be back by Friday," Caleb continued. "Depending on how things go with her mom, obviously."

Friday was five days away. Such a short time to go before Halloween arrived, and whatever skull-duggery their enemies had planned reached its culmination.

"Good," Delia said, even though none of this was good at all.

Caleb's arms tightened around her. "Are you training with Ty today?"

"In an hour. He wants to work on my shields some more." She pulled back so she could look up into his face. "What about you? Are you going to be at the Henderson property today?"

"Yeah. Tony's finishing up the electrical, and I need to sign off on the inspection. It should only take a few hours, though."

A few hours. She could handle a few hours alone. The wards Ty had placed around the house were strong, and he could be over here in less than fifteen minutes if anything went wrong. She was fine. Everything was fine.

But then the flash hit her without warning.

It wasn't a vision, not exactly...more like a photograph burned onto her retinas for a fraction of a second. Flames. Smoke. The Henderson house, its windows blown out and its roof caved in. And underneath it all, a sense of wrongness, of danger, of something terrible about to happen.

She gasped, and Caleb's hands were on her shoulders immediately, steadying her.

"Delia? What is it? What's wrong?"

"I don't know." The image was already fading, slipping away like water through her grasping fingers. "I saw...I think I saw the Henderson house. There was fire, and...." She shook her head, annoyed with herself for not being able to hang onto the vision. “It’s gone. I couldn’t hold onto it.”

Caleb’s expression had gone sharp and focused. “Fire at the Henderson property?”

“Maybe,” she replied. “I don’t know if it was real or just my brain misfiring.” She pressed a hand to her temple, where the ache had intensified. “These flashes have been happening more often. Ty thinks they might be precognition, but I can’t control them or make any sense of what I’m seeing.”

“I’ll be careful.” Caleb cupped her face in his hands and leaned down to touch a gentle kiss against her forehead. “I’ll check everything twice before I go inside. And I’ll call you the second I’m done.”

She wanted to tell him not to go, wanted to keep him here where she could see him and feel him and know he was safe. But they couldn’t put their lives on hold because she was having visions she couldn’t interpret. They had bills to pay and properties to flip and a future to build.

Assuming they survived the next five days, of course.

“Okay,” she said. “Be careful.”

He kissed her, slowly and thoroughly, and she felt his love through their bond like sunlight breaking through clouds. Then he grabbed his keys and headed for the garage, and she was alone with the too-bright morning light and the silence of the empty house.

Ty arrived promptly at ten, carrying a paper bag from the tea shop on Eastern Avenue and wearing his usual expression of calm competence. They worked in the living room, Delia sitting cross-legged on the floor while Ty guided her through exercises designed to strengthen her mental shields.

It was hard, exhausting work. Every time she thought she'd built a wall solid enough to keep the world out, something would slip through. She'd feel the echo of Ty's emotions or the distant hum of a neighbor's frustration, and she'd have to start all over again.

"You're improving," Ty said when they stopped to take a break. He handed her a cup of the ginger tea he'd brought. "Your shields held for almost three minutes that time."

She made a face. "Three minutes isn't going to help me when I'm trying to buy groceries."

He only smiled in response to her obvious frustration. "It's a foundation. We can build from here." He settled into the armchair across from her, his clear blue eyes thoughtful. "The precognitive flashes you mentioned to Caleb. How often are they happening?"

"Two or three times a day, maybe," she said. "Sometimes more." She wrapped her hands around the warm cup, letting the heat seep into fingers that felt perpetually chilled. "They're never clear. Just fragments, images that don't make sense. And they're gone before I can really see them."

"That's common with emerging precognition. The ability develops faster than the mind's capacity to process it." He paused. "Have any of them come true?"

Delia was quiet for a moment as she considered his question. "I'm not sure. Last week, I had a flash of Pru crying, and then two days later, she got the call about her mom. But that could have been a coincidence."

"Or it could have been genuine precognition, filtered through your emotional connection to her." Ty placed his hands on his knees and leaned forward slightly. "Your abilities are developing along multiple axes simultaneously. Empathy, clairvoyance, precognition. That's unusual but not unheard of, especially given the circumstances."

The circumstances. A nice, clinical way of saying that she was pregnant with a quarter demon's baby and her mind was being reshaped by forces she didn't understand.

"Can I ask you something?" she said.

"Of course," he said.

His immediate response should have been

encouraging. However, just because he'd told her she could ask the question, that didn't mean he would necessarily give her the answer she was looking for. But she plunged in anyway and asked, "What happens if I can't control this? If the abilities keep growing and I can't build shields strong enough to handle them?"

Ty was quiet for a moment, his expression unchanged. "That's unlikely. You're stronger than you give yourself credit for."

"But if it did happen," she pressed. "What would it look like?"

Another pause, longer this time. "Psychic burnout is rare, but it does occur. The mind becomes overwhelmed by input it can't process, and it shuts down to protect itself. In mild cases, it results in temporary loss of abilities, headaches, disorientation. In severe cases...."

He didn't finish the sentence. He didn't have to, because Delia already knew that the worst-case scenario was her mind shutting down entirely, becoming basically a vegetable.

"That's not going to happen to you," he continued, his voice firm. "We're going to train every day, and you're going to learn to manage what's happening. The baby's influence on your abilities will stabilize as the pregnancy progresses. Right now, everything is in flux because your body is adjusting. It will get easier."

Delia wanted to believe him. She wanted to believe that this chaos inside her head was temporary, that she would emerge on the other side with her sanity intact and her abilities under control. But she'd felt the power that had surged through her at the warehouse, the barrier she'd created without thinking, and she knew that whatever she was becoming, it wasn't small, and it definitely wasn't safe.

"Okay," she said. "Let's keep going."

They worked for another hour before Ty declared her done for the day. He left with promises to return tomorrow and instructions to rest, to eat well, to practice the breathing exercises he'd taught her whenever she felt overwhelmed.

After he was gone, Delia curled up on the couch with a blanket and tried to nap. The house was quiet, the wards humming at the edges of her awareness like a constant low note. She closed her eyes and let herself drift...

...the sound of her phone ringing jolted her awake.

She grabbed it from the place where it lay on the coffee table, her heart beginning to pound the second she saw Caleb's name on the screen.

"Caleb? Are you okay?"

"I'm fine." But his voice was tight, too controlled in a way that told her he was anything but fine. "There was an accident at the Henderson property. Gas line rupture. The place exploded about ten minutes after I got Tony out."

The image from this morning flashed through her mind. Flames. Smoke. Windows blown out.

"Oh, God." She was on her feet at once. "Are you hurt? Is Tony—"

"We're both okay," Caleb reassured her. "I smelled the gas before it ignited and got us out in time." A pause. "Delia, that gas line was fine yesterday. I checked it myself. Someone sabotaged it."

A chill walked its way down her spine. "Someone tried to kill you."

"I don't think so. An explosion like that would injure me, maybe badly, but it wouldn't kill me. Not with my healing abilities." Another pause, a longer one this time. "I think it was meant to distract me. To keep me busy dealing with the fire marshal and the insurance company while you were alone."

She looked around the empty house, at the wards she couldn't see but could feel, at windows that suddenly seemed too large and too exposed, even though the street outside looked serene and utterly normal, just as it always did. Across the way, Carrie Sneed was walking her miniature schnauzer.

"I'm fine," Delia said, and tried to believe those words. "The wards are holding. Nothing's tried to get in."

Those reassurances didn't seem to mean much

to him. "Stay inside," Caleb admonished her. "I'll be home as soon as I can, but I have to deal with the authorities first. They're going to want a statement, and I need to make sure they don't find anything they shouldn't."

Anything demonic, he meant. Any evidence that the explosion was caused by something other than faulty construction.

"Okay," she said. "Be careful."

"I will. I love you."

"I love you, too."

She ended the call and stood there in the middle of the living room, her hand pressed to her stomach, her heart racing. Outside, the October sun was bright and warm, and somewhere in the distance a dog was barking. Everything looked normal...and everything felt horribly, terribly wrong.

They could attack their properties. They could sabotage Caleb's work, threaten their livelihood, create chaos and distraction whenever they wanted. The surveillance hub had been destroyed, but whoever was behind this had other resources, other ways to strike.

Nothing was safe anymore.

Caleb didn't get home until after dark. By then, Delia had paced the length of the house approximately a thousand times, had checked and rechecked every ward, had called Ty twice for reassurance that the protections were still intact. She'd tried to eat dinner and managed half a sandwich before her stomach rebelled. She'd tried to watch television and couldn't focus on anything for more than a minute at the most.

When she finally heard the garage door open, the relief that flooded through her was so intense that her knees nearly buckled.

Caleb came through the door looking like he'd aged ten years since this morning. His clothes were rumpled and smelled faintly of smoke, and there was a smear of soot on his cheek that he'd apparently missed when cleaning up. But he was whole and alive, and when he pulled her into his arms, she held on like she was drowning and he was the only solid thing in the world.

"I'm okay," he murmured against her hair. "Everything's okay."

It wasn't. They both knew it wasn't. But she let herself believe it for a moment anyway.

They ended up on the couch, her head on his chest and his arm around her shoulders. He told her about the explosion, about the investigation, about the careful lies he'd had to construct to explain how he'd known to get out before the blast.

The fire marshal had ruled it an accident, at least preliminarily. Faulty valve, they said. Could have happened to anyone.

But Caleb and Delia both knew better.

"I can't figure out their game," he said. His voice was hoarse with exhaustion. "If they wanted me dead, they could have used something more effective. If they wanted to hurt you, they would have attacked the house, not a flip property. It's like they're playing with us."

"That's exactly what they're doing," Delia replied. "They want to keep us off-balance and wear us down, make us jump at shadows."

"It's working." His arm tightened around her. "I keep running scenarios in my head. What if they attack the Summerlin house before we close? What if they go after your parents? What if they find a way past the wards?" He paused. "What if I'm not there when they make their move?"

She felt his fear through their connection, the raw terror he was trying so hard to contain. It matched her own, fed it, amplified it until she wasn't sure where his panic ended and hers began.

"Caleb." She pushed herself up so she could look at his face. "You can't protect me from everything. You know that, right?"

His jaw tightened. "I can try."

"And you'll wear yourself out trying. You'll make mistakes because you're exhausted. You'll miss something important because you're so focused on keeping me safe that you can't see what's right in front of you." She reached up to touch his cheek, her fingertips brushing over the smear of soot he'd missed. "We need to be ready. Both of us, not just you."

"I know." But his eyes were dark, haunted. "I just keep thinking about what could have happened today. If I hadn't smelled the gas. If Tony had been closer to the blast. If you'd been with me—"

"I wasn't. And you did smell it, and Tony's fine, and we're both here, right now, together." She held his gaze. "I'm scared, too. I'm terrified of what's happening to my abilities, and I'm terrified of Halloween, and I'm terrified of what's growing inside me and what it might mean. But I can't let that fear paralyze me, and neither can you."

He was quiet for a long moment. Then he pulled her back against his chest, his chin resting on top of her head.

"When did you get so wise?" he asked.

"I've always been wise," she said archly. "You just don't always listen."

He let out a laugh, and some of the tension in his body seemed to ease. "That sounds like something Pru would say."

"Where do you think I learned it?"

Another chuckle. Then they sat there in the

quiet of the living room, the wards humming around them, the October night pressing against the windows. In less than five days, whatever had been building would reach its peak. They still didn't know who was behind it or what they wanted or how to stop them.

But they would face it together. That was the one thing she was sure of.

Even if they were both scared out of their wits.

Chapter Ten

THREE DAYS BEFORE HALLOWEEN, DELIA was in the kitchen, forcing herself to eat a bowl of oatmeal that tasted like wet cardboard and wondering if the universe would judge her for chucking it and driving over to the closest In-N-Out for a single with cheese when her phone pinged. Lately, she'd been getting a lot of spam, so for a second or two, she ignored it. But something made her glance idly down at the screen.

> Does he know what you're carrying?

She stared at the words, spoon frozen halfway to her mouth. Then she set it down and picked up the phone with fingers that had already begun to shake.

The number wasn't one she recognized. No

contact name, no identifying information. Just those six words, stark and black against the white background of her messaging app.

Her first instinct was to show Caleb, who was in the garage installing a new toolbox in his truck. But she hesitated. He'd barely slept since the explosion at the Henderson property, and seemed to spend his nights wandering the house, checking the wards and running through backup plans that grew more elaborate by the hour. The shadows under his eyes had deepened until he almost looked as if he was sporting a couple of shiners, and his temper had grown short in ways that weren't like him at all.

Adding yet another worry to his plate felt cruel.

Delia told herself it was nothing—a wrong number, or some kind of new and disturbing phishing scam. She deleted the message and went back to her oatmeal, which had grown cold and even less appetizing during the interruption.

The second message came about an hour later, while she was sitting on the couch and trying to focus on the book she'd been reading for the past three weeks without making much progress. Everyone had told her she needed to rest and give herself some downtime, but the words on the page kept blurring together as her thoughts wouldn't stop circling back to Halloween and the warehouse and the calendar with its red-circled date.

Her phone pinged again, and she reached to pick it up. The words she saw there made her heart begin to slam against her ribs in slow, heavy strokes.

> Demon babies don't survive in human wombs.

A different number this time, from another unknown sender, a message that seemed calculated to drive straight to the center of her deepest fears. She'd been telling herself that the pregnancy would be fine, that Caleb's mother and the rest of the cambions' wives in Greencastle had carried half-demon children to term without any problems... that whatever was growing inside her was strong and healthy and wanted.

But she didn't know that for sure. No one did. There were no books about demon pregnancies, no websites with helpful tips, no community of experienced mothers she could turn to for advice. She was navigating blind, and every reassurance she'd given herself suddenly felt hollow.

She deleted the message.

The third text arrived while Caleb was in the shower, the water running loud enough that he wouldn't hear her phone ping again, that sharp little chime now like a harbinger of doom.

> You should be afraid of what's growing inside you.

Her hands began to shake. Three messages from three different numbers, all targeted at the same deep-seated fear. This couldn't possibly be random. Someone knew about her pregnancy, knew about the baby's demon blood, and wanted her to be scared.

Well, it was working.

She sat on the edge of the bed, phone clutched in her trembling fingers, and forced herself to think rationally. The surveillance hub they'd destroyed had contained her medical records. Whoever was behind this had known about the pregnancy for weeks, had most likely been planning this kind of psychological warfare from the moment they'd learned she was carrying Caleb's child.

Knowing where all this had probably come from didn't make it hurt any less.

She knew she should tell Caleb. But when he emerged from the bathroom with a towel around his waist and water dripping from his hair, she looked at the exhaustion carved into his handsome, beloved face and couldn't make herself add to it. He was already carrying so much, was already stretched so thin. What good would it do to burden him with something neither of them could control?

"Everything okay?" he asked.

"I'm fine," she said. "Just tired."

He studied her for a moment, and she could

feel him reaching out through the connection they shared, trying to read her emotions. She pushed back gently, not blocking him entirely but muting the sharp edges of her fear. It felt wrong to hide from him, but she told herself this was only temporary, just until he got some rest.

Just until she figured out how to handle this on her own.

"You should try to nap," he said. "Ty won't be here for another couple of hours."

"I will," she promised.

He kissed her forehead and went to get dressed, and she sat on the bed with her phone in her hand, wondering how long she could keep this to herself.

Because of course the messages kept coming.

By the end of the first day, she'd received seven of them. Each came from a different number, one impossible to trace, and each had been carefully designed to burrow into her brain and take root like poison.

> You're not strong enough.
>
> He'll leave you when he sees what you become.
>
> The baby will kill you.

She deleted every hideous text as soon as it appeared, but the words stayed with her, echoing in her mind. When she closed her eyes to take a nap, she saw them floating in the darkness like accusations. When she tried to meditate during her training sessions with Ty, they intruded on her concentration and shattered her focus, sending her carefully constructed shields crumbling into nothing.

Ty immediately noticed something was wrong. Of course he did. His angelic senses were too sharp to miss the way her anxiety was flaring all over the place, the way her hands trembled when she thought no one was watching.

"What's the matter?" he asked during a break in their afternoon session. He handed her a cup of the ginger tea he'd brought, his clear blue eyes searching her face. "Beyond the obvious, I mean."

She almost told him then. The words were right there, filling her mouth, demanding to be spoken. But something held her back, maybe stubborn pride or misguided protectiveness, and she found herself saying, "Just the usual. Pregnancy hormones and impending doom."

He didn't look convinced, but at least he didn't press.

By the second day, she'd received twelve more messages. They were getting progressively worse, even more personal, more targeted. Whoever was sending them knew things they shouldn't know, things about her relationship with Caleb, about her fears for the baby...about the guilt she carried for not being stronger.

> He's only staying because of the baby. Once it's gone, so is he.
>
> Your powers are destroying you from the inside. Can't you feel it?
>
> The child will be born with its father's hunger. It will consume you.

Each message was a knife, sliding between her ribs and twisting. She found herself checking her phone compulsively, unable to stop herself from reading each new horror as soon as it arrived. The rational part of her brain knew she should block the numbers, should stop engaging with the psychological warfare, but the numbers kept changing, and the messages kept finding her no matter what she did.

And then....

> Your mother deserves to know what kind of monster her daughter is creating.

She was sitting in the living room, alone because Caleb had gone to meet with the insurance adjuster about the Henderson property, when the message arrived. She read it three times, and on the third reading, the tears that had been burning in her eyes began to fall.

Her mother, who had been so happy about the pregnancy, so excited to become a grandmother. She'd already started talking about nursery colors and baby showers and all the ways she planned to spoil her first grandchild. She had no idea that her grandchild would be part demon, that the baby growing in Delia's womb carried blood from creatures that existed only in nightmares.

What would her mother say if she knew the truth? Would she still be excited? Would she still look at Delia with that warm pride, still talk about the future with such joy? Or would something in her eyes change, some fundamental trust shattered beyond repair?

Delia had never lied to her mother about anything important. She'd talked to her about the way Bill had broken off their engagement and walked out, had discussed every significant relationship and career decision and life choice she'd ever made. But this, the truth about Caleb, about what he was and what their child would be, she'd kept hidden. She'd told herself it was for Linda's protection, that some truths were too dangerous to share, but the message had stripped away that comfortable justification.

She was lying to her mother. And the lie was only going to grow bigger.

The front door opened, and Caleb walked in.

He took one look at her face and came over in a rush, dropping to his knees in front of her. Voice urgent, he asked, "What happened? Are you hurt? Is it the baby?"

"No, I'm not hurt." She could barely get the words out past the constriction in her throat. "It's nothing. I'm fine."

"You're crying." His hands reached up to touch her face, strong fingers brushing away the tears that wouldn't stop falling. "Talk to me. Please."

She knew she should have told him from the beginning. Keeping all this to herself hadn't protected him, hadn't protected either of them. It had only made her feel more isolated, exactly like whoever was sending the texts wanted.

"I've been getting messages," she said. "Texts from unknown numbers. They started yesterday."

His expression changed at once, concern giving way to something harder and more dangerous. "What kind of messages?"

Without saying anything, Delia handed him the phone.

She watched his face as he scrolled through the texts she hadn't been able to bring herself to delete, even though she'd tried. His jaw tightened as he read each one, the muscles in his neck cording with suppressed rage, and by the time he reached the last message, the one about her mother, his eyes had gone cold in a way she'd never seen before. The warm brown had darkened to something closer to black, and she could feel his fury like heat radiating out from a furnace.

"I'm going to find whoever sent these," he said quietly. His voice was calm, almost gentle, but she could hear the rage underneath. "And I'm going to make them regret it."

"How?" She heard the edge of hysteria in her own voice but couldn't seem to control it. "We don't know who they are. We can't trace the numbers, and we can't track the source. We can't do anything except sit here and wait for the next one to arrive."

"There has to be a way. Pru could—"

"Pru's in California, dealing with her mother's drama. And even if she weren't, she already tried to trace the surveillance network and didn't get anywhere. These people know how to hide."

Caleb's hands were clenched into fists at his sides, and his rage seemed almost like a physical thing, a white-hot fury that wanted an outlet and couldn't find one. He was a man of action, built to fight and protect and solve problems through force of will, and this enemy had found the one way to neutralize him. You couldn't punch a text message. You couldn't burn down a spoofed phone number.

"Why didn't you tell me?" he asked.

The question wasn't accusatory, but she felt the hurt underneath it nonetheless. They were supposed to be partners, supposed to face things side by side, and she'd been hiding something this significant for two days.

She knotted her fingers together, idly noting how thin and pale they looked, and stared down at them as if they belonged to someone else. "Because you're barely holding together as it is. I didn't want to add to all the things you're already dealing with. I thought maybe if I ignored them, they would give up." The tears were flowing freely now, and she didn't try to stop them. "They're in my head, Caleb. They know exactly what I'm afraid of, and they're using it against me. Every fear I've had about this pregnancy, every doubt, every moment of weakness—they know all of it."

He pulled her into his arms and held her while she cried, his hand stroking her hair, his voice murmuring reassurances she couldn't quite hear over the sound of her own sobs. The connection they shared allowed her to feel his helplessness, his desperate need to fix something that couldn't be fixed.

When the tears finally subsided, he pulled back and looked at her face.

"We need to tell Ty," he said. "He might be able to sense something, figure out who's behind this."

She nodded, too drained to argue, even though she wasn't sure Ty could do anything about their unknown troll.

Caleb made the call, and twenty minutes later, Ty was sitting in their living room, scrolling through the messages, brows drawing together in concentration while he read. His dark hair was pulled back in its usual ponytail, and he was dressed simply in jeans and a dark gray Henley, but there was nothing simple about the intensity in his sky-colored eyes as he read each poisonous text.

"Psychological warfare," he said once he'd finished reading. He set the phone down on the coffee table and looked at Delia with something approaching sympathy. "Classic destabilization tactics. They're trying to break you mentally before Halloween."

"But how do they know so much?" Delia asked. "Some of these things, they're not just lucky guesses. They know about the pregnancy, about my worries, even about my relationship with my mother. How?"

Ty leaned back in the armchair, his fingers steepled in front of him. "The surveillance operation we destroyed would have given them extensive information about your daily lives. Your medical records were accessed. They've had weeks to study you and identify your vulnerabilities, to map out exactly which buttons to push." He paused there, then went on, "Just the mere fact that they're resorting to these sorts of tactics suggests they view you as a significant threat. They want you destabilized and unable to mount an effective defense when the time comes."

"So what do we do?" Caleb demanded. "How do we stop them?"

"You can't stop the messages," Ty replied. "Not directly, anyway. The numbers are spoofed, the accounts are disposable, and the senders are almost certainly using multiple layers of anonymization that would take weeks to unravel." His voice was calm but serious, seeming to signal that he'd seen this kind of tactic before. "What you can do is refuse to let them succeed. Recognize the messages for what they are—manipulation, not truth. The fears they're exploiting are real, but the conclusions they're pushing you toward are not."

Delia looked down at the phone on the table, at the screen that had become a portal for poison. "That's easy for you to say. You're not the one getting them."

"No," Ty agreed. "But I've seen this tactic used before, and I've seen it fail. The people who use psychological warfare are counting on their targets to isolate themselves, to push away the people who might help them. The countermeasure is connection. Talk to each other...talk to me. Don't let them convince you that you're alone in this."

She reached for Caleb's hand and felt his fingers close around hers, warm and solid and real.

"From now on," Caleb said, "you tell me when they come. Every single one. No more trying to protect me from things I need to know."

She nodded. "I will."

Seeming to think that the matter was settled, Ty stood, although his expression remained grave. "I'll see what I can learn from the energy signatures on these messages. There may be traces I can follow, threads I can pull. In the meantime, I need both of you to come to my place tomorrow. There's something we need to discuss."

The way he made the request made Delia's stomach tighten in a way that had nothing to do with her pregnancy. "What kind of something?"

"I've been in contact with others on our side. They have some information about what's building toward Halloween." He paused, and something in his eyes made her wish she hadn't asked. "It's not good news."

Of course it wasn't. At this point, she wasn't sure she remembered what good news felt like.

The next day, they headed over to Ty's house.

The half-angel looked exhausted. No, he wasn't sporting the kind of shadows that had marred

Caleb's eyes for the past week—maybe half angels had the kind of genetics that would prevent that sort of thing—but the tension in his shoulders and the stubble on his chin seemed to suggest he hadn't been sleeping very well, either. His small house was as spare and minimalist as Caleb remembered, but today there were papers scattered across the dining table and a map of Las Vegas pinned to one wall, a map marked with symbols Caleb didn't recognize. Red dots were clustered in certain areas, connected by lines that formed patterns he couldn't interpret.

"My people have been tracking supernatural activity across the city for the past two weeks," Ty said. He stood in front of the map, his posture straight despite his obvious fatigue. Caleb couldn't help noting that the half angel was very careful not to call out exactly who he was working with, although it had to be other half angels or people who had at least some angelic blood. "Since the warehouse raid, things have escalated significantly. We're seeing incidents everywhere, with multiple factions that don't normally interact suddenly moving in concert."

"What kind of incidents?" Delia asked. She was sitting next to Caleb on Ty's gray couch, her hand in his, and he could feel her fear through their connection, a steady thrum of anxiety that matched his own.

"Possessions. Hauntings. Demonic infestations

in places that have never shown any sign of supernatural activity before." Ty moved to the map and traced a finger along a series of red marks that formed a rough circle around the city's center. "The pattern suggests coordination. Someone is stirring things up deliberately, creating chaos that's pulling my people's resources in a dozen different directions at once."

Caleb studied the map, his jaw tight. "So while we're dealing with small fires everywhere, whoever's behind this is preparing something big."

"That's our assessment, yes." Ty turned to face them, his expression grave. "The veil between worlds is always thinnest on Halloween. Demon powers are amplified, barriers are weakened, and rituals that would be impossible at other times become possible. Whatever they're planning, they've timed it for maximum effect."

"And your people can't help us?" Delia's voice was steady, but Caleb could feel a shimmer of fear beneath her words.

Ty hesitated, and that hesitation told Caleb everything he needed to know before the other man even spoke. "I'll stay as close as I can. But I may not be able to be with you every moment over the next few days. The incidents are spreading, and I'm being called to respond to situations across the valley. Last night alone, three separate manifestations required intervention." He paused, and when he continued, his voice was heavy with regret. "I'm sorry. I know this isn't what you wanted to hear."

Great. Just great. They were losing their strongest ally at the worst possible time. Pru was still in California dealing with her mother's overdose, and now Ty would be stretched thin, pulled in multiple directions by a threat that seemed designed specifically to isolate them.

"Do your people know what the target is?" he asked. "What are the demons actually planning to do on Halloween?"

Ty shook his head. "Not specifically. The coordination suggests something significant, but we haven't been able to identify the focal point." His gaze moved between Caleb and Delia, and something in his expression made alarm bells go off in Caleb's mind. "However, given the surveillance on you and Delia, given the timing of her pregnancy and the interest they've shown in the baby...."

He didn't finish the sentence. No need to, right?

Delia's hand tightened on Caleb's. "We're the target."

"I believe so, yes." Ty's voice was gentle but unflinching. "The child you're carrying represents something significant. A partial demon born to a psychic mother, conceived during a period of heightened supernatural activity. Some factions would see such a child as a threat to be eliminated.

Others might view it as an opportunity to be exploited."

Neither option sounded at all good, but Caleb thought he'd focus on the one that seemed slightly more ominous. "An opportunity for what?" he demanded.

"Power. Leverage. A weapon to be shaped and wielded." Ty's shoulders lifted, and he went on, "I don't know their specific intentions. But I know they've invested considerable resources in tracking you, studying you, and now destabilizing you. That suggests they have plans, and those plans center on Halloween."

They were all quiet for a moment. Caleb stared at the map on the wall, at all those red marks scattered across the city like drops of blood, and tried to process what they were facing.

They had two days until whatever was coming finally arrived...and they would have to face it with diminished support and no clear understanding of what they were up against.

"So...what should we do?" Delia asked. Her voice was quiet but filled with resolve, and a surge of love went through him as he thought of her courage, her determination to protect the child she carried.

Ty came over to them and knelt in front of the couch, his clear blue gaze meeting each of theirs in turn. "You stay alert, and you stay together. Don't go anywhere without checking in with me first. And always remember that you're stronger than you know, both of you. What you did at the warehouse, the power you manifested"—and now he looked directly at Delia—"that wasn't a fluke. That's who you're becoming."

"That's not much of a plan," Caleb said.

"No," Ty agreed. "But it's what we have. I'll be monitoring the situation continuously, and I'll come the moment you need me. If anything happens, anything at all, you call. Don't try to handle it alone."

He rose and walked them to the door. Before they left, he put a hand on Caleb's shoulder.

"Protect her," he said quietly. "But don't forget to let her protect you, too. That's how you'll get through this."

Caleb nodded, not trusting himself to reply.

During the drive home, neither of them spoke. Delia stared out the window at the passing streets, at the Halloween decorations that had sprouted on lawns and storefronts throughout the city. Carved pumpkins grinned from porches. Fake cobwebs stretched across bushes. Skeleton figures dangled from trees, their plastic bones rattling in the dry desert wind.

Las Vegas was preparing for Halloween, the Strip hotels putting up elaborate displays and the costume shops doing brisk business with tourists who had no idea what was building beneath the surface of their party destination. Soon, the streets would be flooded with people in costumes, celebrating a holiday that had once been about honoring the dead and now was mostly about candy and revelry.

Somewhere in that chaos, their enemies would make their move.

When they got home, they sat in the living room as the afternoon light faded toward evening. Neither of them seemed to have the energy to move, to do anything but exist in the quiet space they'd carved out for themselves.

"I'm scared," Delia said at last. Her voice was almost monotone, as if she didn't have the resources to inject much emotion into those two words.

Caleb pulled her closer and pressed his lips to her hair. "Me, too."

"What if we can't stop them? What if they take the baby, or hurt you, or—"

"Hey." He tilted her chin up so he could look directly into her eyes. "We don't know what's coming. Not exactly. But we know we're going to fight like hell when it gets here."

She studied his face for a moment, and he felt her reaching out to him through their connection, searching for something. Reassurance, maybe. Or possibly just the truth.

"Do you really believe that?" she asked. "That we can get through this, I mean?"

For a second or two, he wondered if he should hand her a little white lie, should give her the confident answer she probably wanted to hear. But she would feel the deception through their connection, and she deserved better than false comfort.

And they'd promised to always be honest with one another.

"I believe that whatever comes through that door on Halloween, they're not taking you or our baby without going through me first," he said. "And I don't plan on making that easy. If they want a fight, they'll get one."

She was quiet for a few beats. Then she leaned up and kissed him, soft and fierce at the same time.

"Then that's what we'll give them," she said.

Outside, the sun finished setting, and the darkness of another night settled over the city. Caleb held Delia close and watched the shadows deepen beyond the window.

They would be ready.

They had to be.

Chapter Eleven

DELIA STOOD AT THE LIVING ROOM window and watched the sun sink toward the western mountains as the sky turned shades of soft orange and dusky purple that should have been beautiful. Instead, all she could see were the wards shimmering at the edges of her vision, the invisible barriers that Ty had strengthened just yesterday, barriers that were meant to keep danger out but increasingly felt like they were keeping her trapped inside.

Behind her, Caleb was prowling restlessly, reminding her of nothing more than a caged jungle cat. He'd been doing that for the past hour, moving from room to room in a circuit that had become numbingly familiar over the past few days. Kitchen to living room to hallway to all four bedrooms and bathrooms and then back again, pausing at each window to scan the street, checking each door to make sure the locks were engaged, touching the ward-points Ty had marked with a kind of compulsive repetition that made her want to scream at him to stop.

Of course, she wouldn't do anything so crazy.

Not yet, anyway.

"The Rodriguezes just pulled into their driveway," she said as she watched their neighbors' minivan ease past the mailbox. "Should I call Ty and report the suspicious activity?"

Caleb stopped mid-pace and stared at her, brows lowering. "That's not funny."

"It wasn't meant to be." She turned away from the window and took in the dark circles under his eyes, the tension in his shoulders, the way his hands kept flexing at his sides as if he was fighting the urge to summon fire, or maybe just punch a demon in the face. He looked like he hadn't slept in days, which was accurate, because he hadn't. Neither had she, really, but at least she'd managed to lie still in bed for a few hours each night. Caleb had spent those hours roaming the house, checking and rechecking protections that were already as strong as Ty could make them.

"I need to get out of here," she said next. "Just for an hour or so. I could drive to my parents' house and have dinner with them. It would be good to pretend things are normal for just one evening."

The word "no" was already forming on his lips before she'd finished speaking. She could see it in the way his jaw tightened, the way his dark eyes went flat and hard.

"It's too dangerous," he said. "We don't know when the people who've been stalking us are going to make their move, and if you're out there, exposed—"

The words tumbled out of her lips. "I'm not asking for your permission, Caleb."

Maybe she shouldn't have said anything, but for some reason, she didn't regret that remark. Something hot and tight had been building in her for days, and she had to let it out or explode.

"I'm just trying to keep you safe." His voice was tight, telling her that he was fighting to keep his own frustration in check. "Halloween is tomorrow. One more day, Delia. That's all. Can't you just give me one more day?"

"And then what?" The pressure in her was spilling over now, hardening her voice with an edge she couldn't seem to soften. "Another threat after Halloween? Another crisis, another enemy, another reason to lock the doors and check the wards and never let me out of your sight? When does it end?"

He crossed his arms, and a hint of red flickered in his dark eyes. "When I know you're safe."

"I'm never going to be safe," she retorted. "Not completely." She moved away from the window, putting a distance between them that felt necessary and painful at the same time. "We fight demons, Caleb, and we're having a baby that's part demon. Safety isn't something we get to have, not the way normal people do."

Those words didn't seem to have much effect. Jaw hardening, he said, "Which is exactly why—"

"Why you've decided you need to control everything? That you get to decide where I go and when and with whom?" She could hear her voice rising, could feel the argument spiraling toward territory they'd both been avoiding, but she couldn't seem to stop herself. Pregnancy hormones, maybe, or simply days and days of building frustration and worry. "I'm not a child, Caleb. I don't need you to protect me from my own choices."

His usually sensual mouth clamped down into a thin line. "Someone has to make decisions around here. You've been avoiding them for months."

She stared at him, disbelieving. "Excuse me?"

"Where to live," he said. "What to do about your mother's business...whether to actually commit to building a life with me or just keep straddling the fence." He was moving toward her now, his pacing transformed into something that looked to her more like stalking, frightening and purposeful. "Every time something comes up that requires you to take a stand, you freeze. You find reasons to wait and see and think about it some more."

A flip answer came to her mind...*well, that's because I'm a Libra*...but she pushed it away. Not that the answer she gave him was much better. "That's not fair."

"Isn't it?" He stopped a few feet away, close enough that she could feel the heat radiating off him, the perpetual warmth born of the fire in his blood. "We've been together for six months. We're having a child together. And you still can't decide whether you want to be all in or keep one foot out the door."

That comment cut deeper than she wanted to admit, mostly because there was a splinter of truth buried in it. She had been avoiding decisions, had been holding back some part of herself even as she'd fallen deeper and deeper in love with him. But having that behavior shoved in her face now, in the middle of a fight that had nothing to do with her commitment issues and everything to do with his need for control, made her want to throw something.

Damn those hormones.

"You don't get to criticize me for being careful when you're the one who can't let me take a single breath without monitoring it," she shot back. "You're not protecting me, Caleb. You're smothering me."

"And you're not being careful. You're being a coward."

He might as well have written that rebuke in fire. The word "coward" hung in the air between them, ugly and irretrievable.

Something cracked inside her, a wall she'd been using to hold back the flood of fear and exhaustion and uncertainty that had been building for weeks. Her eyes burned, and she pressed her lips together hard, refusing to let the tears fall.

She refused to give him the satisfaction of seeing how much that word had hurt.

"Maybe this was a mistake," she heard herself say. "Maybe we weren't ready for any of this."

Caleb went absolutely still, staring at her with eyes that might as well have been tunnels to the underworld, they were so dark, so hopeless.

"What?"

"I don't *know!*" she burst out. The tears were falling now despite her best efforts, hot and silent, tracing paths down her cheeks. She didn't bother to wipe them away and instead let them drip from her face onto her shirt, leaving ugly little stains of smeared moisture and mascara. "I don't know anything anymore. I thought I knew what I wanted, thought I knew who I was, and now everything is just—" She made a helpless gesture that encompassed the house that had become a prison, the baby growing inside her...the man standing in front of her looking like she'd just driven a knife into his heart. "I can't do this. I can't fight with you and fight with myself and fight with whatever's coming tomorrow all at the same time."

The silence that followed seemed to echo in her ears.

Or maybe that was just the frantic beating of her heart.

Caleb's face had gone blank in a way she'd never seen before, all its usual animation shuttered behind a mask of careful neutrality. When he spoke, his voice was monotone, almost mechanical.

"I think I should stay at my house tonight. It sounds like you need some space."

Part of her wanted to take back what she'd said, wanted to close the distance between them and tell him she hadn't meant it, that she was scared and exhausted and taking it out on him because he was the easiest target. But another part, the part that was drowning in all the pressure and the fear and the suffocating weight of being watched and never left alone...that part stayed silent.

"Okay," she said at length.

He nodded once, a sharp jerk of his head that communicated nothing and everything at the same time. Then he turned and walked toward the garage, his footsteps echoing through the too-quiet house.

The sound of the garage door opening was followed by the rumble of his truck engine, then the garage door closing again...and then silence.

Delia stood in the middle of her living room, one hand pressed to her stomach where something miraculous and terrifying was growing, and wondered if she'd just destroyed everything she'd been trying so hard to protect.

Caleb sat in the darkness of his living room, staring at walls he couldn't really see. He hadn't turned on any lights when he'd gotten home. *Home,* as if this place still deserved that word, as if it wasn't just an empty shell he'd been slowly abandoning ever since he'd started spending most of his nights at Delia's house. The furniture was still here, the expensive countertops and hardwood floors still gleaming in whatever ambient light filtered through the windows, but the life had drained out of the space months ago. It was a showpiece now, nothing more.

Maybe this was a mistake. Maybe we weren't ready for any of this.

Her words kept replaying in his head, an endless loop he couldn't seem to shut off. Intellectually, he understood what she'd been trying to say. He knew she'd been talking about the timing, the pregnancy, the chaos that had consumed their lives ever since those three positive tests had appeared in her bathroom. She hadn't meant that *they* were a mistake, that everything they'd built was something she regretted.

But part of him had heard it that way nonetheless.

He looked down at his hands, spread open on his thighs. In the darkness, they looked normal enough, human hands attached to human arms. But he knew what those hands were capable of. He'd felt the fire surge through them just hours ago, responding to his fear and his anger, eager to be unleashed.

You're smothering me.

Maybe she was right. Maybe in trying to protect her, he'd become the very thing he was trying to protect her from. Another cage, another presence that made her feel trapped and controlled.

Just like his father.

The thought hit him like a bucket of ice water thrown at his head. Daniel Lockwood had kept everyone at arm's length, had controlled every interaction and every relationship in his world. He'd built walls around himself so high and so thick that no one could get through them, not his wife, not his son, not anyone who might have gotten close enough to see the demon hiding beneath the banker's cool smile.

And now here was Caleb, building his own walls. Not to protect himself, true, but to protect Delia. He'd convinced himself this was different, that his walls were made of love instead of fear, that his control was protection rather than manipulation.

But the result was the same, wasn't it? He'd pushed her away. He'd made her feel suffocated and trapped, unable to breathe.

He'd called her a coward, and now he wondered if that cruel remark had been him projecting more than anything else. Because he was afraid. Scared shitless, really. Scared of losing her, of losing the baby, of proving that he was exactly what he'd always feared he might be. A monster wearing a human face. A man so damaged by his demon blood that he couldn't love someone without also trying to own them.

He thought about the way his father had looked at his mother, with a cold, assessing gaze that had calculated her value and found it acceptable, but never actually seen her as a person. Daniel had never loved Brooke Lockwood. He'd acquired her because she was beautiful and the kind of woman a successful man would marry. She was an asset to be managed, not a partner to be cherished.

Caleb had sworn he would never be like that.

Even back before he'd fought his way free of his father's clutches, back when he'd still had to do Daniel's bidding, he'd wanted to be the opposite of everything his father represented. After he'd escaped from Hell and started a new life here in Las Vegas, he'd thought maybe he could finally make those hopes and dreams come true. He could be a new man, someone who could love honestly and deeply and not have to hide who he was anymore.

He thought he'd found that with Delia.

And yet here he was, alone in a dark house, replaying a fight that had shattered something precious, wondering if the woman he loved would ever look at him the same way again.

His phone sat on the coffee table, its screen dark. He could call her and apologize, could tell her that she was right and he was sorry, and he would do better.

But what if she didn't answer? What if she looked at the screen and saw his name and decided she didn't want to hear whatever excuse he was about to offer? What if the silence on the other end of that call was worse than the silence of this empty house?

He picked up the phone, turned it over in his hands, and set it back down again.

Tomorrow night, the streets would be flooded with costumes and parties and people celebrating a holiday they didn't understand. They would dress as vampires and werewolves and demons, never knowing that real monsters walked among them, never realizing that somewhere in this city, forces were gathering that could tear the veil between worlds and let something terrible through.

And Caleb would face it alone.

No, that wasn't true. He would face it with Delia, because whatever else had been broken between them tonight, he knew she wouldn't abandon him when the real fight came. She was too strong for that, too committed to protecting the life growing inside her.

But they would face that conflict fractured, their connection strained and their trust damaged in ways that might take months to repair. They would fight side by side without being able to lean on each other, and that might be the most dangerous thing of all.

He let the darkness settle around him and didn't try to push it away.

Delia lay in bed, staring at a ceiling faintly illumined by the glowing numerals of the clock on her nightstand.

12:47 a.m.

The house was far too quiet. She'd grown accustomed to the sound of Caleb's breathing beside her, the warmth of his body, the way he would sometimes murmur in his sleep and reach for her hand, as if making sure she was still there. Now the bed stretched empty on his side, the sheets cold, the pillow untouched.

Her hand rested on her stomach, fingers spread wide over the place where something impossible was growing. Eight weeks along, barely anything, a cluster of cells that had somehow already upended her entire existence. She couldn't feel the baby yet, not the way pregnant women talked about feeling their children move and kick. But she could sense it in other ways—the strange new energy signature that Caleb had detected before she'd even known to look, the demonic power that pulsed beneath her own psychic abilities, amplifying them, transforming them into something she barely recognized.

Her child. Their child. Part demon, part human, part something entirely new.

Maybe this was a mistake.

She hadn't meant that angry remark the way it had sounded. Of course she hadn't. But the words had gotten out there before she could stop them, carried on a wave of exhaustion and fear that had been building for days. And she'd seen the way Caleb's face had changed when she'd said them, the light going out behind his eyes, the walls slamming down with an almost audible crash.

She'd hurt him. She'd taken her frustration and terror, her desperate need for some measure of control, and she'd wielded them like weapons against the person she loved most.

Pru's voice echoed in her memory, gentle but unyielding. *The thing about building a life with someone is that you can't do it alone. You have to let them carry some of the weight.*

Thank God for Pru. And thank God for the text she'd sent Delia a few hours ago, the message simple and reassuring.

Mom's stabilized. I'm heading back to Vegas a few days early. See you soon.

At least tomorrow she'd be able to face all this with her best friend at her side.

Still, Delia also knew she had to acknowledge that Pru was right, that she had to let someone else help with her burdens. She'd been so focused on managing every aspect of her life with the same meticulous attention she brought to her real estate transactions that she'd forgotten partnership meant letting go sometimes. It meant trusting someone else to make decisions, to carry burdens she couldn't carry alone.

Caleb wasn't trying to control her. He was trying to protect her, and yes, he'd gone too far, had let his fear turn his protection into something suffocating, but the impulse behind it had been love. Pure, desperate, terrified love.

And she'd thrown it back in his face.

She reached for her phone on the nightstand, pulling it close enough to see the screen. Now it was 12:49, the numbers echoing those of her bedside clock. Halloween had arrived already, creeping in while she lay here, drowning in regret.

Her gaze locked on the screen as she stared down at Caleb's contact info, that familiar photo of him grinning at the camera during their trip to Mount Charleston, looking happier and more relaxed than she'd seen him in weeks. She could call him and tell him she was sorry, that she hadn't meant what she'd said.

She could tell him that she wanted him to come home.

But how much good would that do? The fight had exposed something real, something they both needed to address. An apology wouldn't fix the underlying problem. She couldn't just take back her words and pretend everything was fine when it so clearly wasn't.

Tomorrow, she told herself. Tomorrow they would talk, *really* talk, the way they should have been talking all along. They would figure out how to be partners instead of adversaries, how to face their fears without letting those fears destroy what they were building.

Assuming tomorrow didn't bring something worse.

She set her phone back on the nightstand and stared at the ceiling again, her hand still pressed to her stomach, and tried not to think about all the ways this could end badly. The demons who were planning something for Halloween...the baby whose power was already transforming her in ways she didn't understand.

And Caleb, alone in his empty house, was probably thinking the same thoughts she was thinking, probably blaming himself for things that were at least half her fault.

I pushed him away, she realized. *I've been pushing him away since the day I found out I was pregnant. Every time he tried to make a decision, I resisted. Every time he tried to plan for our future, I deflected. I told myself I needed time, needed space, needed to think things over. But what I was really doing was keeping one foot out the door, just like he said.*

The tears came again, hot and unwanted, soaking into the pillow that should have cradled his head beside hers.

She'd spent so long being afraid of losing control that she'd forgotten to ask herself what she actually wanted. And now, as she lay there in the darkness in an empty bed with a day of reckoning looming on the horizon, the answer seemed painfully obvious.

She wanted Caleb. She wanted their baby, and

she wanted the life they'd been building, no matter how messy and complicated it might be.

She just had to figure out how to stop being so afraid of letting herself have it.

The clock on her nightstand crept toward one o'clock, and sleep remained stubbornly out of reach.

Tomorrow. Everything would change tomorrow.

She just had to survive long enough to make it right.

Chapter Twelve

THE COMING OF DAY FOUND CALEB exactly where the darkness had left him...sitting on his couch and staring at nothing.

He hadn't slept, hadn't even bothered to try. The hours had crawled past in a blur of self-recrimination and fear, his mind circling endlessly around the same worn tracks. The things he'd said. The things she'd said. The look on her face when he'd called her a coward, that flash of hurt before all expression drained away and her lovely features went blank.

Maybe this was a mistake.

He needed to call her. He'd been telling himself that for hours, had picked up his phone and set it down again what felt like at least fifty times, all the while drafting apologies in his head that never seemed remotely adequate. What could he even say that would undo the damage he'd caused? What words existed that could bridge the chasm he'd helped tear open between them?

Morning light crept across the floor, pale and cold, and Caleb watched it advance like an enemy approaching. Halloween. The day they'd been dreading, the day when whatever forces had been gathering against them would finally make their move. He should be at Delia's house right now, standing guard, preparing for whatever was coming.

Instead, he was sitting here alone, because she'd asked for space and he'd given it to her, even as every instinct he possessed had screamed at him that leaving her unprotected was the worst decision he'd ever made.

His phone rang.

The sound cut through the silence like a machete, and he grabbed for it before the first ring had finished, his heart already hammering against his ribs. Delia's name glowed on the screen, her photo smiling up at him, and he stabbed the reply button with shaking fingers.

"Hello?"

"Caleb." Her voice was tight and breathless, and alarm bells immediately started shrilling in his mind. "Someone's in my house."

He was on his feet before his brain had even finished processing the words, heading toward the garage on pure instinct. "Get out. Get out right now."

"I can't." Those two short words were followed by a sound in the background that might have been glass breaking. "They're blocking the exits. I tried the back door, but there's something out there, and the front—"

"I'm coming." Even as he spoke, he was already yanking open the door to the garage, one hand reaching for his truck's key fob after he was inside. "Stay on the phone with me. I'm coming right now."

"Caleb, I'm sorry." Her voice broke, and he could hear the tears beneath the obvious fear and worry. "I'm sorry about last night, about what I said. I didn't mean—"

"I know. I know you didn't. Just stay hidden, okay? Find somewhere to hide and stay there until I—"

She screamed.

The sound froze him in mid-step, hand already on the driver-side door handle. Chaos echoed through the phone's tiny speaker, crashes and snarls and something that sounded like furniture being thrown, followed by a voice that wasn't Delia's, something deep and inhuman that uttered words he couldn't understand.

"Delia! *Delia!*"

The line went dead.

Caleb stood there for one endless second, the phone still pressed to his ear, his heart beating so hard he could feel it pounding in his temples. Then something inside him pushed through the frozen shock, and he was moving again, throwing himself into the truck, gunning the engine before he'd even gotten the garage door all the way up.

The drive to her house was usually around fifteen minutes, give or take. Caleb made it in less than seven, running red lights and taking corners at speeds that should have flipped the truck, his otherworldly reflexes the only thing keeping him on the road. He didn't think about the other cars he was endangering or what would happen if he was pulled over, didn't think about anything except the echo of Delia's scream still ringing in his ears.

When he reached her street, he knew immediately that he was too late.

The front door stood open, hanging crooked on its hinges like a broken jaw. Even from the curb, he could see the destruction inside, the overturned furniture and shattered glass. The wards that Ty had so carefully constructed were gone, not just broken but obliterated, leaving nothing but a faint residue of scorched energy in their wake.

Caleb was out of the truck before it had fully stopped, hurrying across the lawn in a couple of anguished strides and bursting through the ruined doorway with fire already blooming around his fists. The living room was a disaster zone. The couch had been flipped onto its back, its cushions slashed as if by massive claws, and a faint haze of down hung in the air like unholy fog. A lamp lay shattered on the floor, its shade crushed beneath what appeared to be a cloven hoofprint pressed deep into the rug that covered the hardwood floor. The coffee table had been smashed in half, and the wall where the television had hung was now just exposed drywall and dangling wires.

And standing in the middle of all that destruction, arranged in a loose semicircle as if they'd been waiting for him, were three demons.

They weren't the lesser creatures he'd fought at the warehouse. These were bigger, more solid, with mottled gray skin and eyes that burned like hot coals in faces that were almost but not quite human. Muscles corded beneath their hide like bunched rope, and their hands ended in claws that looked capable of shredding steel. One of them grinned at him, revealing rows of needle-sharp teeth.

"The mate arrives," it said, its voice gravel scraping against stone. "Right on schedule."

No point in wasting time on a reply.

The fire erupted from him in a wave, fed by rage and terror and the desperate need to tear apart anything that stood between him and Delia. The first demon caught the full force of it, screaming as the flames engulfed its torso and face. The creature staggered backward, clawing at the fire that consumed it, and Caleb was already moving past it toward the other two. They dodged in opposite directions, moving with inhuman speed, trying to flank him, but he was faster. He closed the distance before either of them could react, driving his fist into the nearest one's chest with enough force to crack the bones beneath its mottled hide.

The demon doubled over, choking on whatever foul substance passed for blood in its veins, and Caleb grabbed it by the horns and wrenched its head to the side with a wet snap.

The third demon lunged at him from behind, claws raking toward his spine, but Caleb was already spinning, already bringing his elbow around in an arc that connected with its skull. The impact sent the creature staggering, and Caleb followed up with a blast of fire that caught it full in the face. It shrieked, a high-pitched sound that seemed to shred his eardrums, and then it was burning, collapsing in on itself as the flames consumed everything that made it solid.

In less than a minute, the three demons had been reduced to ash and smoke on the living room floor. Caleb stood among the wreckage, his chest heaving, flames still flickering around his hands and forearms. The rage that had carried him through the fight was already ebbing, replaced by something colder and more terrible.

She wasn't here.

He searched the house anyway, tearing through every room, checking every closet and corner and hiding place he could think of. Her bedroom was untouched, the bed still made from when she'd straightened the covers that morning. The kitchen also showed no signs of the struggle. The bathroom, the guest room, the converted bedroom office where she occasionally worked from home.

All of them empty, all silent.

Whatever had happened, it had been fast and brutal, and confined to the living room.

He found her phone on the floor near the front door, its screen cracked and dark. When he picked it up, he saw the last call still displayed, his own name at the top of the call log. She called to warn him, and he'd been sitting alone in the dark, feeling sorry for himself while demons broke down her door.

The phone's case was warm in his hand, still holding a trace of her body heat. Or maybe that was just his imagination, his desperate need to find some connection to her in this wreckage. He slipped the phone into his pocket, unable to leave it behind.

Something on the wall caught his attention.

At first, he thought it was just smoke damage, a

dark smear left behind when the demons died. But as he stepped closer, he realized it was something else entirely. Symbols had been burned into the drywall, black and angular and arranged in a pattern that tugged at something deep in his memory. He couldn't read the demonic script, not really, but he knew enough to recognize one word.

HOME.

The message was meant for him. A taunt, maybe, or possibly an invitation. Either way, he had no idea what it was supposed to mean.

The sound of tires screeching outside made him spin toward the door, fire surging to his hands again before he recognized the vehicles pulling up to the curb. Ty's truck, with Pru's green Mini Cooper right behind it, even though she was supposed to still be in California.

They must have sensed something. Or maybe Pru had tried to call Delia, and when she couldn't reach her, she'd known immediately that something was wrong.

Ty was out of his truck and across the lawn in seconds, his bright blue eyes taking in the scene with a single sweep. Pru was right behind him, her dark green hair still wet from what must have been a very hasty shower, her laptop bag slung over one shoulder. She must have caught a red-eye from California, must have been on her way back already when everything fell apart.

"When?" Ty asked.

"Maybe twenty minutes ago." Caleb's voice sounded strange to his own ears, hollow and distant. "She called me. I heard her scream, and then the line went dead. By the time I got here, they were gone."

Ty moved through the living room, stepping carefully around the piles of demon ash, his eyes narrowed in concentration. He paused near the overturned couch and crouched to examine something Caleb couldn't see. His fingers brushed against the carpet, and a faint glow emanated from his touch, probably some kind of angelic perception at work.

Then he went to the nearest ward-point—the one above the front door, now just a blackened smear on the wall where hammered copper had hung—and his expression darkened. "These wards weren't broken from the inside. They were shattered from a distance, all of them at once. Lesser demons couldn't have done this." He looked at Caleb, and something grim settled behind those bright blue eyes. "Someone with considerably more power cleared the way for them."

That didn't sound good. Actually, it sounded downright terrible.

Before Caleb could respond, the half angel continued. "Multiple demons in a coordinated attack." Ty straightened and moved toward the burned message on the wall, studying the symbols with cool intensity. "They took her alive. There's no blood here, no sign of lethal force. They wanted her intact."

"Where?" The word was barely more than a growl. "Where did they take her?"

"I don't know yet." Ty traced the angular symbols with one finger, not quite touching them. "This is demonic script. Old dialect, pre-Babylonian. It says —"

"Home," Caleb cut in. "I know what it says." His hands were clenched into fists at his sides, the fire threatening to break free again. "What the hell does that mean?"

Ty shook his head, expression puzzled. "I'm not sure. But whoever took her wanted you to find this. They're sending a message...or perhaps issuing a challenge."

Pru had set up her laptop on the kitchen counter, her fingers flying across the keyboard with the speed of long practice. "I'm pulling traffic camera footage from the past hour. If they moved her by car, there might be something we can track."

"They didn't use a car." Ty's voice was grim. "The energy signature here suggests teleportation. They took her somewhere instantly, without leaving a physical trail."

Damn it. No trail, which meant no way to track her. She could be anywhere, in any of the thousand dark places where demons lurked and plotted and did unspeakable things to their captives.

Caleb could feel his control start to slip, the demonic blood inside him surging in response to his fear and rage. Fire crept up his forearms and cast flickering shadows on the walls. His vision narrowed, the world compressing down to a single, terrible point of focus.

He was going to find whoever had taken her. And when he did, he was going to burn them out of existence, was going to destroy them so completely that not even ash remained.

"Caleb." Ty's hands closed on his shoulders, forcing him to meet the half angel's clear blue eyes, a reminder of happier days under sunny skies. "You need to hold it together. We'll find her."

"I should have been here." The words sounded frayed, even to his own ears. "I should have stayed. We fought, and I left her alone, and now—"

"This isn't your fault." Pru looked up from her laptop then, her face pale but determined. "This was planned. They waited until she was alone, until the timing was perfect. They were always going to take her, Caleb. If you'd been here, they might have taken you both...or just killed you to get you out of the way."

But Caleb could barely hear those words. All he could think about was the sound of Delia's scream, the way it had cut off so abruptly, the silence that had followed. She was gone. The baby was gone. He'd failed to protect them both, had let his wounded pride drive him away when he should have been standing guard.

The fire around his hands flared brighter, and somewhere in the house, a smoke detector began to shriek.

"We need to move," Ty said, raising his voice over the alarm. "This location is compromised, and we can't afford to draw attention from the authorities. Pru, can you work from Caleb's place?"

"Already packing up." She closed her laptop and shoved it into her bag. "Let's go."

They hurried out of the house and got in their various vehicles, then drove in a tense convoy back to Caleb's house on Pueblo Street, a journey that felt endless even though it took less than fifteen minutes. Caleb sat behind the wheel of his truck, his hands gripping the steering wheel hard enough to leave dents in the leather, and tried to think. There had to be something he was missing, some clue that would tell him where they'd taken her.

Home.

The word kept circling in his mind, refusing to resolve into anything useful. "Home" could mean anything. Delia's house, which he'd just left? His own house, where they were headed now? Some other location that held a particular significance for the demons who'd orchestrated this attack?

Or maybe it meant something else entirely. Something older and darker, something connected to the forces that had been watching them for weeks.

By the time they reached his place, Caleb had worn grooves into his own thoughts. He sat on the couch where he'd spent the night wallowing in self-pity and watched Ty stand by the big windows in the living room that overlooked the backyard while Pru set up what appeared to be a mobile command center on his dining table. Laptops, tablets, cables running to devices he didn't recognize. She worked with a fierce efficiency that told him she was channeling her own fear into action, refusing to let terror paralyze her.

"Full mobilization," Ty was saying into his phone. "I need every available asset in the Las Vegas area, and I need them now." A pause, during which Caleb could hear the faint buzz of someone speaking on the other end. "I understand the protocols, but this is a coordinated demonic attack. One of our allies has been taken. The protocols can wait." He ended the call there and turned to face Caleb, his expression grave. "They're sending help. It's going to take time to coordinate, though, and we don't know how much time we have."

"What about you?" Caleb's voice was flat, the

voice of a man who no longer had anything left to lose. "Can you sense her, maybe use your angelic abilities to find where they're holding her?"

Ty closed his eyes, his body going still in a way that suggested he was reaching out with senses that had nothing to do with the physical world. Caleb watched him, hope warring with despair, and tried not to think about all the things that could be happening to Delia while they sat here waiting.

After an agonizing moment, Ty opened his eyes. His expression told Caleb everything he needed to know even before he spoke.

"Nothing. Whoever took her is shielding her location, and the shielding is stronger than anything I've encountered before." He paused, then added, "This isn't amateur work, Caleb. Someone with significant power is protecting this operation."

Pru looked up from her laptop. "The Styx Group? We know they're behind the surveillance. Maybe they have resources we haven't accounted for."

"Maybe," Ty replied, although he didn't sound convinced. "But this level of shielding requires more than just resources. It requires power. *Real* power, the kind that usually belongs to demon lords or those who serve them directly."

Demon lords. The words sent a chill down Caleb's spine that had nothing to do with the temperature inside the house, which was always set at a pleasant seventy-two degrees. He'd faced a demon lord before, had helped Delia destroy Vinea in the wedding chapel showdown that had nearly killed them both. The memory of that fight, of the raw power Vinea had commanded, made every muscle in his gut want to clench.

"So we're dealing with something big," he said. "Something bigger than we thought."

"We're dealing with something organized." Ty came over and stood next to the couch where Caleb sat, although his gaze was still fixed on the serene morning scene outside, as if he was seeing something beyond the carefully landscaped backyard and the expanse of green golf course beyond the back wall. "The surveillance...the psychological warfare...it was all building toward this. They wanted Delia isolated and vulnerable, and they wanted you distracted by the conflict between you. They've been planning this for quite a while."

Caleb stared at the floor, at the expensive hardwood he'd installed during the renovation, and the weight of his failure seemed to press down on him like a physical thing. Every moment with Delia flashed through his mind, a highlight reel of everything they'd built together. Seeing her that first time back in January, when she'd walked into his life with her copper hair and her skeptical smile and had turned his world upside down. Fighting

Calach together, learning to trust each other with their secrets. The poker tournament where he'd realized he was falling for her. Laughlin, where she'd nearly died, and he'd understood for the first time how much he had to lose.

The night of their battle with Vinea, when they'd fallen into each other's arms after her cousin's wedding reception and sealed the bond they knew they already shared.

Every battle they'd fought, they'd fought together. And every time, they'd won because they'd had each other.

Now she was alone, pregnant and terrified, in the hands of enemies they couldn't even identify. And the last thing she'd heard from him was a word that had cut her to the bone.

Coward.

He should have told her the truth, should have said what he'd been too proud and too afraid to admit during their fight. She needed to hear that she was the best thing that had ever happened to him, that she'd saved him in ways she didn't even realize, that he loved her more than he loved his own safety and his own survival. He should have told her every single day how much she meant to him.

But he hadn't.

"We're going to find her." Pru's voice cut through his spiral, and he looked up to find her standing in front of him, her dark eyes fierce with resolve. "I don't care what it takes. I don't care how many demons we have to kill or how many leads we have to chase down. Delia is my best friend, and I am not about to let her die in some demon's lair."

The question escaped his lips before he could stop it, his voice raw and broken, sounding like someone else's entirely. "What if we can't? What if they kill her? What if they kill the baby? What if the last thing I ever said to her was—"

He somehow managed to stop there. He couldn't bring himself to say the word again, to acknowledge the poison he'd put into the air between him and the woman he loved.

Pru sat down beside him on the couch, close enough that their shoulders almost touched. She didn't try to hug him or offer empty comfort. No, she only sat there, solid and real, refusing to let him drown alone.

"Then we'll make them pay," she said. "But we're not there yet. She's alive, Caleb. Ty said there was no blood at the scene, no sign of lethal force. They took her for a reason, and whatever that reason is, they need her alive. That gives us time."

Time. A handful of hours, maybe, before whatever ritual or plan the demons had in motion reached its culmination. The veil between worlds was thinnest on Halloween night, Ty had said. Demon powers amplified, barriers weakened. If they were going to use Delia for something, they'd do it when their power was at its peak.

Which meant they had until sundown. Maybe less.

Across the room, Ty was back on his phone, still trying to find any thread he could pull. Pru gave his hand a reassuring squeeze and returned to her laptop, her fingers beginning to move across the keyboard with renewed urgency. They were doing everything they could, throwing every resource they had at the problem.

All while Caleb sat on his couch, paralyzed by fear and guilt and a despair so complete that it felt like drowning.

I should have stayed. I should have protected her.

The thoughts circled endlessly, a loop of self-recrimination that led nowhere except deeper into the dark. He could feel his demon blood surging beneath his skin, fire and rage demanding release, and he forced it down with an effort that left him shaking.

He couldn't afford to lose control. Not now. Not when Delia needed him to be strong, needed him to find her and bring her home.

But strength felt very far away, and the silence where her voice should have been was louder than any demon's roar.

Chapter Thirteen

Delia came back to consciousness in stages, awareness seeping in like water through cracks in stone. First came the pain, a dull throb at the base of her skull that sharpened when she tried to move. Next was the disorientation, the sense of being somewhere unfamiliar, somewhere wrong. And finally, there was fear, cold and immediate, sending ice water through her veins.

Her hands were bound behind her back. She could feel rough cord biting into her wrists, tight enough to restrict circulation but not tight enough to cut off the blood flow entirely. Whoever had tied her knew what they were doing. They wanted her restrained, not damaged.

She forced herself to breathe, to think past the panic clawing at her throat. The air around her was cool and still, with a faint mustiness that seemed to tell her that wherever she was, it had stood empty for a while. When she shifted slightly and tested her bonds, the sound of her movement echoed back to her from what seemed like a significant distance. A large room, then. High ceilings. Empty, or nearly so.

The baby.

At once, she reached inward, searching for that familiar flicker of alien energy that nevertheless had become as natural to her as her own heartbeat. For one horrible moment, she felt nothing, and panic stole her breath.

Then...there it was. Faint but unmistakable, a tiny pulse of power nestled deep within her. Still alive, still fighting.

The relief that flooded through her was so intense that it brought tears to her eyes. The baby was okay. Whatever had happened, whatever was still happening, they hadn't hurt her child.

Yet.

She pushed the terrible thought away and forced herself to focus on her surroundings. The darkness was complete, the kind of black that pressed against your eyes and made you question whether you'd gone blind. But she wasn't helpless. Her psychic abilities were still there, thrumming beneath her skin like a live wire, and she reached out with them now, trying to get a sense of where she was and what she was dealing with.

The space around her was huge. She could feel its boundaries, walls that seemed impossibly far away and a ceiling that soared overhead like the vault of a cathedral. There were other presences in the building, demonic signatures scattered throughout the structure. And surrounding everything, woven into the very fabric of the space, were wards, layer upon layer of protective sigils designed to contain and conceal.

But they weren't designed for her.

The realization came slowly, a puzzle piece sliding into place. The wards were strong—devastatingly strong, capable of blocking even Ty's angelic senses. But they were calibrated for demonic energy, for the kind of power that Caleb wielded. Her psychic abilities operated on a different frequency entirely, and while the wards dampened them somewhat, they didn't block them altogether.

Whoever had taken her apparently had underestimated her.

She filed that information away for later use and kept probing, trying to build a mental map of her prison. The room she was in seemed to be some kind of converted hotel suite, the dimensions wrong for a standard room but right for something that had been modified, walls knocked out to create a much larger space. There were shapes around her that might have been furniture, bulky shadows her senses couldn't quite resolve.

Where am I?

The demons had moved so horribly fast. She remembered the sound of glass breaking, the wards around her house collapsing like wet paper, and then they were everywhere, gray-skinned nightmares with burning eyes and claws that reached out for her. She'd fought, had even managed to throw one of them back with a psychic blast that surprised even her, but there had been too many. Something had hit her from behind, a blow to the head that dropped her like a puppet with cut strings, and then...nothing.

Until now.

Had Caleb been taken, too? Was he somewhere in this building, bound and helpless just like her? Or was he still out there, searching, tearing apart the city to find her?

The last thing she'd said to him echoed in her memory, sharp as broken glass.

Maybe this was a mistake.

God, she hadn't meant it. She'd been scared and overwhelmed, lashing out because that was easier than admitting how frightened she truly was. And now she might never get the chance to take those words back, might die with that terrible lie hanging between them.

Stop it. The voice in her head was sharp and practical, the kind of voice that refused to let her wallow in her terror. *You're not dead yet. Focus.*

Footsteps.

Delia went still, every muscle in her body tensing. The sound was coming from somewhere to her left, a measured tread that grew steadily louder. Heels on hard flooring, expensive shoes by the sound of them, approaching with the unhurried confidence of someone who had all the time in the world.

Then the lights came on.

They weren't bright at all—just a dim amber glow that filtered down from fixtures somewhere far overhead—but after the absolute darkness, it felt like staring into the sun. She squeezed her eyes shut and waited for the pain to subside, for her vision to adjust.

When she opened them again, she saw where she was.

A hotel room, just as she'd sensed. But not any hotel room. This space had been gutted and rebuilt, the original walls torn out to create a single vast chamber. The décor was all dark wood and deep red upholstery, expensive and tasteful in a way that felt out of place, given the circumstances. Sigils covered every surface, carved into the walls, painted on the floor, even etched into the high ceiling overhead. They pulsed with a faint crimson light, the wards she'd sensed from inside the darkness made visible.

She was sitting in a heavy wooden chair in the center of the room, her wrists bound behind her, her ankles tied to the chair legs. The rope was ordinary cord, nothing special about it, but the chair itself had been bolted to the floor. They weren't taking any chances.

And standing in the doorway, watching her with an expression of mild interest, was a man.

He was maybe in his late fifties or early sixties, with dark hair silvering at the temples and features that would have been handsome if not for the wrongness behind his eyes. He wore a charcoal suit, bespoke by the look of it, cut so perfectly that it might have come straight from a fitting room in London or Milan. His shoes were Italian leather, his cufflinks were platinum, and his pale blue gaze shimmered with the kind of power that made her skin crawl.

He looked human. But Delia could feel what lurked beneath that polished surface, a darkness so vast that it seemed to bend the very air around him.

"Delia Dunne." His voice was cultured, pleasant, the kind of voice that belonged in boardrooms and country clubs. A slight smile curved his lips as he stepped into the room. "Welcome. We have so much to discuss about that baby you're carrying."

She said nothing. Her heart was beating against her ribs as if it wanted to escape her chest, but she kept her face blank, refusing to give him the satisfaction of seeing her fear.

He didn't seem bothered by her silence. Instead, he moved to a sideboard against one wall and poured himself a drink from a crystal decanter, his movements elegant and unhurried. Ice cubes clinked against glass, and he took a sip of what she thought was probably Scotch before he turned back to face her.

"You're wondering who I am," he said. It wasn't a question. "You're wondering why you're here, what I want, how long it'll be until your very impressive boyfriend comes charging to the rescue." Another sip of his drink. "All reasonable questions. I'd be happy to provide the answers...in time."

"Where am I?"

The words sounded much steadier than she'd expected, although her voice was hoarse with thirst. The man's smile widened fractionally.

"Straight to the point. I appreciate that." He set his drink down and moved closer, then stopped a few feet from her chair. "You're in a place I've spent considerable resources preparing. The wards you can feel"—he gestured at the glowing sigils—

"are designed to prevent any interference with our conversation. No angels can sense this location. No demons can enter without my permission. We're quite alone."

She lifted her chin. "My boyfriend will find me."

"Oh, I'm counting on it." Something flickered in those pale eyes, something that might have been amusement. "In fact, his arrival is rather the point of all this. Everything I've done—the surveillance, the psychological games, even the timing of your capture—has been designed to bring him to me."

A shiver of ice worked its way down her spine. "Why?"

"Because he has something I need. Or rather, he *is* something I need." The man began to walk, glass of Scotch still in his hand, his steps slow and measured, like a professor delivering a lecture. "You see, I've been watching your Caleb for some time now. Ever since he escaped from Hell, in fact. I was quite impressed by his resourcefulness, his determination...his willingness to embrace his demon blood when necessary. He has such potential."

Escaped Hell. Although she couldn't move, Delia could still feel how her entire body wanted to clench in shock. This man knew about Caleb's time in Hell, knew details he hadn't revealed to her until months into their relationship.

"Who are you?" she asked, and this time she could hear the edge in her own voice.

The man stopped and turned to face her directly. That smile was still in place, but now there was something darker beneath it, something ancient and hungry.

"My name is Daniel Lockwood."

Hearing those words, Delia thought it was probably a good idea that she was bound. Otherwise, she might have collapsed from sheer shock.

Daniel Lockwood. Caleb's father. The half-demon who was supposed to be trapped in Hell, who had been caught there when Belial fell... the cambion whom Caleb had believed would be stuck in that blasted, infernal plane forever.

But Daniel Lockwood wasn't trapped. He was here, very much alive, standing in front of her with a drink in his hand and a plan she couldn't begin to understand.

"I see you recognize the name." His smile widened a fraction. "Good. That will save us some time." He moved to an armchair near the window and settled into it with a kind of casual unconcern that felt woefully out of place, considering their surroundings. "Yes, I'm Caleb's father. And yes, I was in Hell for quite some time. But circumstances have changed. When Belial fell"—he paused there, savoring the word like fine wine—"his power had to go somewhere. I am the son of his lieutenant, his most trusted servant. So the power flowed into me."

Belial's power. Nausea churned in Delia's stomach as she recalled what Caleb had told her about demon lords, about the hierarchy of Hell and the vast power that beings like Belial wielded. If Daniel had absorbed that power....

"You're not just a cambion anymore," she said.

"Clever girl." He raised his glass in a mock toast. "No, I'm considerably more than that now. More than any cambion has ever been. I have resources, connections, and abilities that make your old adversary Vinea look like a minor functionary." He took a sip of his drink and was silent for a moment as he appeared to consider its taste. "Which brings us to you...and that very interesting child you're carrying."

Her hand instinctively tried to move to her stomach, but the bonds held her fast. "What do you want with my baby?"

"'Want'?" Daniel repeated, then paused again, as if to consider the question. "I want what any grandfather would want. To secure my legacy. To ensure that the Lockwood bloodline continues, stronger and more powerful than ever before." His pale gaze dropped to her midsection. "A part demon with psychic abilities? That's quite a combination. The potential is remarkable."

"He's not yours," Delia said fiercely. "He'll never be yours."

"'He'?" Daniel's eyebrows rose. "Ah. You assume it's a boy. All the offspring of demons have been male, so I understand the assumption. But I suppose we'll just have to wait and see." He waved a dismissive hand. "Regardless of gender, the child is of my blood. That makes it my concern. But you have questions...and I have answers, even if they might not be the ones you want to hear."

He spoke then, recounting the tale, and Delia listened and tried to piece together the scope of what they were facing.

He'd escaped Hell at the same time Caleb had, riding the chaos of Belial's death to slip through the barriers between worlds. But where Caleb had gone to Indiana to check on his mother before settling in Las Vegas, Daniel had gone to California, to a hidden cache of wealth no one in his family knew about. Millions of dollars, squirreled away over decades of careful planning.

He'd used that money to build the Styx Group, a corporate shell that allowed him to operate openly while pursuing his true goal of opening a permanent gateway between Hell and Earth. It was the same goal Belial had worked toward for centuries, and now Daniel intended to finish the job.

"The wedding chapel ritual was a test," he

explained as he swirled the last of the drink in his glass. "Vinea was overeager, as always. He moved too quickly, drew too much attention. But his failure taught me valuable lessons about what would and wouldn't work."

Delia thought about all the attacks they'd faced over the past months, all the demons they'd fought and defeated. "Calach," she said slowly. "And the demon who took over August Sellers' body. They were working for you?"

"Indirectly," Daniel replied. "The demonic world operates through hierarchies and alliances. I didn't command them directly, but I encouraged certain lines of attack." His smile turned cold. "Caleb has been very useful, actually. He eliminated my competition, cleared the board of demons who might have challenged my authority. Every victory he won made my position stronger."

Once again, her stomach churned. All those battles, all those close calls...they'd thought they were protecting Las Vegas from demonic incursion. Instead, they'd been pawns in a game they hadn't even known they were playing.

"Why tell me all this?" she asked. "What's the point?"

Daniel went over to the sideboard and set down his empty glass, then turned around, his pale eyes—so unlike Caleb's warm, friendly brown—fixed on her face with unsettling intensity.

"Because I want you to understand the situation you're in. I'm not some minor demon with delusions of grandeur. I am the most powerful being you have ever encountered, and I have plans for this family that extend far beyond your limited imagination."

"Caleb will come for me." She said those words again, clinging to the certainty like a lifeline. "He'll find me, and when he does—"

"Oh, I know he'll come." Daniel's smile returned, broader now, showing too many teeth. "That's rather the point, as I said. My son will walk through that door, driven by love and fear and righteous fury, and he'll find himself exactly where I want him."

His son. She'd known for some time who Caleb's father was. But hearing the half demon say those words, seeing the casual possessiveness in his expression....

"Caleb will destroy you," she said.

That comment only earned her another unpleasant smile. "He's welcome to try." Daniel rose from his chair and straightened his jacket. "But I suspect he'll find me somewhat harder to destroy than the lesser demons he's used to fighting. Belial's power runs through me now. I am more than half demon, more than cambion. I am something new." He paused at the door and looked back at her. "Rest now, Ms. Dunne. Save your strength. The real entertainment will begin when my son arrives."

Then he was gone, the door closing behind him with a soft *click,* and Delia was alone with the pulsing wards and the terrible knowledge of who their adversary actually was.

She tested her bonds again, more carefully this time. The rope was tight, but the knots had been tied by someone who knew methods for containing demons, not humans with psychic abilities. They'd left her hands far enough apart that she could move her fingers, and while the chair was bolted down, the rope wasn't.

Her psychic abilities surged within her, amplified by fear and rage and the fierce, desperate need to protect her child. She could feel them straining at the boundaries of her control, power that had grown exponentially since the pregnancy began. The wards covering the walls were designed to contain demonic energy, to prevent demons from teleporting in or out. But she wasn't a demon.

She might be able to break free. The question was whether she'd have time to do anything useful before Daniel or his minions caught her.

Caleb will come for me.

The thought was both comfort and terror. She wanted him here, wanted to feel his arms around her. God, she wanted to tell him all the things she should have said last night instead of that awful, untrue accusation. But she also knew what walking into this trap would mean. Daniel was counting on Caleb's love for her and was using it as a weapon.

And Caleb would come anyway. Because that was who he was. Because he would burn down the world to keep her safe, even if it meant walking into the jaws of a trap he could see closing around him.

She just had to make sure that when he got here, she would be ready to fight beside him.

The sun set over Las Vegas, and the city began to transform.

Caleb stood at the window of his living room, watching the Strip light up in the distance like a carnival of lost souls. Halloween night. The streets were probably already filling with revelers in costumes, tourists and locals alike pouring out of hotels and houses to celebrate the one night of the year when everyone pretended to be something they weren't. Vampires and witches and sexy nurses and zombies, thousands of them streaming through the neon glow, drunk on candy and alcohol and the electric thrill of the holiday.

None of them knew what was coming. None of them could feel the weight pressing down on the city, the sense of something vast and hungry gathering at the edges of perception.

Somewhere out there, Delia was being held. Somewhere in that glittering maze of light and shadow, the woman he loved and the child she carried were in the hands of enemies he couldn't identify and couldn't find.

Behind him, he heard the soft chime of Pru's laptop and the low murmur of Ty's voice as he made yet another call to his unnamed contacts. They'd been at this for hours, chasing every lead, pulling every string, and they were no closer to finding Delia than they'd been when this nightmare started.

"Nothing." Ty's voice cut through his thoughts, heavy with frustration. "The shielding is too complete. I've reached out to every resource I have, and no one can penetrate it."

Caleb didn't turn from the window. "So we're back to square one."

"Not quite." Footsteps approached, and then Ty was standing beside him, his reflection ghosting across the glass. "We know more than we did this morning. We know the attack was planned well in advance and that whoever is behind this has significant power and resources. That narrows the field considerably."

"It doesn't give us a location."

"No," Ty agreed. "It doesn't." He was quiet for a moment, watching the city lights the same way

Caleb was. "There's something I need to say to you."

Caleb's jaw tightened. "If this is another speech about hope and perseverance—"

"It's not." Ty moved so he stood in front of him now, those bright blue eyes seeming to bore into his brain. "I need you to listen to me, Caleb. *Really* listen."

Something in the half angel's tone made Caleb pause, made him meet Ty's gaze despite the hollow ache in his gut that made everything feel distant and unreal.

"You're obsessing," Ty said. "I can see it. You're blaming yourself for not being there when the demons came, and you're telling yourself that if you'd been a better man, a better partner, then none of this would have happened."

"Ty—"

"I'm not finished," the half angel broke in, his voice firm but not unkind. "You're also telling yourself that you're turning into your father, that you're controlling and cold. I can see it in your face, Caleb. You're waiting for the other shoe to drop, waiting for the moment when you prove yourself to be exactly the monster you're afraid of becoming."

Damn. Each word seemed to land in a place that was already bruised. Caleb wanted to argue, wanted to deny all of it, but the truth was too raw to hide from.

"You're not Daniel Lockwood." Ty didn't move, but a sense of furled power seemed to hover around him nonetheless. "You know how I know that? Because Daniel never loved anyone the way you love Delia. He never allowed himself to need someone so much that their absence felt like dying."

Caleb's throat tightened, but he made himself say, "That doesn't feel like much of a strength right now."

"That's because you're using it against yourself." Ty's voice softened as he went on. "You and Delia are strongest when you're together. You've proven it again and again—against Calach, against Sellers, against Vinea. When you work together, when your powers combine, you're nearly unstoppable. That's not a coincidence, Caleb. That's your connection, the love you share."

Pretty words, but that was all they were. "I can't connect with her if I can't find her."

"Yes, you can." The half angel reached out to grip Caleb's shoulder, his hand warm and somehow steadying. "Stop trying to find her the conventional way. Stop relying on traffic cameras and digital trails. Those are all external methods, and they're being blocked. But there's one thing they can't block, one connection they can't sever, no matter how strong their wards might be."

Caleb stared at him, not understanding...or maybe understanding and not wanting to believe it.

"Your bond," Ty said. "The link between you and Delia, the one that formed when you thought she was lost to you in Laughlin and strengthened when she conceived your child. It's not demonic energy, and it's not angelic perception. It's something else entirely, something that exists outside the normal categories they're warding against."

"I've tried reaching for her." The words were ragged. "All day, I've been trying to feel her, to sense her presence. There's nothing."

"Because you're trying to control it." Ty's grip on his shoulder tightened. "That's not how this kind of connection operates. You have to let go. Trust it. Trust *her.*"

Let go. Easy enough for Ty to say. He wasn't the one who'd spent his whole life running from who he truly was.

"I don't know how," he said.

"Yes, you do." Ty released his shoulder and stepped back. "You've done it before. Every time you've trusted Delia with your secrets, every time you've let her see the parts of yourself you're ashamed of—that's letting go. This is just...more."

Pru spoke up then. "Ty's right." She'd closed

her laptop and was watching them, dark eyes fierce and determined. "You two have something special. I've seen it from the beginning, that weird connection that lets you finish each other's sentences and know what the other one's thinking. If anyone can break through whatever shields these bastards have set up, it's you."

Caleb looked between them—Ty with his calm certainty, Pru with her stubborn faith—and something shifted inside him. He wouldn't call it hope. That seemed too presumptuous.

Maybe hope's second cousin once removed.

He turned back to the window, to the city sprawling in the distance. Somewhere out there, Delia was waiting. She was alive; he had to believe that. Alive and fighting and counting on him to find her.

He closed his eyes.

The demon inside him stirred, restless and eager, sensing what he was about to do. For months, he'd kept it on a tight leash, afraid of what would happen if he let it loose. But Ty was right. The control he clung to so desperately wasn't protecting anyone. It was just another wall between him and the people he loved.

He stopped fighting.

It was like releasing a held breath, like unclenching a fist that had been closed so long that the muscles had forgotten any other shape. The power rushed through him, his demon senses expanding outward in a wave of perception that had nothing to do with sight or sound. He felt the city around him, felt the thousands of lives going about their Halloween celebrations, felt the demonic presences scattered throughout Las Vegas like sparks from a fire.

But that wasn't what he was looking for.

He reached deeper, past the external noise, searching for something quieter and deeper. The connection he shared with Delia, the bond that had formed in blood and battle and love. It was there—he *knew* it was there, buried beneath layers of fear and self-doubt and the terrible weight of the day's events.

Delia.

He thought her name, not as a word but as a feeling. He let go of his terror that she might be hurt, his guilt over their fight, his desperate need to control the outcome of this nightmare. He let all of it fall away until there was nothing left but the simple, overwhelming truth of how much he loved her.

And then he felt her.

Just a tiny flicker at first, like a candle flame glimpsed through fog. But as he focused on it, let himself move toward it without trying to force or direct, the connection grew stronger. Fear. She was afraid. But underneath that fear was something harder, something fierce.

Resolve.

She hadn't given up.

And beneath all of that, beneath the fear and the fight, was love. Vast and complex and shot through with regret for words spoken in anger, but love nonetheless. Love for him, for their child, for the future they'd planned to build together.

She was alive. And she was waiting for him.

He pushed deeper into the connection, and now he could feel not just her emotions but her location. Not coordinates on a map, not an address he could plug into his truck's GPS. Something more instinctual, a sense of direction and distance that pulled at him like a compass needle pointing north.

Where are you?

The answer came not in words but in images. Darkness. High ceilings. Glowing sigils. And beyond the walls of her prison, visible through some window or gap in the wards, a shape he recognized instantly.

A pyramid. Black glass and spotlights, iconic and unmistakable.

His eyes snapped open.

"The Luxor," he said, his voice sure and strong. "She's at the Luxor."

Ty had gone pale under what seemed to be a perpetual tan. "You're sure?"

"Yes. I can feel her there." He turned from the window, and something must have shown in his face, because both Ty and Pru took half a step back. The demon was close to the surface now, fire flickering at the edges of his vision, but he didn't push it down. He let it burn. "Someone's using the pyramid as a base. That's where they've taken her."

Pru was already at her laptop, fingers flying across the keyboard. "The Luxor's been closed for renovations for months. If someone's been using it as a stronghold without anyone noticing...." She looked up, her expression grim. "That takes serious resources and serious power."

"I don't care how powerful they are." Caleb started moving toward the door to the garage. "She's there. I'm bringing her home."

Ty caught his arm before he could leave. "We need a plan. We can't just storm in blind—"

"Then plan on the way." Caleb wouldn't stop, wouldn't allow himself to slow down. The connection to Delia burned in him like a second heart, pulling him forward with an urgency that wouldn't be denied. "But I'm not waiting another second while she's in danger. Are you coming or not?"

A moment's hesitation. Then Ty nodded, something like respect flickering in his eyes. "We're coming."

Pru had already grabbed her bag and was shoving her laptop inside. "I'll coordinate with your contacts from the car. Maybe we can get backup in place before we arrive."

They moved together toward the garage, three people against an enemy they still didn't fully understand. The odds were terrible, and the risks astronomical, and they didn't have even the beginnings of a plan.

But Caleb didn't care about any of that.

The woman he loved was waiting for him. His child was in danger. And for the first time since this nightmare began, he knew exactly where he needed to be.

He was going to bring them home.

Whatever it took.

Chapter Fourteen

THE LUXOR LOOMED AGAINST THE NIGHT sky, a dark pyramid of wrongness.

Caleb stared at it through the windshield of Ty's truck as they drove south on Las Vegas Boulevard, the building's black glass surfaces swallowing the light from the Strip behind them. The iconic spotlight that normally shot from its apex into the heavens was still operational, a single beam cutting through the darkness like a beacon, or maybe a warning. Everything else about the building was dark, dead, the windows that should have glowed with the warmth of occupied rooms showing nothing but black.

The Luxor had been closed for renovations for months now. That's what the signs said, anyway, the ones posted on the temporary fencing that surrounded the property. *Coming Soon: A New Era of Entertainment.* Caleb had driven past the property dozens of times since the shutdown and had never thought twice about it. Lots of places in Vegas put things on pause to get a glow-up.

Now, though, he understood what that closure really meant.

"The pyramid is thirty stories tall," Ty said as he maneuvered his truck through the cloggy Halloween traffic. He sounded calm and measured...but then, he almost always did. "Over four thousand rooms in the original configuration, plus casino space, restaurants, theaters, and convention areas. Finding one person in there could take hours we don't have."

"I can feel her." Caleb's connection to Delia still thrummed in his chest like a second heartbeat. "She's high up. Near the top, maybe. The pull is stronger now that we're closer."

"That helps." Ty turned onto Reno Avenue, circling around toward the back of the property, away from the Strip's crowds and the cheerful chaos of Halloween night. "But we still need a way in that doesn't announce our arrival to every demon in the building."

From the back seat of the extra-cab, Pru looked up from her laptop, her face illuminated by the screen's glow. "There's a service entrance on the east side. Security cameras show it's been used recently—tire tracks in the dust, fresh scratches on the door frame. That's probably how they've been moving in and out."

"So they'll be expecting us to use it," Caleb said.

"Maybe." Pru shrugged, and her dark green hair shimmered like shattered tourmalines in the light from the laptop's screen. "But our other options are the main entrance, which is definitely monitored, or trying to break through the construction fencing somewhere else, which would take time and make noise. The service entrance is our best shot."

Ty nodded, his jaw tight. "Once we're inside, we'll need to move fast. The casino floor will be the most direct route to the elevators, but it's also the most exposed. If they have demons stationed there—"

"Then we'll go through them." Fire flickered at Caleb's fingertips, a reflection of the rage burning deep within him. "I'm done planning around obstacles. Delia's in there, and our baby's in there. Anyone who gets between me and them dies."

Ty glanced at him, and something in his expression—not exactly disapproval, but a kind of cautious assessment—made Caleb force the flames back down. He was on edge, running hot in more ways than one, and he knew that losing control now would only make things worse. But the connection to Delia was pulling at him constantly, her fear and determination bleeding through their bond, and every second he and Ty and Pru spent talking was a second she remained in enemy hands.

"The Luxor's shape isn't just architectural," Ty continued, his tone turning more serious. "Pyramids have symbolic significance across multiple spiritual traditions. They channel energy upward, concentrating power at the apex. If someone's using this building as a demonic stronghold, they're tapping into that geometry. The wards inside will be stronger than anything we've encountered before."

"Then we'll break them," Caleb said simply.

Ty was quiet for a moment. Then he nodded, something almost like respect flickering in his eyes. "We'll need to stop at my place first so we can pick up some weapons and supplies. We can't walk into the Luxor empty-handed."

Another delay was the last thing he needed. Voice a harsh rasp, Caleb asked, "How long?"

"Ten minutes," Ty replied, imperturbable as always. "Maybe less."

Ten minutes. Caleb's hands clenched into fists on his thighs, but he nodded. Ten minutes to arm themselves properly was worth it, even if every instinct screamed at him to drive straight to the Luxor and start tearing the place apart brick by brick.

Ty's house was dark when they pulled up, the quiet residential street a stark contrast to the neon chaos they'd left behind. Inside, he moved quickly and calmly. Lights came on, closets opened...and Caleb found himself staring at an arsenal that would have made a small militia jealous.

Weapons lined one wall of what had probably been intended as a guest bedroom. There were blades of various sizes, from combat knives to something that looked almost like a short sword; a few firearms, all of them modified in ways Caleb couldn't immediately identify; containers of what he recognized as holy water, ranging from small vials to gallon jugs; bundles of dried herbs tied with silver cord; and several items he couldn't name at all, objects that hummed with power he could feel even from across the room.

Ty moved along the collection as if there was nothing particularly strange about having such an evil-fighting arsenal in his home, selecting items and handing them out.

"Holy water for you both." He pressed two plastic bottles into their hands. They were the kind you might see at any convenience store, unremarkable except for the faint blessing Caleb could feel humming against his skin. "It probably won't kill the kind of demons we'll be facing, but it should hurt them enough to slow them down."

"Got it," Pru said. She'd used holy water before, back in the warehouse raid, although those demons had been much lower level than the ones that were most likely infesting the Luxor. Her aim had been good then. Caleb hoped it would be just as good tonight.

"Blessed ammunition." Ty handed Pru three additional magazines for the Glock she was sporting in a shoulder holster, the bullets gleaming with a faint silver sheen. "These will do real damage, not just annoy them. Center mass or head-shots—don't waste rounds on extremities."

She nodded, her face pale but determined as she loaded the first magazine into her weapon with the kind of smooth, practiced motion that told Caleb she'd probably spent plenty of time at the range. "Got it."

Ty produced a small leather pouch next, the kind that might hold coins or jewelry. "Protective charms. Wear them around your necks, against your skin. They won't make you invulnerable, but they'll give you some resistance to demonic influence—possession attempts, psychic attacks, that sort of thing."

Caleb took the charm Ty offered and slipped it over his head, feeling the leather cord settle against his throat. The object inside the pouch was small and hard, roughly circular, and it seemed to pulse with a warmth that had nothing to do with body heat.

Pru did the same, tucking hers beneath her black shirt. "What about you?"

Ty smiled, but there was no humor in that lift at the corners of his mouth. "I have my own protections."

Well, that was true. If he unleashed a blast like the one he'd used to blow the doors off the Angel's Dream Wedding Chapel, he'd probably vaporize any demons in a ten-foot radius.

He turned to Caleb last, and his expression turned deadly serious. "You don't need weapons, because you are one. But take these anyway." He pressed two small vials into Caleb's palm, the glass cool against his skin. Inside each one, a faint golden light swirled like liquid sunshine.

"Angelic essence," Ty explained. "If you find yourself overwhelmed, if the wards inside are too strong for your demon abilities to penetrate, break one of these. It'll give you a burst of power that should cut through most demonic protections."

Caleb studied the vials, watching the light move inside them. "What's the cost?"

Ty sent him a direct look, his gaze unflinching. "A lot of pain. Angelic energy and demon blood don't mix well. Your body will reject it even as it uses it. You'll feel like you're burning from the inside out." A pause, and then he added, "But it won't kill you, and it might be the edge you need to reach Delia when everything else fails."

Caleb tucked the vials into his jacket's inner pocket, where they'd be protected but accessible. "Understood."

They finished arming themselves in near-silence, each of them lost in their own thoughts. Pru checked her weapon twice, ejecting the magazine and reseating it, racking the slide to ensure a round was chambered. Ty gathered a few more items—a flask of something that definitely wasn't water, a thin silver chain he wound around his left wrist, a knife with a blade that seemed to shimmer between states of matter—and secured them in an almost casual way, his movements making it plain that he'd done the same thing at least several times before.

When they were finished suiting up, Pru turned to Caleb and pulled him into a fierce hug.

The gesture startled him. Pru wasn't usually the demonstrative type, preferring sarcasm and practical support to physical affection. But her arms locked around his back with surprising strength, and her voice was hoarse as she murmured into his chest.

"Bring her home. Whatever it takes."

He hugged her back, feeling the tremors in her slender frame, the desperate hope she was trying so hard to contain. Pru and Delia had been friends since high school, had been through things together that he probably didn't even know about. If something happened to Delia tonight, Pru would never forgive him.

He knew he wouldn't forgive himself.

"I will," he said. "I promise."

She pulled back and swiped at her eyes with the back of her hand. Almost at once, her expression hardened, her eyes now glinting and her chin determined. "Okay. Let's go storm a demonic stronghold and ruin some asshole's Halloween."

Despite everything, Caleb almost smiled.

The Luxor's service entrance was exactly where Pru had said it would be—a loading dock on the east side of the property, hidden from the Strip by a concrete barrier and accessible through a narrow access road that wound between construction equipment and temporary fencing.

They'd left Ty's truck a block away, approaching the final distance on foot to minimize noise. The night air was cool, the kind of desert autumn that reminded you how quickly the temperature could drop once the sun went down. The sounds of Halloween celebrations drifted toward them from the Strip; distant music, the occasional burst of laughter, the ever-present hum of a city that never really slept.

Here, in the shadow of the black pyramid, none of that seemed to matter a single bit.

Caleb's demon senses were screaming at him before they even reached the door, and he set his jaw. He hadn't expected this to be a picnic, but a part of him had been hoping it might not be as difficult as he'd feared.

No such luck.

"Multiple presences scattered throughout the building," he said in an undertone. "Maybe a dozen, maybe more. It's hard to tell with the wards dampening everything."

Ty nodded, gaze scanning the dark bulk of the pyramid rising above them. The spotlight beam cut through the sky overhead, impossibly bright against the darkness of the building itself. "I'm getting the same read. They know we're coming."

Caleb sent the half angel a grim smile. "Then let's not keep them waiting."

The service door was unlocked—an invitation or a trap, impossible to tell—and they slipped inside with weapons drawn and all their senses on high alert. The corridor beyond was industrial and utilitarian, nothing like the Egyptian-themed opulence Caleb remembered from the casino floor above, just a series of bare concrete walls with exposed pipes running along the ceiling and the faint drip of water coming from somewhere in the darkness ahead. Emergency lighting cast everything in a dim red glow, enough to see by but not enough to reveal what might be lurking in the shadows.

Maybe that was a good thing.

They moved in formation. Caleb was on point, his demon senses reaching out to probe for threats, with Ty directly behind him, his angelic abilities providing a different kind of awareness. Pru brought up the rear, her weapon drawn and her eyes constantly scanning their surroundings. The silence was oppressive, broken only by the soft sounds of their footsteps and the distant hum of machinery somewhere deep in the building's guts.

The service corridor wound through the Luxor's backstage areas—storage rooms, maintenance closets, what looked like an employee break room with tables still littered with abandoned coffee cups and magazines. Everything was covered in a layer of dust and neglect, the detritus of a building that had been officially empty for months but was clearly being used for purposes its original architects had never intended.

They passed through a set of double doors and found themselves at the edge of the casino floor, and Caleb stopped dead.

A vast space stretched out before them in the dim emergency lighting, a cathedral of abandoned excess. Slot machines stood in silent rows like tombstones, thousands of them, their screens dark and their coin trays empty. Gaming tables occupied the center of the space, their felt surfaces gray with dust, the dealer positions empty, the chairs pushed back as if their occupants had simply vanished mid-hand. The carpet beneath their feet was thick with grime, and the air had the stale quality of a place that hadn't been properly ventilated in months.

The Egyptian theming was everywhere. Hieroglyphics carved into fake stone columns, statues of Anubis and Horus and other animal-headed deities standing sentinel at the ends of gaming aisles. Reproductions of ancient artifacts were displayed in glass cases that had grown cloudy with neglect, and an enormous replica of Tutankhamun's death mask hung on one wall, its golden surface tarnished, its hollow eyes seeming to track their movement across the floor.

In the darkness, with the red emergency lights casting long shadows, it all looked less like a casino and more like a tomb.

"Fitting," Ty murmured, echoing Caleb's thoughts. "They've turned a temple of greed into a temple of something far worse."

"She's above us," Caleb said, and tilted his head back to stare at the slanted glass walls that rose toward the pyramid's apex. The Luxor's unique architecture meant the guest rooms were arranged around the hollow core of the pyramid, their windows facing inward rather than out. From here, he could see the dark rectangles of those windows climbing toward the summit, story after story of emptiness rising into the dark. "High up. Near the top."

"Penthouse level," Ty responded. "That's where they'd put a ritual chamber. Maximum height, maximum symbolic power. The pyramid shape channels energy upward toward the apex."

Caleb didn't care how much energy their foes might be channeling. He just wanted to get up there and get Delia out. "Then that's where we're going," he said shortly.

They crossed the casino floor quickly but carefully, weaving between the dead slot machines and empty gaming tables. Their footsteps seemed too loud in the silence, the sound echoing off the high ceiling in a way that made it impossible to tell if anyone—or anything—was moving nearby.

Caleb's senses were stretched to their limits, probing the darkness for any sign of ambush. He could feel the demonic presences scattered throughout the building, some close and some far, but none of them were moving to intercept. They were being watched, he was certain of it. But the watchers weren't attacking. It was like walking through a haunted house where the ghosts were content to observe rather than engage.

That should have worried him more than it

did. But his connection to Delia was growing stronger with every step, her fear and determination bleeding through their bond. She was alive, and she was waiting for him.

Nothing else mattered.

The elevator bank stood at the far end of the casino floor, a row of brass-doored portals beneath an enormous re-creation of an Egyptian sunburst. The fixtures were tarnished, the once-bright metal now dull with age and neglect. Most of the elevators showed no power, their call buttons dark and unresponsive.

But one—the one on the far left, slightly larger than the others, probably intended for VIP access to the upper floors—glowed with a faint light.

"Convenient," Pru muttered in a wry whisper.

"Too convenient," Ty agreed. His hand rested on the hilt of something beneath his jacket, ready to draw at a moment's notice. "They want us to use it."

Caleb was already pressing the call button. "Then let's not disappoint them," he said.

The elevator arrived with a soft chime that seemed too cheerful for the circumstances, and its doors slid open to reveal an interior that had been thoroughly modified from its original tourist-friendly configuration. The brass walls were covered in sigils, a demonic script that made Caleb's skin crawl with recognition, symbols he'd seen in Hell during his time there, symbols that spoke of binding and containment and power. The floor was marked with a pattern that looked disturbingly like a summoning circle, its lines scored deep into the metal beneath the carpet.

He stepped inside anyway.

"Caleb —" Ty began, a warning note in his voice.

"It's the fastest way up. And it's obvious they're expecting us." He met Ty's eyes, letting the fire flicker openly in his gaze, allowing some of the demon he usually kept leashed to show through. "I'm done playing their game. It's time to start playing mine."

After a moment's hesitation, Ty and Pru followed him into the elevator. The doors slid shut behind them, and the car began to rise, smooth and silent despite the obvious age of the mechanism. The sigils on the walls pulsed faintly as they ascended, responding to Caleb's demonic presence, but they didn't seem designed to trap or harm. Maybe they were more like sensors, announcing their arrival to whatever waited above.

Let them know he was coming. He didn't give a shit. It wouldn't matter in the end.

The power saturating this place was immense, though, pressing against his senses like a hand against his chest. It reminded him of something—a flash, sudden and disorienting, that hit him between one heartbeat and the next. White fire...a blade that blazed with light. A woman's scream, and the sound of something ancient shrieking as it died.

Then the image was gone, slipping from his mind before he could begin to make any sense of it, leaving nothing behind but a sick, dizzy feeling and the certainty that he'd just glimpsed something important.

He shook his head and pushed the vision away. Now wasn't the time. Delia was above him, and nothing else mattered.

The numbers climbed. Ten. Fifteen. Twenty.

On the twentieth floor, the elevator stopped.

Caleb had a heartbeat's time to register that they hadn't reached the top before the doors opened onto chaos.

Three demons were waiting for them in the corridor. These weren't the kind of lesser creatures he'd fought at the warehouse near the airport, but something larger and more formidable, with mottled gray skin and eyes that burned like hot coals in faces that were just enough off from human to be truly disturbing. They were already moving as the doors parted, claws extended, mouths open to reveal rows of needle-sharp teeth.

Caleb met them with fire.

The flames erupted from his hands in a concentrated burst, a wave of orange and gold that caught the lead demon full in the chest. The creature shrieked, a sound that seemed to come from somewhere beyond its throat, and it staggered backward as the fire ate into its flesh. But it didn't fall. These weren't the weaklings from the warehouse. These were soldiers, bred for combat, and one blast of fire wasn't going to be enough.

The second demon tried to circle around him, going for his flank, but Ty was there. A blade of pure white light manifested in the half angel's hand—something that seemed to exist somewhere between physical weapon and divine force—and he intercepted the creature's charge with a sweeping cut that opened its shoulder to the bone. The demon howled and fell back, black ichor spraying from the wound.

Pru's gun fired twice, the sound deafening in the enclosed space. Her blessed bullets found their mark in the third demon's knee and hip, and the creature stumbled, its leg giving out beneath it. She followed up with two more rounds to its chest, and it collapsed, twitching and smoking where the holy ammunition burned in its flesh.

Caleb finished the first demon with a second blast of fire, this one concentrated into a spear of flame that punched through its chest and out its back. The creature came apart around the wound, its physical body losing shape and form, collapsing into ash and sulfurous smoke. He was already turning as it fell, already targeting the one Ty had wounded.

But the half angel was faster. That impossible blade swept down in a clean arc, severing the demon's head from its shoulders. The body dissolved before it hit the ground.

Pru put another two rounds into her target, and it stopped moving entirely.

The whole fight had taken maybe thirty seconds.

"That was too easy," Ty said, his voice tight with residual adrenaline. The blade in his hand flickered and vanished like a candle being blown out. "They weren't really trying to stop us."

"Gatekeepers," Caleb agreed as he stepped over the pile of ash that had been the first demon. His jacket was singed where claws had gotten too close, but the wounds beneath were already healing, his demon blood working to repair the damage. "They were testing us...or maybe just trying to slow us down."

Pru tilted her head at him. "Why would they want to slow us down?"

Caleb looked at the elevator doors, still standing open behind them, and then at the corridor stretching ahead toward another bank of elevators that would take them higher still. The connection to Delia was pulling at him harder now, her fear surging through their bond in a way that made his bones ache.

"Because something's happening up there," he said. "Something they need time to finish."

They started moving.

More demons appeared at the twenty-fifth floor, two of them this time, larger than the first three. Caleb and Ty took them apart in a brutal exchange that left ichor splashed across the walls and another tear in Caleb's jacket. At the twenty-eighth floor, three more were waiting, and Pru had to reload in the middle of the fight, her hands surprisingly steady despite the chaos around her.

By the time they reached the thirtieth floor, Caleb had lost count of how many of their adversaries they'd killed. His arms were streaked with ichor and his own blood from wounds that had already closed. Ty was limping slightly from a slash across his thigh, the wound healing visibly but not fast enough to completely erase the pain. Pru was pale but steady, her weapon down to its last magazine, her dark eyes hard with a determination that bordered on fury.

The elevator they'd been using couldn't go any higher. Above them, the apex of the pyramid waited, accessible only by a final set of stairs that wound upward into darkness.

Caleb could feel Delia so clearly now that it was almost like having her there beside him. Her fear, her determination, her love...all of it flowed through their connection in an unbroken stream. She knew he was coming. She was waiting for him.

Hold on, he thought, pushing the message through their bond as hard as he could. *I'm almost there.*

He didn't know if she could hear him. He didn't know for sure if their connection even worked that way. But he had to try.

"This is it," he said as he looked up the stairs. "Whatever's at the top, whatever we're facing—it ends here."

Ty gripped his shoulder, his hand warm and steady despite everything they'd been through. "Then we'll face it."

Pru checked her weapon one last time, ejecting the magazine to count her remaining rounds before she slammed it back into place. "Let's go get her."

Caleb started up the stairs, fire dancing at his fingertips, the woman he loved waiting somewhere above him in the dark.

Chapter Fifteen

THE STAIRWELL ENDED AT A SINGLE DOOR that was heavy, reinforced steel painted matte black. It stood open about six inches, as if someone had left it ajar deliberately. Beyond the door, Caleb could see faint light spilling through the gap, warm and golden, utterly at odds with the darkness they'd been fighting through for the past hour.

The connection to Delia was a physical ache now, so strong that he could almost feel every breath she took. She was there, just past that door, and every instinct he possessed was screaming at him to throw it open and rush in.

Somehow, though, he made himself stop and think.

"A trap," Pru said in an undertone, her Glock trained on the door. She was down to three rounds in her magazine, but her voice was calm. "It has to be."

"Obviously," Ty replied. He was studying the doorframe, eyes narrowed in concentration. "But I'm not sensing any wards. Either they're beyond my ability to detect, or—"

"Or they want us to walk in," Caleb cut in. He knew the answer already. Whoever had taken Delia, whoever had orchestrated all of this, they weren't trying to keep him out. They were sending him a goddamn invitation.

Fine. Then he'd accept.

He pushed the door open and stepped through, then stopped.

Inside was a penthouse suite—or at least, it had been once, before someone had torn out most of the interior walls and converted the entire floor into a single massive chamber. The slanted glass walls of the Luxor's apex rose around them on all sides, and through them, Las Vegas spread out in every direction, a glittering carpet of light and color. The Strip blazed in the middle distance, its gaudy excess somehow small from this height, its Halloween crowds reduced to anonymous specks moving between the casinos. The entire city was celebrating below them, thousands of people in costumes and masks, laughing and drinking and utterly oblivious to the evil lurking above their heads.

But Caleb only had a second for that view, because he'd found Delia.

She was in the center of the room, bound to a high-backed chair with restraints that looked like they'd been designed for exactly this purpose. Her wrists were locked to the armrests, her ankles were bound to the legs of the chair, and a web of silver chains crisscrossed her torso. Her red hair was tangled, her face pale, and her smeared mascara had left dark smudges under her eyes.

But she was alive. She was breathing. And when her gaze met his, the relief and love that flooded through their connection almost brought him to his knees.

"Delia—" he breathed, and began to move toward her.

"Hello, Caleb."

The voice stopped him cold.

He knew that voice, had hoped never to hear it again.

A man stepped from the shadows at the edge of the room, moving into the golden light with an easy confidence Caleb remembered all too well. The man was impeccably dressed, his charcoal suit cut from fabric that looked like it had been tailored on Savile Row, his silver tie knotted in a perfect Windsor. He could have been any wealthy businessman, any corporate executive, any of a thousand men who held power in cities around the world.

Including the town where Caleb had grown up.

His eyes were wrong, though. They'd always been icy blue, striking against his dark hair, but now they were even paler, the irises the color of bleached bone ringed with darkness. They seemed to swallow the light around them even as they reflected it.

It was his father...but something else at the same time, something far worse than the cambion Daniel Lockwood had been.

"You're gone," Caleb heard himself say, and his own voice sounded distant, disconnected from the roaring in his ears. "You were trapped in Hell."

Daniel smiled. The expression was as glacial as those unnatural eyes.

"So were you," he replied. "And yet, here we both are."

His gaze shifted from Caleb to Delia, tracking down to her midsection, to the place where their child grew, still barely visible but undeniably present to anyone who knew what to look for.

"And you've been busy," Daniel continued, that predatory smile widening. "A grandson. How...unexpected."

A fresh wave of horror hit Caleb, washing away everything else. His father was alive and free, and was standing in front of him in a bespoke suit with Las Vegas spread out behind him like a conquered kingdom. His father had taken Delia.

His father had been behind everything.

Ty and Pru had come through the door as well, and he could feel their shock without looking, could sense the moment they understood what they were facing. Ty's hand went to the hilt of his blade, and Pru raised her weapon, training it on Daniel with rock-steady aim.

But he didn't seem concerned. He simply stood there, drink in hand—Caleb hadn't noticed the crystal tumbler of amber liquid until now—and regarded them all with an expression of vague amusement.

"Don't bother," he said, then gestured lazily at Pru's gun with the hand that held the glass of Scotch. "Your blessed bullets are effective against common demons, but I'm considerably more than that now." His gaze moved to Ty, and he added, "And your angelic trinkets might sting, but they won't kill me. Nothing in this room can kill me."

"We'll see about that," Caleb growled.

Daniel laughed. It was a soft sound, almost genuinely amused. "There's the fire I expected. The famous Lockwood temper. You got that from your mother, actually, not from me. I was always more...methodical."

The words ground themselves past his clenched teeth. "Let her go."

"Why would I do that?" Daniel raised his glass, studied the liquid within, and then took a small sip. The casual gesture was somehow more infuriating than anything he could have said. "She's carrying my grandson—a child with your blood and her abilities. That baby will be powerful, Caleb. More powerful than either of you could imagine. Under my guidance—"

"He'll never be yours," Delia said.

Her voice was steady, far steadier than Caleb would have expected, given everything she must have been through during the past few hours. He turned to look at her, and despite the restraints, despite the exhaustion in her face, her eyes were clear and fierce. The woman he loved was still fighting.

"Neither will I," she continued. "And neither will Caleb."

Daniel regarded her for a long moment, those bone-pale eyes unreadable. Then he set his drink on a small table near the windows and turned back to face them, his hands clasped behind his back like a professor about to deliver a lecture.

"I imagine you have questions," he said. "About how I survived. About what I'm doing here. About what happens next." That thin smile appeared again. "I'll answer them, because I believe in being civilized, and because you're going to need to understand your situation before you can make intelligent decisions."

"We don't want your explanations," Caleb said. Fire was flickering at his fingertips now, barely controlled.

"Of course you do. You've always wanted explanations, Caleb. Even as a child, you needed to understand things. It was one of your more admirable qualities." Daniel began to walk, circling slowly around the perimeter of the room. "When Belial died, his power had to go somewhere. That's the nature of power—it doesn't simply disappear. And I was there, the son of his most trusted lieutenant, the cambion who had served him faithfully for longer than you've been alive, who'd kept the faith knowing that one day, Belial would return to this world. And so...the power flowed into me."

He paused and studied his own hand as if seeing it for the first time. The air around his fingers seemed to darken slightly, shadows gathering where none should exist.

"It made me more than a simple half demon," he continued. "More than anything I'd been before. I came to Las Vegas with a purpose—to open a permanent gateway to Hell, to let our people through. The Greencastle demons still trapped on the other side, the allies who served Belial, everyone who's waiting for a chance to walk freely in this world again." He gestured at the windows, at the city sprawling hundreds of feet below. "I intend to build Hell on Earth, Caleb. Starting here."

"You built the Styx Group," Ty said. His voice was calm, analytical, as if he were working through a complex equation. "The shell company behind the attacks. The real estate purchases near ley lines. The recruitment of other demons."

Daniel acknowledged all this with a slight nod. "Your people are smarter than I gave them credit for. Yes, the Styx Group is mine. Every acquisition, every asset, every subsidiary—all were designed to position me for the final ritual."

Pru had lowered her gun slightly, although Caleb could see the tension in her shoulders, the readiness to snap it back up at a moment's notice. "Every attack against us, every plot. That was you."

"Not all of them." Daniel's smile was now glacial, almost a grimace. "Some of my subordinates showed initiative. Vinea, for instance, was overeager with his wedding chapel scheme, and he moved too quickly, ensuring that he would not succeed. But the overall structure? The strategy?" He spread his hands. "Mine." He turned to face Caleb, and something flickered in those unnaturally pale eyes that might have been pride. "And you, my son, were useful. Every demon you eliminated—Calach, Sellers, Vinea—cleared the board for me." The smile returned, sharp and self-satisfied. "Every victory you won made my position stronger."

The fire in Caleb's hands flared brighter, and he had to fight to keep his voice level. "I'm not your pawn."

"No," Daniel agreed. "You're something better. You're my contingency plan. If I can't have your cooperation, I'll have your son. A partial demon with his mother's psychic gifts—now, that's a legacy worth cultivating."

The anger that surged through Caleb was white-hot, so intense that for a moment, the edges of his vision went red. This man—this creature wearing his father's face—had orchestrated every attack, every danger, every moment of fear Delia had suffered. He'd used Caleb like a piece on a chess board, manipulating him into eliminating rivals without ever knowing he was serving his father's agenda. And now he wanted their child, wanted to twist an innocent baby into another weapon for his hellish plans.

Through their bond, Caleb could feel Delia's emotions surge in response to his own—her fear spiking, yes, but also her resolve, her refusal to let this monster anywhere near their family. She was reaching for him through the connection, trying to anchor him, to remind him that he wasn't alone.

I'm here, he felt her think, the message pushing through their bond. *We're in this together.*

He let her presence steady him, and the fire at his hands settled down from wild flickering to a controlled burn.

"You don't know anything about connection," Delia told Daniel. Her voice was stronger now, fed by her certainty, by the love flowing through the connection she and Caleb shared. "You don't understand what it means to trust someone completely. You've never loved anyone in your entire miserable existence."

Daniel's expression flickered. Just for a moment, something crossed his face that might have been irritation—or possibly something much darker.

"Love is a weakness," he said. "A vulnerability that stronger beings learn to excise. Your connection to my son might feel like strength, but it's really just another point of attack. I've already demonstrated that by using you to lure him here."

"You're wrong." Delia met his pale eyes without flinching. "And that's going to be your undoing."

For one agonizing moment, no one moved. The penthouse was silent except for the faint hum of the building's climate-control systems and the distant sounds of Halloween celebration drifting up from the Strip far below. Daniel stood by the windows, backlit by the glow of Las Vegas, his expression unreadable. Caleb remained near the door with fire dancing at his fingertips. Ty and Pru flanked him, weapons ready, waiting for the signal to act.

And Delia sat in the center of it all, bound but unbroken, her eyes fierce with a determination that made Caleb's heart ache with love and fear in equal measure.

Daniel broke the silence with a soft laugh.

"Such faith," he said, and there was something almost wistful in his tone. "I remember what that felt like once. Before I learned better." He picked up his drink again and swirled the amber liquid in the glass. "You think your love makes you strong. You think your connection gives you power. But all it really does is give me leverage. You've already proven how easy you were to manipulate, since all I had to do was send some threatening texts, texts designed to cause a rift between the two of you... which they obviously did."

He took a sip of his Scotch, savoring it, then set the glass down with a soft *click*.

"Here's what's going to happen," he continued, his voice hardening. "You're going to surrender. All of you. You're going to put down your weapons and your fire and your righteous anger, and you're going to listen very carefully to what I tell you. Because if you don't"—his gaze moved to Delia, and something hungry flickered in those pale eyes—"I'll take what I want anyway. And it will be considerably less pleasant for everyone involved."

Caleb's hands clenched into fists, the fire at his fingertips flaring brighter. "You're not taking anything. Not Delia. Not our baby. Not one goddamn thing."

"Caleb." Daniel shook his head slowly, almost sadly. "You always were stubborn. It's another trait you got from your mother. But stubbornness isn't the same as strength, and right now, you're badly outmatched." He lifted a hand to indicate the penthouse, the sigils Caleb could now see had been carved into the floor beneath the expensive carpet, the wards humming at the edges of his perception. "This is my territory. My stronghold. Every advantage here belongs to me."

"Then we'll take it from you," Ty said quietly.

Daniel's smile widened. "You're welcome to try."

The tension in the room ratcheted up another notch. Caleb could feel it building, that moment before violence erupts, when everything seemed to slow down and speed up at the same time. His demon blood was singing with the need to attack, to protect, to burn this monster to ash and scatter the remains across the desert.

But he forced himself to wait. Forced himself to *think.*

Daniel was powerful, more powerful than anything they'd faced before. Rushing in blind would only get them killed. They needed a plan. They needed to find the weak points in his defenses and had to work as a team if they had any hope of getting Delia out of there alive.

Together, he thought, pushing the word through his bond with Delia. *We do this together.*

He felt her response, a surge of warmth and determination that steadied him more than any words could have.

Daniel watched the silent exchange with something that might have been curiosity, his head tilting slightly to one side like a predator observing unfamiliar prey.

"Interesting," he murmured. "That connection of yours is stronger than I expected. I'll have to study it more closely once this is over." His pale gaze moved back to Delia, and the hungry look returned. "The combination of demon blood and psychic ability really is remarkable. Our little family is going to accomplish great things."

"We're not your family," Caleb said. "We never were."

Something shifted in Daniel's expression—a flicker of genuine emotion breaking through the mask of cold amusement. For just a moment, he looked almost human.

Then the mask was back, and he was smiling again, a predator's smile with no warmth.

"We'll see about that," he said. "We have all night. And I've waited a very long time for this reunion." He spread his arms wide, encompassing the penthouse, the city, the future he was so certain belonged to him. "Welcome to my home, son. I hope you'll learn to love it here."

Caleb didn't respond. He just stood there, fire burning at his hands, his eyes locked on the monster wearing his father's face.

Whatever happened next, whatever it cost him, he was going to burn this place to the ground along with anyone in it who stood between him and the woman he loved.

Daniel seemed to read the thought in his expression. His smile widened.

"There it is," he said softly. "That's the fire I've been waiting to see. That's the Lockwood legacy." He picked up his drink one more time and raised it in a mocking toast. "To family."

Delia spoke then, her voice cutting through the tension like a blade.

"You think you understand us," she said. "You think you know what we're capable of. But you've spent so long without anyone who actually cares about you that you've forgotten what real strength looks like." She met Daniel's pale gaze without flinching, without fear. "We're going to show you."

Daniel regarded her with what appeared to be pity, as if she were a child who had said something foolish but endearing.

"My dear," he said, "you don't have a choice.

"None of you do."

Chapter Sixteen

CALEB MOVED.

He didn't think about it, didn't weigh options or calculate odds. He simply saw Delia bound to that chair and Daniel standing between them wearing that predator's smile, and something inside him snapped loose from whatever chains had been holding it back.

Fire erupted from his hands as he charged, and Daniel met him halfway across the room.

It was like hitting a wall of solid darkness. Daniel's fist connected with Caleb's jaw, and the blow sent him staggering sideways, stars exploding behind his eyes. He'd been hit by demons before, had taken punishment that would have killed a normal man, but this was something else entirely. Daniel moved with the kind of speed and power that made everything Caleb had faced before seem like sparring practice.

But he wouldn't allow that to stop him.

He caught himself against an overturned couch and launched back into the fight. Fire wreathed his fists as he swung, and this time, he connected, his knuckles slamming into Daniel's ribs with enough force to crack bone. Flames seared into the expensive suit, and he grunted in pain, but he didn't fall. He barely even flinched.

"Better," he said, something almost approving in his tone. He blocked Caleb's next strike with his forearm and countered with an elbow to Caleb's temple that made the world go gray around the edges. "It seems your time in Hell taught you something after all."

Caleb snarled and threw more fire, a concentrated burst aimed at Daniel's face. His father batted it aside like he was swatting a fly, shadows gathering around his hand to absorb the flames.

"But you're still fighting angry," Daniel continued. He moved in close...too close...and drove his knee into Caleb's stomach. The air left his lungs in a rush, and he doubled over, gasping. "Anger makes you sloppy. I thought I taught you better than that."

Caleb forced his next words out through clenched teeth. "You never taught me anything."

Then he grabbed Daniel's arm before the next

blow could land and channeled fire directly into his grip, pouring heat into his father's flesh. Daniel hissed and jerked back, and Caleb used the momentary opening to drive his shoulder into Daniel's midsection, tackling him backward across the room.

They crashed into the small table where Daniel had set his drink, shattering it into splinters of expensive wood and shards of crystal. Caleb ended up on top, raining down blows with fists that burned bright enough to leave afterimages in the air. Each impact drew a grunt of pain from his father, and each strike left scorched marks on his suit and the skin beneath.

But he was smiling.

Even as Caleb pounded him into the floor, even as fire seared his flesh and demon strength drove each blow home, Daniel Lockwood continued to smile that cold, predatory smile.

"There it is," he said softly. "There's the monster I knew was hiding inside you."

He moved so fast that Caleb barely registered what was happening before he was airborne. Daniel had planted both feet against Caleb's stomach and kicked, launching him across the room like a rag doll. He hit the slanted glass wall hard enough to crack it and then slid down to the floor in a shower of broken glass, his vision swimming.

"You think you're different from me." Daniel rose to his feet and brushed debris from his shoulders with casual disdain. His suit was ruined, his face burned and bloody, but he moved as if none of it mattered. "You think your pretty little psychic and your unborn child have changed you into something better. But I know what you really are, Caleb. I know because I made you."

A blade of pure white light sliced through the air where Daniel's head had been a heartbeat before, signaling that Ty had entered the fight.

The half angel's light blade hummed as it cut through the darkness, and Daniel was forced to retreat, shadows gathering around his hands to parry each strike. The collision of angelic and demonic energy sent sparks scattering across the room, bright flares of light that strobed against the slanted windows.

"Go," Ty called out to someone behind him. "Free her. I'll keep him occupied."

Caleb looked up in time to see Pru sprinting toward Delia's chair, her empty gun abandoned in favor of a set of lockpicks she must have grabbed from Ty's arsenal...or maybe they were her own, since she seemed to have an arsenal of interesting skills at her disposal. Either way, she slid to her knees beside the chair and went to work on the restraints, her fingers moving deftly to spring the locks.

Daniel obviously saw what she was doing, because he snarled something in a harsh, guttural language and hurled a bolt of concentrated darkness at Pru.

But Caleb intercepted it.

He didn't know how he'd moved that fast, didn't know where the speed had come from. One moment, he was on the floor with glass embedded in his back, and the next, he was standing between Pru and that killing bolt of shadow, his hands raised to catch it.

And then the darkness hit him.

It was cold, so cold it burned, and it brought with it whispers of things Caleb had tried very hard to forget. Hell. The endless darkness of the pit. The screaming of the damned and the laughter of those who tormented them. His time trapped in that place came flooding back, and for a moment, he was there again, lost in the darkness with no hope of escape.

Then he felt Delia.

Through their bond, through a connection that had only grown stronger since she'd conceived their child, he felt her reaching for him. Her love was a warm light cutting through the shadows, her determination a steady anchor holding him in place. She couldn't speak aloud, couldn't move from the chair where Pru was still working to free her, but she was there with him nonetheless.

I've got you, he felt her think. *You're not alone.*

Caleb roared and pushed back against the darkness.

Fire erupted from his entire body, not just his hands this time, but his arms, his torso, his legs, every inch of him blazing with heat that burned away the shadows Daniel had thrown at him. The bolt of darkness shattered like glass, and Caleb stood in its aftermath, wreathed in flames that licked harmlessly against his skin.

Daniel's eyes widened. For just a moment, something that might have been surprise flickered across his features.

"Interesting," he murmured.

Then Ty was on him again, light blade flashing, and Daniel had to turn his attention back to the half angel or risk losing his head. The two of them clashed in a fury of light and shadow, divine power against demonic corruption, and the room shook with each impact of their blows.

Caleb wanted to join the fight, wanted to tear his father apart for everything he'd done, but he forced himself to hold his position. Pru needed protection while she worked on Delia's restraints, and that mattered more than simple revenge.

"How many of these goddamn locks are there?" Pru muttered, her picks scraping against metal.

"The wards are layered into the chains," Delia

said. Her voice was strained but steady. "They're designed to dampen psychic energy. Ty might be able to—"

"A little busy right now," Ty called to her, sounding breathless. He ducked under a swipe of Daniel's shadow-wreathed hand and retaliated with a thrust that opened a gash across Daniel's shoulder. Black blood welled from the wound, smoking where it dripped onto the floor. "But I'll try to work on weakening them from here."

The light emanating from Ty's blade seemed to pulse brighter for a moment, and Delia gasped as something seemed to shift in the energy around her.

"That helped," she said quickly. "The wards are flickering. Pru, try the left wrist again."

Pru's picks found something, and there was a *click* as the first restraint fell away. Delia immediately used her freed hand to start working on the chains across her torso, her fingers finding the clasp while Pru attacked the other wrist restraint.

But Daniel had noticed what was happening. He disengaged from Ty with a burst of shadow that drove the half angel backward, and he turned toward the chair where Delia was being freed.

"No," he said. His voice echoed with something old and terrible, something that sounded nothing like Daniel Lockwood. "She stays."

He raised his hand and darkness gathered

around his fingers, coalescing into something that looked disturbingly like spears of solidified shadow.

Caleb moved to intercept, but he knew he wouldn't make it in time. Daniel was too fast, the distance too great, and those shadow spears were already flying toward Delia and Pru.

The spears shattered against a wall of shimmering silver light.

Caleb stared. The barrier had materialized out of nowhere, a dome of psychic energy surrounding Delia's chair, with Pru still crouched beside it. It was barely visible, a faint shimmer in the air that you probably wouldn't notice unless you were looking directly at it.

Delia's eyes were closed, her freed hand pressed flat against her stomach where their baby grew.

She'd done that. Even still partially restrained, even exhausted from hours of captivity, she'd manifested a psychic shield strong enough to stop Daniel's attack.

"Impossible," Daniel breathed. His bone-pale eyes were fixed on the barrier with something that looked almost like hunger. "That level of power shouldn't be possible without decades of training."

"You don't understand anything about her," Caleb snapped. He gathered his fire and pulled it inward, condensing it into something hotter and brighter than he'd ever managed before. "You don't understand anything about us."

And then he threw everything he had at his father.

The fire hit Daniel's center mass and drove him backward across the room. For the first time since the fight had begun, Daniel screamed—not in anger, but in genuine pain, his composure cracking as the flames ate into his stolen power.

Ty pressed the advantage immediately. His light blade swept down in a devastating arc that would have bisected Daniel from shoulder to hip if the cambion hadn't twisted away at the last second. Even so, the blade carved a deep furrow across Daniel's back, and more of that smoking black blood sprayed across the floor.

"The last restraint," Pru announced. There was a final *click,* and Delia lurched forward out of the chair on unsteady legs.

She was free.

Delia stumbled to her feet, every muscle screaming in protest after too many hours bound to that chair. Her ankles ached from the restraints, her wrists were raw, and her entire body was weighed down with the kind of exhaustion that made it hard to think straight.

But she was free, and Caleb was fighting for her, and their baby's energy was humming through her like an electric current, amplifying everything she felt and sensed and could do.

Across the room, Caleb and Ty were pressing Daniel back toward the shattered windows. Fire and light combined in devastating waves, and Daniel was actually giving ground, his shadows struggling to re-form fast enough to block the onslaught. Blood dripped from a dozen wounds on his body, and his expensive suit had been reduced to charred and tattered scraps.

But he was still standing, unfortunately. And through her connection to Caleb, Delia could feel something that made cold fear pulse in her veins. He was tiring. The fire he was throwing took energy to produce, energy he'd been burning through at an unsustainable rate ever since he'd charged into this fight. He had minutes left before he hit the wall.

Ty was in better shape, his angelic heritage giving him reserves that Caleb didn't possess, but even he was showing signs of strain. The light blade in his hand flickered occasionally, and his movements were a fraction slower than they'd been at the start.

Daniel, on the other hand, seemed to be drawing strength from somewhere beyond himself. The shadows around him were thicker now, darker, and his wounds were healing even as Delia watched, flesh knitting back together with unnatural speed.

They were losing.

Pru grabbed her arm. "We need to get out of here. Caleb and Ty can cover our retreat—"

"No." Delia shook her head. "We don't retreat. We end this."

And she reached out for Caleb.

It was different from the other times she'd done this, the accidental moments when their connection had flared and she'd felt his emotions or seen through his eyes. This time, she reached deliberately, consciously, pushing her awareness toward him with all the psychic strength she possessed.

The connection flared like a match touching gasoline.

She felt Caleb gasp, felt his surprise as her mind touched his in a way it never had before. Their bond had always been there, humming in the background, but now it was a bridge, a conduit, a pattern of silver light connecting them across the chaos of the battle.

I'm here, she thought, and she knew he heard her.

I know, he thought back. *I can feel you.*

Without discussing it, without planning it, they moved toward each other.

Caleb disengaged from Daniel with a final blast of fire that bought him a few seconds of space. He all but ran across the room, and then his hand was in hers, their fingers interlocking, and the world changed.

The psychic lattice she'd sensed during their fight with Vinea blazed back into existence, but stronger now, brighter. It was visible to everyone in the room—a web of shimmering silver and gold light that surrounded Caleb and Delia like a cocoon, pulsing in time with their heartbeats.

Caleb's fire surged brighter within that network, the flames taking on a golden quality they hadn't possessed before. Delia's psychic energy wrapped around him like armor, protecting and amplifying and channeling in ways she hadn't known were possible. And beneath it all, thrumming between them like a third heartbeat, was the baby's power—untrained, untapped potential that was nonetheless lending its strength to theirs.

The exhaustion she'd felt moments ago vanished, and the ache in her muscles faded. Even the raw skin of her wrists stopped hurting. The lattice was doing something to them, *for* them, filling them with energy that neither of them could have accessed alone.

Daniel stared at them with those eerily pale eyes, and for the first time since Delia had met him, he looked uncertain.

"What is this?" he demanded. "What are you doing?"

"Something you'll never understand," Delia said.

She and Caleb moved as one.

Fire erupted from their joined hands—not Caleb's fire alone, but something new, something that burned with both his demonic heat and her psychic energy. The flames were shot through with silver threads, and they moved with an intelligence that normal fire didn't possess, seeking out Daniel's shadows and burning through them like acid through paper.

Daniel threw up defenses, layers of darkness that should have been impenetrable. The combined fire tore through them anyway. He tried to retreat, to gain distance and regroup, but Ty was there, his light blade cutting off the escape route.

"Impossible," Daniel snarled. He hurled bolt after bolt of shadow at them, but the lattice absorbed each attack, converting the dark energy into fuel for its own radiance. "You're just children. You can't—"

The next wave of fire slammed into him.

He staggered backward, and for the first time since the fight began, real fear flickered across his haughty features. This wasn't the controlled battle of a moment ago, the careful exchange of attacks and counters. This was overwhelming force, power beyond anything he'd anticipated, and it was tearing him apart.

Caleb pushed harder, and Delia pushed with him, and together they poured everything they had into the attack. The penthouse began to come apart around them. Windows shattered, spraying glass out into the cool night air. Cracks spiderwebbed across the walls and ceiling. The sigils carved into the floor blazed bright and then went dark as the power feeding them was overwhelmed.

Daniel screamed.

It wasn't a human sound. It was something older and darker, the cry of a being that had believed itself untouchable suddenly discovering its mortality all over again. He fell to one knee, his arms raised in a desperate attempt to block the onslaught, and black blood poured from his eyes and nose and mouth.

"Enough," Caleb said, and his voice rumbled with undertones that made the very air vibrate. "It ends here."

He raised his free hand, fire blazing at his fingertips, ready to deliver the killing blow.

Caleb looked down at his father and felt nothing.

Not the rage that had driven him into this fight, not the old pain of a childhood spent trying to earn approval from a man who had none to give.

Daniel knelt before him, broken and bleeding, and Caleb felt only a cold certainty that this had to end.

The fire at his fingertips burned brighter than it ever had, fueled by the web that connected him to Delia, amplified by their child's untapped potential. One strike. That's all it would take. One concentrated blast, and Daniel Lockwood would be nothing but ash.

He drew his arm back.

Daniel looked up at him with those bone-pale eyes, and something like a smile touched his bruised and bloody mouth.

"Do it," he said. "Prove that you're my son after all."

The words hit Caleb like a bucket of ice water splashed in his face, cutting through the battle haze that had descended over his mind. He hesitated, his arm still raised, the fire still burning.

Was this what Daniel wanted? Had this whole confrontation been designed to push Caleb to this moment, to force him to embrace the darkest parts of his demon heritage? If he killed his father in cold blood, even after everything Daniel had done, would he be proving Daniel right?

Would he become the monster Daniel had always known was hiding inside him?

Delia's hand tightened on his. He could feel her love and her trust and her absolute faith that he would make the right choice. She wasn't trying to influence him, wasn't pushing him one way or the other. She was simply there, a steady presence at his side, reminding him that he wasn't alone.

He'd spent his whole life afraid of what he might become, afraid that the demon blood in his veins would turn him into something cold and cruel, something like his father. He'd hidden from that fear, suppressed it, tried to control every aspect of his power so that it could never control him.

But standing here now, with Delia's hand in his and their child's energy thrumming through both of them, he realized something.

He wasn't afraid anymore.

Not because he'd conquered the darkness inside him, but because he'd finally understood that the darkness wasn't all he was. He was demon, yes, a quarter of his blood inherited from things that had crawled out of Hell. But he was also human. He was also the man who loved Delia Dunne, the man who would do anything to protect his family.

The monster Daniel wanted him to be would have struck without hesitation. He would have reveled in the killing, in the power, in the final victory over an enemy who had caused so much pain.

Caleb wasn't that monster.

But he wasn't about to let Daniel walk away, either.

He brought his hand down, and the fire struck Daniel full in the face.

The cambion flew backward, crashing through what remained of the shattered windows and out into the night. For a heart-stopping moment, Caleb thought he'd killed him after all—but then he saw Daniel catch himself in midair, hovering on wings of shadow that hadn't been there a moment before. His face was a ruin of burned flesh and black blood, his composure finally and completely shattered.

"This isn't over," Daniel snarled. Blood dripped from his broken features, and his voice was a rasp of pain and fury. "That child is mine by blood. This fight has only begun."

Caleb raised his hand again, fire already gathering, but Daniel was melting away even as he watched, dissolving into shadow, and retreating into the darkness of the Vegas night. In seconds, he was gone, leaving nothing behind but a few drops of smoking black blood on the window frame.

Ty moved toward the broken window, his light blade still blazing. "I can pursue—"

The building groaned around them.

Caleb felt it first, a deep vibration that ran through the floor and up into his bones. The battle had done more damage than he'd realized. The penthouse was destabilizing, its structure compromised by the forces that had been unleashed inside it.

"We have to go," Ty said then, his head snapping toward the ceiling as another groan echoed through the space. "Now."

Caleb wanted to chase his father, wanted to hunt Daniel down through the darkness and finish what they'd started. The need burned in him, almost as hot as the fire still flickering at his fingertips.

But Delia was swaying on her feet, exhaustion finally catching up with her now that the battle was over. She was pale, her copper hair tangled and dirty, her eyes shadowed with more than just sleeplessness. She'd given everything she had to that fight, and she needed rest, needed safety.

Their baby needed safety.

The choice wasn't even a choice.

Caleb let the fire die and pulled Delia close, one arm wrapping protectively around her shoulders. "All right," he said. "We run."

And they did.

Chapter Seventeen

Delia's legs felt like they belonged to someone else, moving through sheer force of will rather than any physical capacity they actually possessed. The battle with Daniel had drained her in ways she hadn't known were possible, her psychic reserves scraped down to almost nothing, and the only thing currently keeping her upright was Caleb's hand locked around hers, pulling her forward through the darkness.

The stairwell glared with baleful emergency lighting and groaning metal. Somewhere above them, the penthouse was collapsing, the damage from their fight finally catching up with the building's structure. Each step sent vibrations through the floor, and dust sifted down from the ceiling in thin streams that caught the red glow of the exit signs.

"Keep moving," Caleb told her. His voice was hoarse, strained, but his grip on her hand never wavered. "Don't stop."

She didn't have the breath to answer, so she just kept running.

The stairs seemed to go on forever, flight after flight spiraling down through the guts of the pyramid. Ty was ahead of them, his light blade still glowing in one hand, casting dancing shadows on the walls. Pru brought up the rear, her empty gun replaced by a knife she must have grabbed from Ty's arsenal. None of them spoke.

There wasn't anything to say.

Delia's thought kept flashing back to the penthouse, to the moment when she and Caleb had joined hands, and the lattice had formed around them. She'd never felt anything like that before, a complete merging of power and purpose, her psychic energy intertwining with his demonic fire until she couldn't tell where she ended and he began. It had been exhilarating and terrifying in equal measure, and now that it was over, she felt hollowed out, as if someone had scooped everything vital from inside her and left only the shell behind.

The baby's energy flickered weakly against her awareness, a reminder that she wasn't the only one who had given everything to that fight.

Hold on, she thought. *We're almost out. Just hold on.*

At the twenty-fifth floor, the stairwell door burst open.

Demons poured through, three of them, smaller than the soldiers they'd fought on the way up but still dangerous enough to kill. Their eyes burned red in the darkness, and their claws scraped against the concrete as they charged.

Ty's blade swept through the first demon before it could even raise its bony hands, white light slicing through corrupted flesh like it was made of paper. The creature dissolved into ash and sulfur, and Ty was already pivoting to face the second one, his fluid movements betraying nothing of the exhaustion that must be weighing on him.

Caleb released Delia's hand just long enough to throw fire at the third demon. The flames caught it mid-leap, and it shrieked as it tumbled past them down the stairs, burning while it fell. The sound of its demise echoed off the concrete walls and mixed with the groaning of the structure above them.

"Go," Ty called out as he finished the second demon with a thrust through its chest. "I'll hold the rear."

Caleb grabbed Delia's hand again, and they kept running.

The building creaked around them, a deep, ominous sound that seemed to come from everywhere at once. Delia could feel the structure shifting, stressed beyond its tolerances by the supernatural forces that had been unleashed in the penthouse. The Luxor was a pyramid, designed to distribute weight and stress in specific ways, but it hadn't been built to withstand the kind of power she and Caleb had channeled through its apex.

Twentieth floor. Fifteenth. Tenth.

Her lungs were burning, each breath a ragged gasp that never seemed to bring enough oxygen to do much good. The muscles in her legs had progressed from aching to screaming to a kind of numb agony that she was trying very hard not to think about. She'd never been much of a runner, had always preferred yoga and a fast walk on her treadmill to anything more strenuous, and now her body was making her pay for that lack of training.

More demons appeared at the eighth-floor landing, but Caleb barely slowed down. Fire erupted from his free hand, a wave of orange and gold that drove the creatures back long enough for them to push through. One of them managed to rake its claws across Caleb's shoulder as they passed, tearing through his leather jacket and the flesh beneath, but he didn't even flinch. He just kept pulling Delia with him, moving down and down and down, with Pru's light footsteps pattering behind them.

Still, the pain of his new wound hit her

through their bond, a sharp flare of heat and agony that made her stumble. She caught herself on the railing and forced her legs to keep moving. Thanks to their connection, she could feel Caleb's determination like a physical force, his absolute refusal to stop or slow down or let anything stand between them and safety. He was running on fumes and willpower, the same as she was, but he wouldn't stop. Not until they were safe.

"Almost there," he said. "Almost there."

She believed him because she had to.

Fifth floor. Third. Second.

The stairwell ended at a heavy fire door marked with a sign that read CASINO LEVEL in faded letters. Caleb hit it at full speed, his shoulder slamming into the metal hard enough to send it crashing open, and they spilled out onto the casino floor.

The space had been transformed since they'd passed through it on the way up.

The emergency lights were flickering now, some of them dead entirely, casting the vast room in a strobing red glow that made everything look like a fever dream. The slot machines that had stood in silent rows were toppled and scattered, knocked over by something Delia didn't want to think about too closely, not when she guessed it must have been bigger than anything else they'd encountered so far. Glass from shattered display cases crunched under their feet, and the Egyptian statues that had lined the gaming aisles were cracked and broken, Anubis missing an arm, Horus lying face-down in a pile of debris.

The enormous replica of Tutankhamen's death mask had fallen from the wall and lay in pieces across a blackjack table, its golden surface reflecting the emergency lights in fragmented patterns.

And there were demons everywhere.

Not the organized soldiers from before, but a mass of chaotic creatures fleeing the collapsing upper levels just as desperately as Delia and her companions were. They scurried through the darkness like rats abandoning a sinking ship, most of them ignoring the humans in their midst, too focused on their own survival to bother with a fight.

Most of them.

One of the larger demons spotted them and changed course, its burning eyes fixed on Delia with a hunger that made her skin crawl. It was moving fast, faster than something that size should have been able to move, and she was too drained to do anything about it. Her psychic abilities were gone, emptied in the penthouse, and she had nothing left to defend herself with.

Pru stepped in front of her.

The knife in her friend's hand wasn't anything special, just steel and an edge, but Pru wielded it like she'd been training for this her whole life. She ducked under the demon's first swipe and drove the blade into its throat, then twisted and pulled, opening a wound that sprayed black, gooey blood across the dusty casino carpet.

The demon staggered, clutching at its neck, and Ty finished it with a sweep of his light blade that took its head clean off.

"The exit," he called out, pointing toward the far side of the casino floor. "Thirty seconds."

Thirty seconds. Delia could do thirty seconds.

They ran.

The casino floor seemed to stretch forever, an endless maze of overturned tables and scattered chips and broken glass. Delia's lungs were on fire, her legs screaming with every step, and she could feel the baby's energy flickering inside her, the little life that had given so much of itself to the fight now running on empty, just like its mother.

Hold on, she thought, pressing her free hand against her stomach as she ran. *Just hold on a little longer.*

A demon lunged at them from behind an overturned craps table, and Caleb incinerated it without breaking stride, the flames so hot that the creature didn't even have time to scream before it was ash. Another came at them from the left, and Ty cut it down with a backhanded sweep of his blade, not breaking stride.

The exit materialized out of the darkness, a rectangle of light that seemed impossibly bright after the gloom of the casino. There were the emergency doors, propped open by a fallen statue of some Egyptian deity Delia couldn't identify, leading out onto the service road they'd used to enter what felt like a lifetime ago.

They were going to make it.

And then the floor began to buckle beneath them.

Delia stumbled, her ankle turning on a piece of debris, and she would have fallen if Caleb hadn't caught her. He swept her up without breaking stride, one arm under her knees and one behind her back, carrying her the last twenty feet to the exit like she weighed nothing at all.

At last, they burst through the doors and into the night.

Fresh air surrounded her, cool and clean after the stale atmosphere inside the pyramid. The sounds of the city crashed over her in a wave—music from the Strip, laughter and shouting, the distant wail of sirens, the constant hum of a city that never stopped moving. Halloween was still in full swing, thousands of people celebrating in costumes and masks just a few hundred yards away, completely unaware of the nightmare that had been playing out inside the dark pyramid behind them.

Caleb set her down gently, although he kept one arm around her waist to steady her. They stood in the shadow of the Luxor's eastern face, the black glass walls rising above them toward the apex where the spotlight beam still cut through the sky, impossibly bright against the darkness of the abandoned building.

For a moment, no one spoke. They just stood there, breathing hard, letting the reality of their survival sink in.

Then Ty pulled out his phone, his fingers flying across the screen. "I need a full team at the Luxor," he said, sounding far less exhausted than he should have been. "Yes, now. I'll explain everything when you get here, but the short version is this—Caleb's father is the head of the Styx Group, he has Belial's power, and he's been using the Luxor as a base of operations."

A pause while whoever was on the other end responded.

"No, we didn't kill him. He escaped." Another pause. "Yes, I'm sure. I watched him dissolve into shadow and disappear. He's wounded, but he's alive." Ty's jaw tightened. "Just get the team here. We need to secure this location before he has a chance to regroup." He ended the call and turned to face them, his expression grim. "My people are mobilizing. They'll have a containment team here within the hour."

"What will they do?" Pru asked. She'd moved so she stood next to Delia, knife still in one hand, her dark eyes scanning the shadows around them. "Can they track him?"

"They'll try." Ty didn't sound very optimistic, though. "But Daniel has Belial's power now. That includes the ability to move through shadows, to hide from conventional detection. If he doesn't want to be found...." He shook his head, then added, "We'll find him eventually. But it might take time."

Time. Delia thought about what Daniel had said in the penthouse, about his plans to open a permanent gateway to Hell, about the army of demons he wanted to bring through. They didn't have time.

But that was a problem for tomorrow. Right now, she was too exhausted to think about anything beyond the next few minutes.

Pru turned to her, one hand reaching out to grip her arm. "Are you hurt? The baby?"

The question cut through the fog of exhaustion, and Delia forced herself to focus. She reached inward with what little remained of her psychic senses, searching for that familiar pulse of energy, the second heartbeat that had become as natural to her as her own.

It was there.

Thank God. The baby's energy signature

pulsed beneath her hand, steady and strong despite everything they'd been through. Relief washed through her, so intense that her knees nearly buckled.

"We're okay," she said, and her voice wasn't much more than a harsh whisper. "Shaken, but okay."

Pru's face crumpled with relief, and she pulled Delia into a hug that was fierce enough to hurt. "Don't you ever scare me like that again," she said against her shoulder. "I mean it. Never again."

Delia hugged her back, drawing strength from her friend's familiar presence. They'd been a part of one another's lives for so many years now, had been through things that would have broken most friendships, and Pru had never once let her down. Even now, even after everything, Pru was here, solid and real and refusing to let go.

"I'll do my best," Delia replied.

"You'd better." Pru pulled back and swiped at her eyes with the back of her hand. "Because if you make me storm another demon stronghold, I'm going to be seriously pissed."

Despite everything, Delia almost smiled.

When Pru finally released her, Delia turned to find Caleb.

He was standing apart from the group, his back to them as he stared up at the dark pyramid that had almost become their tomb. The spotlight beam cut through the sky above the apex, unchanged, eternal, as if nothing had happened. But Delia could see the tension in his shoulders, the rigid set of his spine, the way his hands were clenched into fists at his sides.

She went to him.

Her legs protested every step, but she made them carry her anyway, crossing the distance between them until she was near enough to touch him. Up close, she could see the damage the fight had done, the tears in his leather jacket, the blood seeping through his shirt where the demon had clawed him, the bruises already forming on his jaw and temple. His demon blood would heal the wounds eventually, but right now, he looked like he'd been through a war.

Which, she supposed, he had.

But it was his eyes that worried her most. When he finally turned to look at her, she saw a different kind of war raging behind them, emotions churning so fast and fierce that she couldn't separate one from another. Rage and pain and betrayal...and underneath it all, a grief so profound that it made her breath catch in her throat.

His father was alive, had been alive this whole time, had orchestrated every attack and every danger they'd faced since Caleb had returned from Hell. His father had tried to take her, tried to claim their baby, had revealed himself to be a monster beyond anything they'd imagined.

And somewhere in the darkness of Vegas, wounded but not defeated, Daniel Lockwood was already planning his next move.

"Hey," Delia said softly. She reached up and touched Caleb's face, her palm cool against his bruised cheek. "Look at me."

He did. Those brown eyes, usually so warm, were haunted now, shadowed by things he probably couldn't even put into words.

"We're alive," she said. "All of us. We made it out."

"He's still out there." Caleb's voice was scraped raw by smoke and screaming and all the fire he'd thrown. "He's still alive, and he's going to come after us again. After you and the baby."

"I know," she said quietly.

"I should have killed him when I had the chance." His jaw tightened, a muscle jumping beneath the bruised skin. "I had him on his knees. I could have ended it."

"Maybe." She kept her hand on his face, fingers gently stroking his cheekbone. "But you didn't, and that doesn't make you weak. It makes you human."

Something flickered in his expression, too fast for her to catch.

"He wanted me to do it," Caleb said. "That's

what I keep thinking about. Right at the end, when I had him beaten, he smiled. He smiled and told me to prove I was his son." His voice dropped. "He wanted me to become a monster. He wanted me to prove that I was just like him. And I almost gave him exactly what he wanted."

"But you didn't."

"No." He let out a breath that seemed to hold years of pain within it. "I didn't."

"Because you're not like him." Delia stepped closer, close enough that she could feel the heat radiating from his body, the warmth that came from the fire that lived inside. "You never were. Daniel Lockwood spent his whole life alone, using people and even his fellow cambions like pieces on a game board. You're nothing like that. You never have been."

Caleb was quiet for a long moment, his haunted gaze searching her face as if he was looking for something. Proof, she supposed, confirmation that she believed what she was saying.

"He's my father," he said at last. "His blood is in my veins. His demon heritage is part of who I am."

"So is your mother's humanity, and the humanity from the woman who was Daniel's mother. So is every choice you've ever made to be something better than what he wanted you to be." She went up on her toes and kissed him.

It wasn't gentle. There was nothing gentle about the fear and relief and desperate love that surged through her as her lips met his. She kissed him like she was claiming him, like she was reminding them both that they were alive and whole and still standing despite everything the universe had thrown at them. His arms came around her, pulling her close, and she felt some of the tension drain out of him as he kissed her back.

When they finally broke apart, both of them breathing hard, she kept her forehead pressed against his.

"He'll come after us again," she said. "I know that, and you know that. But not tonight. Tonight, we survived. Tonight, we won."

Caleb was silent for a moment, his arms still wrapped around her, his breath warm against her skin.

"We won," he repeated, like he was testing the words, trying to see if they felt true.

"We did. And we'll keep winning, because that's what we do." She pulled back just far enough to meet his eyes. "You and me, Caleb. Whatever comes next, we face it. And we won't stop fighting until our family is safe."

Something shifted in his expression. It wasn't quite peace she saw there, not yet, but it looked like something close to it. This was an acceptance of the battle that lay ahead and the strength they'd need to face it.

"Whatever comes next," he agreed.

Behind them, sirens were growing closer, and Delia could hear Ty talking on his phone again, coordinating with his mysterious compatriots, who appeared to be on their way. Pru stood, her knife still in her hand, watching the shadows around them with eyes that wouldn't rest until they were somewhere truly safe.

The Luxor loomed above them, dark and damaged and no longer quite so threatening now that they'd escaped its depths. The spotlight beam still cut through the sky, but it seemed dimmer somehow, less ominous. Just a light, pointing at the stars.

Tomorrow they'd start planning their next move, would sit down and attempt to figure out how to stop Daniel before he could try again.

The war would continue.

But tonight, as she stood in the shadow of the pyramid with Caleb's arms around her and her friends at her back, Delia let herself breathe.

Chapter Eighteen

Five days since their confrontation with Daniel Lockwood at the Luxor.

Delia stood in her living room—*their* living room now, she reminded herself—and watched Caleb hang a new ward above the front door. The first one had been destroyed in the demon attack, shattered along with half the furniture and most of her sense of security. But they'd put it back together as quickly as they could, Caleb insisting that they go out shopping as soon as they both felt physically able. Now the living room sported a new couch and a new coffee table, with a brand-new rug covering the wood floor...and with new protections layered into every corner of the space.

She'd thought about making a claim with her homeowner's insurance—although she had no idea how she'd ever be able to explain how the damage had occurred—but Caleb had shot that notion down right away. He was the one who'd paid for all the new furniture, telling her that if he hadn't gotten involved with her, there wouldn't have been any reason for a bunch of demons to rampage through her house. And although she'd come up with several arguments to counter that view of the situation, one look at his face had told her she should just go with the flow on this one.

"A little to the left," she said, tilting her head to study the ward's placement.

Caleb shifted it a quarter inch. "Better?"

"Perfect."

He got down from the stepladder and surveyed his work. The ward was a simple thing to look at—just a piece of hammered copper etched with symbols she couldn't read—but she could feel the power thrumming through it. Ty had provided the ward, along with half a dozen others, and the result was a house that felt safer than it had any right to feel.

Safer, but not completely safe. Nothing was truly safe anymore.

To be honest, those five days since Halloween had gone by much more quickly than she'd thought they would. She and Caleb had recorded statements that Ty passed along to his people, whoever they really were. More half angels? True angels? He hadn't said, and she hadn't asked.

Pru recovered the footage from the surveillance hub, and they'd all examined it frame by frame until Delia's eyes had ached from staring at the laptop screen. The rest of the time...well, when she and Caleb weren't furniture shopping...had been taken up by planning sessions that went deep into the night as they mapped Daniel's known operations and identified weak points in his network, preparing for what they all knew was coming.

Daniel Lockwood was still out there. Wounded, yes—she knew they'd hurt him in that confrontation at the Luxor—but not broken. He was hiding somewhere in the pyramid's depths, licking his wounds and planning his next move. Ty's people had established a perimeter, had been monitoring the building around the clock, but they hadn't been able to flush him out. The Luxor was too big, too full of hidden spaces and forgotten corners, and Daniel had clearly been preparing it as a stronghold for months.

He would come for them again. The only real question was when.

"You're thinking too loud," Caleb said as he came over and stood next to her.

"Sorry." She leaned into him, letting his warmth seep into her bones. "I'm trying not to."

"How's that working out?"

"Not great."

His arm came around her shoulders, and they

stood there in silence as they looked at the room they'd reclaimed. New furniture, yes, but the throw blankets were the same ones she'd always had, rescued from the bedroom where they'd escaped the destruction. Family photographs still lined the mantel, a few of the frames replaced, but the pictures themselves were unchanged. Her grandmother's antique clock sat on the bookshelf, still ticking steadily, unmarked by the chaos that had erupted around it.

The bones of the place were good. That's what she'd thought when she'd first bought the house a few years ago—a Mediterranean-style home in an upscale Henderson neighborhood, twenty-five hundred square feet of warm stucco and clay tile roofing. The house was smaller than Caleb's modernized mid-century place by about a thousand square feet, but it had never felt cramped. It had felt like hers, and now it was starting to feel like theirs.

It had weathered this storm. They would weather the next one, too.

"I heard from Lisa about the Mersault Court property," Delia said next. Lisa Alexander was their real estate agent, the one who'd been helping them navigate the purchase of the Summerlin house, since she and Caleb had agreed that it would be better to let a third party handle the transaction rather than doing it themselves.

Caleb's arm tightened slightly around her. "And?"

Delia allowed herself a sigh. This sort of thing cropped up all the time, but it still annoyed her that they'd have to deal with these sorts of mundane complications when they already had so much occupying their time and energy. "Title issues. The sellers' grandmother apparently died intestate in 2010, and there's some question about whether the current owners actually have a clear title. Lisa says it could take weeks to sort out, maybe even months."

She felt him absorb this information, the slight tension in his muscles as he processed the disappointment. They'd both fallen in love with that house—the courtyard entry, the mature landscaping, the two-story living room with its curved staircases. It had felt like a place where they could build a future.

"Weeks," he repeated.

"At least. The title company is trying to track down some distant cousin in Ohio who might have a claim. It's a mess."

Caleb was quiet for a moment. Then he surprised her by laughing, a short huff of breath that seemed to contain more amusement than frustration.

"What?" she asked.

"Nothing. It's just—" He shook his head, even

as he smiled a little. "A month ago, this would have felt like a disaster. The house of our dreams, snatched away by legal complications. I probably would have spent a week trying to fix it, calling lawyers, tracking down that cousin myself."

"And now?"

"Now it feels like a blessing." He turned her in his arms so they were facing each other, his hands settling on her hips. "We've got enough on our plate without adding a two-million-dollar real estate transaction to the mix. And honestly?" He glanced around the living room, taking in the arched doorways, the warm terra-cotta accents, the afternoon light streaming through the windows. "I like it here. It's you. It feels like home."

Something warm and happy seemed to come alive within her. "It does now that you're here."

"Was that cheesy?" His brown eyes crinkled at the corners. "That felt cheesy."

"Maybe a little." She rose on her toes to kiss him, brief and sweet. "I didn't mind."

They'd get their house eventually, the courtyard and the staircases and the room they'd already started planning as a nursery. When this was over—when Daniel was dealt with, when they could breathe again—they'd pick up where they'd left off. Lisa would sort out the title issues, and they'd close escrow, and they'd start the next chapter of their lives in a home they'd chosen together.

But for now, this house with its reinforced wards and its patchwork of old and new, familiar and rebuilt, was exactly what she needed.

"We should eat something," she said. "Pru's bringing dinner later, but I could make sandwiches."

"In a minute." Caleb hadn't released her, his hands still warm on her hips, and there was something in his expression that made her pause.

"Caleb?" she asked, knowing how hesitant she sounded.

He took a breath. "I've been carrying something around for the past few days, waiting for the right moment."

Her heart began to beat a little faster as soon as she heard those words. Now she knew what was coming—had known, on some level, since the moment she'd watched him choose her over pursuing Daniel in the Luxor, since she'd felt his fire wrap around her in that penthouse suite, protective rather than destructive, his power joined with hers in a way that had felt like a promise.

"Carrying what?"

Instead of replying immediately, he reached into his pocket and pulled out a small box. It was black velvet, the type that could only mean one thing. He didn't kneel—they were past the kind of relationship where those sorts of grand gestures felt necessary—but the look in his eyes was far more serious than she'd ever seen it.

"I asked you once before," he said. "You told me to ask again when we weren't both freaking out."

"I remember." Her voice was steady, which surprised her. Inside, her pulse was racing, but it wasn't from fear. Not this time.

"I'm not freaking out now," he said quietly, and opened the box.

The ring inside caught the lamplight and threw it back in a thousand tiny fractals. It was simpler than she might have expected from him, given his taste for expensive things—a square-cut diamond in a platinum setting, clean lines, no unnecessary flourishes. It was the kind of ring that said he'd been paying attention all along, had noticed that she preferred elegant simplicity to ostentatious display.

The kind of ring that looked like it belonged on her hand.

"I'm not asking because I'm scared," Caleb said. "I'm not asking because we're about to go to war, or because I'm trying to lock you down before something happens to one of us." His voice lowered but was no less intense for all that. "I'm asking because I choose you, no matter what's coming. Marry me, Delia."

She looked at his face—the face she'd been

waking up next to for months, the face she'd learned to read like a familiar book. The stubborn set of his jaw when he was determined, the way his eyes softened when he looked at her, the faint lines at the corners of his mouth that deepened when he smiled. She thought about everything they'd been through to get here, all the way back to the first time she'd met him, when she'd thought he was nothing more than a client looking for a house to flip, and then the slow realization that he was something else entirely—something complicated and damaged and determined to be better than his blood suggested he should be.

And she couldn't help thinking about the night he'd proposed the first time, both of them reeling from the pregnancy news, terror and hope tangled together until neither of them could think straight. She'd told him no. Not because she didn't want to marry him, but because she'd wanted it to mean something more than panic and obligation.

Now, here they were, not quite a week later, having survived everything their enemies had thrown at them. She'd watched him face his father—the father he'd thought was safely trapped in Hell, the half demon who'd orchestrated months of attacks against them—and choose her, choose the family they were building over the family that had failed him.

She thought about what it meant to say yes.

This was about agreeing to build a life together, choosing to build something permanent with someone who could summon fire from nothing, who had demon blood flowing in his veins, who would spend the rest of his days fighting to protect the people he loved.

"Yes."

No hesitation, no doubt. Just yes.

Caleb's expression transformed. The careful control he'd been holding onto so tightly seemed to break into pieces, and underneath was something raw and open, a relief so profound that it looked almost like pain, joy so bright that it made her eyes sting. He'd been afraid, she realized then. Despite everything, despite the confidence in his voice when he'd asked, some part of him had been braced for rejection.

"'Yes'?" he repeated, as though he needed to hear it again to believe it.

"Yes." She laughed, the sound wet with tears she hadn't even realized were forming in her eyes. "Did you really think I'd say no?"

"I thought—" He shook his head, unable to finish the sentence. His hands were trembling slightly as he took the ring from the box, and she held out her left hand, watching as he slid the platinum band onto her finger. It fit perfectly, the diamond catching the light like a captured star.

"You had it sized," she said.

"I borrowed one of your other rings, the silver one with the green tourmaline that you wear on your right hand sometimes." He looked almost sheepish. "Pru helped."

Of course Pru had helped. Delia made a mental note to interrogate her best friend about how long she'd been keeping this secret.

"It's beautiful," she said, and meant it. The ring was elegant and understated and exactly what she would have chosen for herself if she'd been the one doing the choosing. Which, she supposed, was the point.

"You didn't even really look at it," Caleb said, laughter at the edges of his voice despite the emotion that still roughened it.

"I don't need to look at it." She grabbed the front of his shirt and pulled him down to her. "I just need you."

There was heat in that kiss, of course—there was always heat between them—but underneath the passion was something steady and strong. His arms came around her, and he lifted her slightly, her toes leaving the floor, and she wrapped herself around him like she never wanted to let go.

Because she didn't. That was the simple truth of it. Whatever came next, she wanted to face it with this man...this infuriating, protective, stubborn, loving man who had somehow become the center of her world.

When they finally pulled apart, both of them breathless, she kept her arms around his neck and looked at his face. That was the face she'd wake up next to for the rest of her life, the face of the man she loved, the father of her child, her partner in every sense of the word.

"We're really doing this," she said.

"We're really doing this," Caleb repeated. He was smiling now, that full smile she loved, the one that made him look younger and less burdened by the weight he could never quite let go of. "You're stuck with me now."

She smiled back at him. "I think I can live with that."

He kissed her again, more softly this time, and she felt the last of the tension drain out of both of them. They'd been running on adrenaline and fear for so long that she'd almost forgotten what it was like to just be still, to exist in a moment without waiting for the next attack.

"Your father is going to lose his mind," she said when they separated. The words had slipped out before she could stop them, and she watched his expression flicker. "Sorry. I shouldn't have—"

"No, you're right." Caleb's jaw tightened, then released. "Daniel thought he could use us. He thought I was just a tool and you were just a vessel for something he wanted to control. He doesn't understand what we are...what we have." His hand moved to her stomach, pressing flat against the place where their child was growing. "He'll never understand it. That's why we beat him."

Delia covered his hand with hers. Seven weeks now, still no visible sign of the pregnancy, but she could feel the baby's energy pulsing beneath their joined palms. Demonic and human and something entirely new, a spark of potential that had already proved stronger than either of them had expected.

The shield she'd thrown in the Luxor—that had been partly the baby's power, channeled through her own expanding abilities. She'd felt it in the moment, that surge of energy rising from her core, demonic fire mixed with something else. Ty had confirmed it afterward, his expression carefully neutral in a way that told her he was more concerned than he wanted to show.

The baby was far more powerful than anyone had anticipated. And that power was only going to grow.

"He's still out there," she said. She didn't bother to say who; they both knew who she was talking about.

Caleb's expression darkened, but he didn't look away. "I know. He'll come for us again. For the baby."

"But not today."

"Not today," he agreed.

They stood there for a while longer, hands

joined over the life they were protecting, in the living room of the house that had become their home. Hunkered down in the damaged Luxor, Daniel Lockwood was plotting his next move, gathering his strength for another assault.

But that was tomorrow's battle. Next week's war.

Right now, in this moment, Delia let herself luxuriate in the weight of the ring on her finger and the warmth of Caleb's body against hers. She let herself imagine the future they might have—the house in Summerlin once the title cleared, a nursery painted in soft colors, a child with her eyes and his powers, growing up surrounded by people who would fight to keep it safe.

They'd earned this moment of peace.

Whatever came next, they would face it the way they'd faced everything else, side by side, ready to fight.

"I love you," she said.

Caleb's smile was like the sun coming up. "I love you, too."

Chapter Nineteen

Someone knocked at the door just as the sun had sunk behind the Spring Mountains.

Caleb was sitting on the couch with Delia, her head resting against his shoulder, both of them content to simply exist in the quiet afterglow of his proposal. The ring on her finger caught the lamplight every time she moved, and he found himself watching those small flashes of brilliance with something like wonder. She'd said yes. After everything they'd been through, after all the fear and uncertainty, after knowing exactly who and what he was...she'd still said yes.

He should have known this fragile peace wouldn't last.

The knock came again, more insistent this time, and Caleb felt the familiar prickle at the back of his neck that signaled a supernatural presence.

This one wasn't hostile, though. He'd learned to read the difference over the past seven or eight months, to distinguish between the cold dread that signaled demons were nearby and the warmer, brighter sensation that told him Ty was somewhere in the vicinity.

"That's them," Delia said, straightening and lifting her head from Caleb's shoulder. "Pru texted earlier that they were coming over after dinner."

Caleb rose from the couch and went over to the door, pausing to look through the peephole out of habit even though he already knew who was waiting at the front door. Ty stood outside, his dark hair pulled back in its usual ponytail, the porch lights illuminating a serious expression that immediately put Caleb on edge. Pru was right behind him, her laptop bag slung over one shoulder, her dark green hair gleaming in that same warm light.

Neither of them looked like they were here for a casual visit. Of course, Caleb had already known they weren't coming over for tea and crumpets.

He opened the door and stepped aside to let them in. "What's wrong now?"

"Nothing's wrong...exactly." Ty went past him into the living room, his gaze sweeping the space as if scanning for threats, even though they all knew things had been utterly quiet the past couple of days. "But we have some new information. My people have been analyzing everything we gathered from the Luxor, and they've put together a more complete picture of what we're facing."

Pru followed, already pulling her laptop from its bag. "Hey, lovebirds. Nice ring, by the way." She shot Delia a quick grin that didn't quite reach her eyes, as if she was waiting for her friend to give her some grief about hiding such a big secret. "It's about time he made an honest woman of you."

"You helped pick it out," Delia replied, mouth twitching a bit.

"Which is why it's so tasteful instead of some gaudy monstrosity with diamonds the size of golf balls. There is some seriously tacky bling to be had in this town." As she spoke, she got her laptop set up on the coffee table, and her fingers began moving across the keyboard with their usual sure speed. "But we can talk about wedding plans later. Right now, we've got other things we need to worry about."

Caleb and Delia sat back down on the couch, while Ty took the armchair across from them. Pru seemed to choose efficiency over comfort and perched on the edge of the coffee table next to her laptop.

"My people have been going through the intelligence we recovered," Ty began. He sounded calm enough, but Caleb could see the tension in his shoulders and hear the careful way he chose his words. "Combined with what they already knew about the Styx Group's operations, they've been able to piece together Daniel's plan."

In a way, it felt better to think about their adversary as Daniel Lockwood rather than his father. The word still felt wrong in Caleb's mouth, still held too many echoes of a childhood spent trying to earn approval from a man who had none to give. It had been almost comforting to know that Daniel was trapped in Hell and had finally been excised from his life. Learning the truth—that he had not only survived but had been orchestrating attacks against their little group for months—had torn open wounds he'd thought had long since scarred over.

"What kind of plan?" Delia asked. Her hand found his, and he could practically feel her steadiness flowing into him, anchoring him against the anger that threatened to rise.

Ty leaned forward. "When Belial died, his power had to go somewhere. Daniel was the son of his lieutenant, his most trusted servant on Earth. The power flowed into him, made him something more than a simple half demon." He paused, and worry flickered in those bright blue eyes. "My people have confirmed it now. Daniel doesn't just have some of Belial's power. He has *all* of it. He's essentially become a demon prince in human form."

Caleb forced himself not to react. After all, he'd already suspected as much after the confrontation at the Luxor, had felt the weight of his father's power pressing against him, implacable, massive, so much more than a half demon should have been able to summon. Hearing those suspicions confirmed, knowing that Daniel had absorbed the full might of one of Hell's most powerful beings, made the threat feel suddenly, terrifyingly real.

"That's why we couldn't beat him," he said. The words sounded almost clinical, as if he were discussing a theoretical problem rather than a very real menace that threatened all their lives. "We hurt him, but we couldn't finish it."

"You hurt him badly," Ty replied. "The combined force of your fire and Delia's psychic abilities, amplified by the baby's power—that was enough to wound him, to force him to retreat. But you're right. It wasn't enough to destroy him."

As he finished speaking, Pru turned her laptop so they could all see the screen. A map of Las Vegas filled the display, dotted with red markers that clustered in certain areas, connected by lines that formed patterns Caleb couldn't quite interpret.

"This is everything we've been able to track," she said. "Styx Group properties, known demon activity, energy signatures Ty's people have picked up over the past few months. Daniel hasn't just been sitting in the Luxor, waiting for us to come to him. He's been building infrastructure for himself. Safe houses, supply caches, recruitment networks. The Styx Group is just the tip of the iceberg."

Caleb studied the map, his jaw tightening as he took in the scope of what they faced. There were dozens of locations spread across the entire valley, from downtown to Henderson to Summerlin to North Las Vegas. His father had been a busy little bee.

"He's got millions and millions," Pru continued. "Hidden accounts, shell companies, assets we're still trying to trace. And he has connections everywhere. I'm pretty sure that some are demons who owe him favors, while others are ordinary humans who work for the Styx Group without knowing what they're really serving. This isn't just one half demon with delusions of grandeur. This is a full-on demonic organization."

"What's his endgame?" Delia asked. Her voice was steady, but Caleb could feel her fear, the cold thread of dread that wound its way through that practiced composure. "What's all this building toward?"

Ty's expression turned grim. "The same thing we've been trying to prevent this whole time—a permanent gateway. That's what Belial wanted, what he'd been working toward for centuries before he was killed, and it's what Vinea was attempting as well, of course. A stable portal between Hell and Earth that would allow demons to pass through freely, whenever they chose. Daniel intends to finish what Belial started."

"The Greencastle demons," Caleb said. Vinea had teased him with that possibility, and now it seemed as if it might finally come to fruition. "The half demons and quarter demons still trapped in Hell. He's going to bring them through this time."

"Them, and worse." Ty met his eyes, and there was no comfort in that gaze. "Anyone who served Belial, anyone who's been promised a place in the new order Daniel's planning to build. If that gateway opens, it won't just be a few demons slipping through during Halloween or on other nights when the veil is thin. It'll be an invasion."

A heavy silence followed those words. Yes, they'd faced a threat like this before, when Vinea had come so close to opening such a gateway, but this was far worse. Vinea was one of many lords of Hell, while Daniel...now embodying all the powers Belial had bequeathed him...was an order of magnitude greater, for all intents and purposes now one of Hell's seven princes. Caleb felt Delia's hand tighten on his, felt the weight of her engagement ring against his palm, and something cold and heavy settled in his gut like a lump of lead. They'd just promised each other a future. Now they were facing the possibility that there might not be a future to have.

"When?" he asked, hearing how tight that single syllable sounded. "When is he planning to do this?"

"The black moon," Ty replied. "November eighth. That's only three days from now."

Three days. Caleb knew a lot could happen in three days, but he still didn't know if it would be enough time to stop a demon lord from tearing open a hole between worlds.

"The veil between worlds is always thin at the new moon," Ty continued. "Demons like to operate in the dark, and with no moon to expose their deeds, they're going to throw everything they have at opening the gate. If Daniel attempts the ritual on that night, with Belial's power backing him, he might actually succeed."

"So we'll stop him before then," Caleb said. Anger was rising in him now, burning away the cold dread. His father had threatened Delia, threatened their child, built an empire of darkness with the intention of unleashing Hell on Earth. There was no room for the complicated feelings of abandonment and betrayal that had plagued him ever since their confrontation at the Luxor. There was only the simple, clarifying certainty that Daniel Lockwood needed to be stopped.

"That's the plan." Ty nodded. "My people are mobilizing. They've authorized a full coordinated strike against Daniel's operations, his resources, everything. We'll hit him as hard as we can, weaken his position, and try to destroy the infrastructure he's built. If we can do enough damage, he won't be able to complete the ritual even with the dark of the moon amplifying his power."

"And if we can't weaken him enough?" Delia asked quietly.

The question hung there for a moment before Ty answered. "Then we'll face him directly on the night of the new moon. We have to do whatever it takes to prevent that gateway from opening."

Pru looked up from her laptop, slender dark brows pulling together. "Your people are willing to commit full resources to this? That doesn't sound like their usual M.O. Aren't they all about being hands-off?"

"This isn't a usual situation," Ty said, his voice hard. "Daniel with Belial's power, opening a permanent gateway to Hell? That's an apocalyptic-level threat. My people don't have a choice. If they don't stop this here, there won't be anything left to protect."

Caleb absorbed those words, turning them over in his mind. He still didn't have a clear picture of who or what those involved actually were, beyond Ty's off-hand references to an organization that monitored supernatural activity. Ty had always been purposely vague, and Caleb had never pushed. But if they were willing to throw everything they had at Daniel, the threat must be even worse than he'd imagined.

"What do you need from us?" he asked.

"Everything you can give." Ty got up from his chair and went over to the fireplace, as if he needed to move and burn off some of the restless energy all of them were probably grappling with right then. "We have less than three days, since the exact time of the new moon is two minutes after six, local time. We'll need to gather intelligence on Daniel's operations, identify targets for my people to strike, and strengthen the wards on this house and any other location where you might take shelter. Delia, you'll need to do whatever you can to continue your training. Your abilities have grown exponentially, but you still need to learn to control them, to use them deliberately instead of instinctively."

Delia nodded, her graceful jaw set. "I can do that."

"Caleb." Ty turned to face him, and something in those sky-blue eyes made Caleb's spine straighten. "You need to fully integrate your demon powers. I know you've been holding back, trying to control the fire instead of embracing it. But against Daniel, half-measures won't be enough. You'll need everything you have."

Those words sent a chill through Caleb, even as he recognized their truth. He'd spent so long fighting against his demon blood, terrified of what he might become if he let it take over. But in the Luxor, when Delia's life and their baby's life had been on the line, he'd stopped fighting. He'd chosen to use his power instead of being used by it.

He could do that again. He *would* do that again. For Delia, and for their child. For the future they'd promised each other.

"I understand," he said.

Pru cleared her throat. "I've been going through the financial records we recovered from Daniel's surveillance hub. There's a pattern here, a schedule of payments to various locations around the city. I think these might be his safe houses, places where his people are stationed. If we can verify the addresses, your people could hit them simultaneously."

Ty nodded. "Good. Send me what you have, and I'll pass it along to the strike coordinators."

He returned to his chair and sat back down, and they spent the next hour going over as many details as possible—target locations, timing, resources. Pru pulled up schematics and satellite images, her fingers flying across the keyboard as she cross-referenced data and built out a picture of Daniel's network. At the same time, Ty provided some context for all that information, explaining how the organization he worked with would approach each target and what kind of resistance they might expect.

Caleb listened, absorbing the tactical information, but part of his mind seemed to be elsewhere. Something was nagging at him, a half-remembered thought that tugged at the edges of his consciousness. It felt important, but every time he tried to focus on it, it slipped away like water through his fingers.

What the hell was he forgetting?

"The Luxor itself is the biggest problem," Ty was saying. "Daniel's fortified it with wards and demonic energy. My people have had teams monitoring the perimeter since Halloween, but we haven't been able to penetrate the building's defenses. Whatever ritual space he's constructed inside, it's protected by some of the strongest shielding I've ever encountered."

"So even if we destroy everything else, he can still complete the ritual if he has the Luxor," Delia said, frowning.

"Yes. Which means ultimately, we'll need to breach the pyramid and stop him directly." Ty sent them all a bleak look. "We're working on a way to get through the wards, but it won't be ready until the black moon itself. We'll have one chance to stop the ritual. If we fail...."

He didn't need to finish the sentence. They all knew what was at stake here.

"Then we won't fail," Caleb said.

The certainty in his voice surprised even him.

But as he looked at Delia, at the ring on her finger and the determination in her blue-gray eyes, a cold resolve seemed to settle within him. They'd faced demons before. They'd faced his father before. And they'd survived because they'd faced those threats together, their powers combining into something greater than either could achieve alone.

They would survive this, too.

No matter what.

Ty smiled, a small, tight expression that had no real warmth in it. "I believe you. Both of you have already accomplished things that should have been impossible. But don't underestimate Daniel. He's not like the other demons you've fought. He's been planning this for months, probably ever since the moment he escaped from Hell. He has contingencies we haven't thought of, resources we haven't discovered yet. And with Belial's power now residing within him...."

The words trailed off. They all knew what that meant.

"We understand what we're facing," Delia said. "But we're not running. Not anymore."

She reached over and slipped her hand into Caleb's. He could feel the resolve practically glowing inside her, the fierce protectiveness that had grown stronger every day since they'd learned about the baby. She wasn't the same woman who'd deflected his first proposal because she wasn't ready to commit.

She was a mother defending her child, a psychic whose powers had grown beyond anything she'd imagined, learning to wield them like weapons.

She was magnificent.

"Then we'll start planning," she said. "Right now. We have work to do."

Their meeting continued as they went over intelligence reports, training schedules, contingency plans. Pru identified six more potential safe houses from the financial records she'd accessed, and Ty marked them on the map for the strike teams. They discussed Delia's training regimen, the specific exercises that would help her control her expanding abilities. They talked about wards and weapons, about angelic essence and demonic fire.

Through all of this, though, that nagging feeling persisted in the back of Caleb's mind. Something he'd forgotten, something important. It tickled at his consciousness, refusing to resolve into anything concrete.

Finally, near midnight, Ty and Pru prepared to leave. The atmosphere in the house felt somehow different now, filled with purpose. They weren't hiding anymore. No, this time they'd be taking the fight to Daniel Lockwood.

"Get some rest," Ty said as he finally headed for the door. "Tomorrow, the real work begins."

Caleb nodded and watched them go, Pru's little green Mini Cooper pulling away from the curb behind Ty's truck. The street was quiet, the neighbors' houses dark, the suburban silence broken only by the distant hum of traffic on the main road.

He closed the door and reset the wards, feeling the protective energy hum against his fingertips. When he turned, Delia was waiting for him, her arms crossed and her expression thoughtful.

"You've been distracted all evening," she said. "What's bothering you?"

He shook his head, frustrated with himself. "I don't know. There's something I'm supposed to remember, something important. But I can't figure out what it is."

Her brows drew together, but she sounded calm enough as she asked, "About Daniel? About the black moon?"

"Maybe." He ran a hand through his hair as he tried to chase down the elusive thought. "It's like when you walk into a room to get something and then forget why you're there. I know there's something, but I can't...."

He trailed off, the thought he was trying to wrangle still maddeningly out of reach.

Delia went over to him and took his hands.

"It'll come to you. Don't force it. Right now, we should sleep. Tomorrow's going to be a long day."

She was right. They had less than three days to prepare for what might be the most important battle of their lives. They needed to get some rest.

But as they climbed the stairs to the bedroom and then lay down together in the darkness with the weight of the coming confrontation pressing down on them, that nagging feeling refused to fade. Something was slipping through the cracks of his memory, something he should have remembered, should have addressed.

Something vitally important.

He'd figure it out eventually. He had to.

For now, though, he pulled Delia close and let her presence anchor him. They had only seventy-two hours to prepare for the black moon and whatever horrors it would bring.

Seventy-two hours to save the world.

No pressure.

Chapter Twenty

All around her was more evidence of the way hers and Caleb's lives had meshed together. His battered copy of *The Count of Monte Cristo* sat on the shelf next to her real estate exam prep books from eight years ago. His leather jacket hung in the coat closet next to her own outerwear, which usually only saw about three months of use each year, if even that much. And his favorite coffee mug—a truly hideous monstrosity he'd bought at the Caesar's Palace gift shop before they'd even met—occupied the prized spot in the cabinet next to her own favorite, a handmade mug from a former client who'd gifted it to Delia after they closed on his house.

On the surface, these were small enough things, the kinds of odds and ends that always seemed to accumulate when two lives began to merge into something new.

But there were other new items as well, ones that were impossible to ignore. A go-bag by the front door, packed with holy water and blessed salt and a silver knife Caleb had bought for her recently, telling her that silver weapons weren't just for werewolves.

She wasn't sure whether he was joking—after all, once you'd admitted the presence of demons, who knew what else might come into play?—so she'd smiled weakly and hadn't asked any questions.

Wards hummed at every window and every threshold, all of them reinforced daily by Ty's angelic energy. Weapons were staged near exits—nothing obvious, of course, nothing that would alarm the neighbors if they happened to glance through a window and caught a glimpse of them, but within easy reach if something came through the door that shouldn't.

They were living their lives...but they were also preparing for war.

Delia stood in the doorway of her home office and studied the small room with new eyes. The desk was still there, flanked on either side by a pair of filing cabinets, and bookcases lined one wall. But she'd already started measuring for a crib, researching paint colors that were supposed to be soothing for infants. Sage green, maybe. Or a soft yellow. There was no reason to believe that the title issues with the Summerlin house wouldn't get worked out in plenty of time, and yet she thought it wasn't a bad idea to start thinking about converting the office to a nursery.

Just in case.

Now she was eight weeks pregnant. Still not showing much—her jeans were starting to get tight, and she had a feeling she had a few more weeks at most before she needed to size up or maybe get some of those waistband extenders that might give her a few more weeks of use out of her regular clothes. Most people probably wouldn't even guess that anything had changed. But she could feel the difference now whenever she reached inward with her psychic senses. That second heartbeat was growing stronger every day, although she had a sense of quiet, of almost peace from the child, as if it somehow understood that now was the time to focus on its own development and not to worry too much about what might be happening in the outside world.

The strikes had begun yesterday, right after Ty and Pru had left. One of Daniel's safe houses, a nondescript office building in North Las Vegas that had been crawling with lesser demons, was hit in the early hours of the morning. Two more locations were raided immediately afterward, and financial pressure was mounting on the various Styx Group accounts as Pru worked her digital magic, freezing assets and disrupting transfers.

They were making progress, chipping away at the empire Daniel Lockwood had built, all the while understanding how quickly time was slipping away from them.

The man himself remained elusive, though. They knew he was somewhere in the Luxor, planning his next move, but getting any more information than that was proving to be impossible.

Now there were only two days left until the black moon. So little time remained until they had to make their move.

She heard footsteps coming down the corridor that led to the secondary bedrooms, and then Caleb appeared in the hallway behind her. He was wearing one of his old Henley shirts, the gray one that had seen better days, and his hair was still damp from the shower. A flash of the old familiar smile, but she could still feel how tense he was, keyed up and ready to go.

He'd never been very good at waiting.

"Ty just called," he said. "His people have confirmed that Daniel's ritual chamber is somewhere in the upper levels of the pyramid. They're working on a way to breach the wards, but it's tough going, and they say it won't be ready until the black moon itself."

About what she'd been expecting. "So we get one shot."

Caleb nodded. "Right." He came into the room and went to her, then wrapped his arms around her waist. One hand settled over her stomach, protective and gentle. "How are you feeling?"

Wound tight as a spring. But she managed a smile of her own and said, "Tired, I suppose." She leaned back against him, drawing comfort from the strength of his presence, the warmth of his body against her back. "Ready for this to be over."

He brushed his lips against the top of her head. "Two more days."

Two more days. Strange how three words could feel so heavy, as if they held the weight of the entire world within them. So little time until they either stopped the black moon ritual or failed, and the world changed forever.

"We'll stop him," Delia said. She believed it. She *had* to believe it.

Caleb's arms tightened around her. "I know we will."

Later that afternoon, Caleb sat on the couch in their living room, staring at the far wall without really seeing it.

That nagging feeling was only getting worse.

Ever since their confrontation at the Luxor, ever since Daniel had revealed himself and they'd barely escaped with their lives, something had been tickling at the edges of Caleb's consciousness. Something important. Something he'd forgotten.

It was maddening, like having a word on the tip of his tongue that refused to materialize, or a dream that slipped away the moment he opened his eyes. He knew it was there, but he just couldn't reach it.

From the kitchen, he could hear Delia talking quietly on the phone with Pru, going over tomorrow's reconnaissance schedule. Ty was due any minute with the latest intel on Daniel's fortifications. The whole house hummed with purpose, with the energy of people preparing for battle.

And Caleb just sat there like a lump, chasing shadows in his own mind.

Daniel has Belial's power.

That was the problem they kept coming back to. They'd hurt Daniel at the Luxor—hurt him badly, according to Ty. The combined force of Caleb's fire and Delia's psychic abilities, amplified by the baby's latent power, had been enough to wound him, to force him to retreat. But it hadn't been enough to destroy him.

Nothing in this room can kill me, Daniel had said, standing in his penthouse suite with shadows gathering around his fingers and that cold smile on his face. *Your blessed bullets are effective against common demons, but I'm considerably more than that now.*

And he'd been right. Everything they'd thrown at him—fire and light and psychic force—had driven him back but hadn't finished the job. Daniel had absorbed a Prince of Hell's power. He was something new now, something that straddled the line between cambion and demon lord, and none of their usual weapons seemed capable of ending him permanently.

Caleb closed his eyes and tried to focus on that elusive notion, the one that had been tickling his brain for far too long. What was he missing? What did he know that he wasn't remembering?

He let his thoughts drift back to Hell, to the endless darkness and the desperate struggle to survive in a realm that wanted nothing more than to swallow him whole. He'd spent two years there, although they'd felt like two hundred. Two years of fighting and hiding and clawing for every moment of continued existence.

And then Belial had died.

He remembered the exact moment when it had happened. So many demons flowing toward the gateway that offered the freedom they all so desperately craved. Flashes of images that hadn't made much sense—several red-haired women lying apparently dead on the floor of a huge room that flickered with candlelight and trembled with all the energy that had been summoned there to open the hellmouth and bring Belial to the physical plane.

The barriers between realms had weakened for just a moment, just long enough for Caleb to fight his way through, to claw his escape while hordes of hungry demons panted at his heels. But before he'd made it out, before the barriers between worlds had sealed again, he'd caught a glimpse of something.

The memory surfaced out of nowhere, sharp and clear after weeks of frustrating fog, a flash that lasted much longer than that one tantalizing, frustrating glimpse he'd gotten in the elevator at the Luxor.

A woman.

Red hair, blazing like copper in the hellfire that illuminated the space between worlds. The strange woman's hair was a lot shorter than Delia's, not much more than chin-length. She was tall and slender, and she held a blade in her hand, a short sword that gleamed with an inner light, white fire crackling along its edge as she drove it deep into the chest of something massive and scaled and terrible.

That monster had been Belial in his true form, towering and hideous, with eyes like burning coals and power radiating from every inch of his scaled hide.

And this woman—this human woman with her fiery hair and her impossible sword—had driven that blade directly into his heart.

White fire had surrounded him, penetrated him. Caleb still didn't know whether that fire had come from the blade or energy the mortal wound had unleashed, but something had consumed Belial from the inside out, draining his life force, reducing a Prince of Hell to ash and memory.

Caleb's eyes snapped open.

That's it.

The sword. The weapon that had killed Belial. It hadn't hurt him, nor banished him, nor driven him back to Hell to lick his wounds and plot revenge. No, it had *killed* him...had given him the kind of death that even a demon lord couldn't escape from.

If that blade could destroy a Prince of Hell, it might be the only weapon capable of destroying Daniel now that he held Belial's power within him.

"Caleb?" Delia was standing in the doorway, phone still in her hand, her copper hair catching the lamplight. Different from the red hair of the woman in his vision, long and sleek rather than short and wavy, but he thought the two of them shared something in common nonetheless. Her head tilted to one side, and her expression seemed to indicate that she'd noticed something had changed about him. "What is it?"

He was on his feet before he even realized he'd moved. "I know how to stop Daniel."

Twenty minutes later, they were all gathered in the living room—Caleb and Delia on the couch, Ty in the armchair by the window, Pru perched on the ottoman with her laptop balanced on her knees. The atmosphere was heavy, expectant, like the moment before a storm broke.

Caleb explained what he'd remembered—the vision he'd glimpsed during his escape from Hell, of the red-haired woman and the sword that had killed Belial.

"If that blade could destroy a Prince of Hell," he concluded, "it might be the only weapon that can kill Daniel now that he has Belial's power."

A moment of silence followed his words. Pru was wide-eyed, while Ty only nodded, as though all this wasn't a complete surprise.

"My people have records of Belial's death," he said slowly. "It happened in Colorado nearly two years ago. A small group confronted him during a summoning ritual—a mix of witches, psychics, and demon hunters, if I remember correctly."

Pru's dark eyebrows rose. "Demon hunters? What kind of demon hunters?"

"The kind who could prove to be useful." Ty pulled out his phone and began scrolling, clearly on the trail of something. "There was a witch involved. A lodestone—that's someone who instinctively attracts magical objects. She was the one who struck the killing blow."

Caleb felt hope kindling in him for the first time in days. "Where is she now? Where's the sword?"

"Santa Fe, last we heard." Ty looked up from his phone. "The woman's name is Penny Zamora —Penny Briggs before she got married. Her husband is a *brujo* named Isaac Zamora. He runs a metaphysical shop called The Enchanted Circle."

Delia's hand found Caleb's, her fingers threading through his, slender and warm. "Can we contact them and ask to borrow the sword?"

"It's not that simple." Ty's jaw tightened slightly as he went on, "That blade is a powerful artifact. Penny Zamora has proven she can wield it effectively, but we don't know if it would work the same way in someone else's hands. The sword might be bonded to her somehow, or it might require specific magical conditions to function." He paused, and something flickered across his features. "There's also a complication. According to the records I just pulled up, she's expecting. Nearly six months along."

A pregnant woman. Caleb thought of Delia, of the baby growing inside her, of everything he would do to protect them both. Asking another expecting mother to face a demon prince felt wrong on every level.

But what other choice did they have?

"Then we'll go to her and explain what's happening," he said. "Daniel isn't just a threat to Vegas—if he opens that gateway, it's a threat to everyone in the world, Santa Fe included." He met Ty's eyes as he added, "Penny Zamora and her husband deserve to know what's coming, even if they choose not to fight."

Pru looked up from her laptop. "I can make the drive in under eight hours. If we leave tonight—"

"No," Caleb broke in. "Delia needs protection here, and you're the best tactical support we have. You need to keep feeding information about Daniel's operation to Ty's people. He and I will go."

Through their connection, Caleb could sense Delia's immediate resistance—her fear, her reluctance to let him out of her sight with the black moon closing in. But he also felt her understanding, her recognition that this might be their only chance.

"Bring her back," Delia said. Her voice was steady, but her grip on his hand was almost painful. "Bring the sword back. And then we'll end this."

Caleb pulled her close and touched his lips to her forehead. He let himself feel her for a moment —the warmth of her body, the familiar rhythm of her heartbeat, the faint pulse of their baby's energy humming beneath her skin.

His family. Everything he was fighting for.

"I will," he said. "I promise."

He met Ty's gaze over Delia's fiery hair. The half angel nodded, his expression grim but determined.

"We'll leave in an hour," Ty said. "I'll contact my people and have them reach out to the Zamoras and smooth the way for our arrival." He paused. "If we're lucky, they'll be willing to help. And if we're very lucky, they'll bring the fight to Daniel themselves."

An hour later, Delia stood on her front porch and watched Ty's truck pull away from the curb. They wouldn't be driving the whole way, of course. That would take too much time, and time was the one thing they didn't have.

This was Las Vegas, and in Vegas, it wasn't so hard to book a private jet...as long as you had the necessary funds.

And Caleb had plenty of those.

The truck's taillights glowed red in the darkness, and his familiar silhouette was visible through the passenger-side window—the set of his shoulders, the way he held his head. He turned to look back at her as they reached the corner, and she felt his love flowing toward her, warm and fierce and absolute.

Then the truck turned, and the taillights disappeared, and she was alone.

No, not alone. Pru stood behind her, a steady presence at her back. And inside, beneath her heart, the baby's energy signature pulsed, reminding her of everything they were fighting for.

"You okay?" Pru asked quietly.

"No." Delia wrapped her arms around herself against the cool November air. "But I will be."

Two days until the black moon.

But now they had a plan. Now they had hope.

Soon, Ty and the man she loved would take flight over the desert, heading east toward Santa Fe. The flight itself wouldn't be very long, just about an hour and a half, because Caleb had booked the fastest plane he could get, expense be damned.

What she didn't know was how long it would take for him and Ty to convince this Penny Zamora and her husband that the fight wasn't over yet, and that the magical sword they possessed needed to be pressed into service once more.

Delia placed her hand over her stomach, feeling the familiar pulse of energy beneath her palm.

"Your father's going to save the world," she whispered. "Again."

Behind her, Pru snorted. "Let's hope that

witch in Santa Fe agrees to help, or we're all screwed."

They went inside together and closed the door against the darkness. Even with Caleb and Ty gone, there was still plenty of work to do—preparations to make, contingencies to plan. They couldn't afford to assume success.

But for the first time since that terrible confrontation at the Luxor, since discovering just how powerful Daniel had become, Delia felt something other than dread when she thought about the black moon.

Now, she felt ready.

Hold on, she thought, sending those words out along the bond she shared with Caleb, toward the man driving through the desert night toward the airport and an uncertain alliance. *Come back to me.*

And faintly, distantly, she felt his response. Not in words, exactly, but something much deeper than that, a promise that seemed to resonate in her very bones.

Always.

Vegas Slayers continues in The Devil's Due.

Also by Christine Pope

LEGENDARY

(Urban Fantasy/Paranormal Romance)

Silver Linings

Lion's Share

Trial by Fire

Here Be Dragons

VEGAS SLAYERS

(Urban Fantasy/Paranormal Romance)

Speak of the Devil

Devil in the Details

The Devil Went Down to Laughlin

Devil May Care

Devil to Pay

The Devil's Due

The Devil Next Door (December 2026)

THE WITCHES OF MINGUS MOUNTAIN

(Paranormal Romance)

Stolen Time

Borrowed Time

Killing Time

Wind Called

Demon Loved

Christmas Past

Season of Magic

Healer's Heart

PROJECT DEMON HUNTERS*

(Paranormal Romance)

Unquiet Souls

Unbound Spirits

Unholy Ground

Unseen Voices

Unmarked Graves

Unbroken Vows

Unholy Night

THE DJINN WARS*

(Paranormal Romance)

Chosen

Taken

Fallen

Broken

Forsaken

Forbidden

Awoken

Illuminated

Stolen

Forgotten

Driven

Unspoken

Hidden

Written

Given

Mistaken

FAMILIAR SPIRITS*

(Cozy Mystery/Paranormal Romance)

Spells and Spaniels

Cauldrons and Cats

Hexes and Hedgehogs

Charms and Chihuahuas

Runes and Ravens

LATTES AND LEVITATION*

(Cozy Mystery/Paranormal Romance)

Caffeine Before Curses

Muffins After Magic

Pastries and Prophecies

Eclairs and Ectoplasm

Sugar Skulls and Specters

Wedding Cakes and Wishes

HEDGEWITCH FOR HIRE*

(Cozy Mystery/Paranormal Romance)

Grave Mistake

Social Medium

Household Demons

Perpetual Potion

Jingle Spells

Wandering Monsters

Uninvited Ghosts

Prophet Motive

Ballroom Bits

Spell Check

Brew Confessions

Charm School

UNEXPECTED MAGIC*

(Urban Fantasy/Paranormal Romance)

Found Objects

Finders, Keepers

Lost and Found

Finding Destiny

THE WITCHES OF WHEELER PARK*

(Paranormal Romance)

Storm Born

Thunder Road

Winds of Change

Mind Games

A Wheeler Park Christmas

Blood Ties

Healing Hands

Wishful Thinking

Smoke and Mirrors

MISS PRIMM'S ACADEMY FOR WAYWARD WITCHES*

(Fantasy/Academy Romance)

Misspelled

Dispelled

Expelled

THE DEVIL YOU KNOW*

(Paranormal Romance)

Sympathy for the Devil

Charmed, I'm Sure

A Wing and a Prayer

Wish Upon a Star

THE WITCHES OF CANYON ROAD*

(Paranormal Romance)

Hidden Gifts

Darker Paths

Mysterious Ways

A Canyon Road Christmas

Demon Born

An Ill Wind

Higher Ground

Haunted Hearts

THE WITCHES OF CLEOPATRA HILL*

(Paranormal Romance)

Darkangel

Darknight

Darkmoon

Sympathetic Magic

Protector

Spellbound

A Cleopatra Hill Christmas

Impractical Magic

Strange Magic

The Arrangement

Defender

Bad Blood

Deep Magic

Darktide

Star Bright

THE WATCHERS TRILOGY*

(Paranormal Romance)

Falling Dark

Dead of Night

Rising Dawn

THE SEDONA FILES*

(Paranormal/Science Fiction Romance)

Bad Vibrations

Desert Hearts

Angel Fire

Star Crossed

Falling Angels

Enemy Mine

TALES OF THE LATTER KINGDOMS*

(Fantasy Romance)

Dragon Rose

Ashes of Roses

One Thousand Nights

Threads of Gold

The Wolf of Harrow Hall

Moon Dance

The Song of the Thrush

THE GAIAN CONSORTIUM SERIES*

(Science Fiction Romance)

Beast (free prequel novella)

Blood Will Tell

Breath of Life

The Gaia Gambit

The Mandala Maneuver

The Titan Trap

The Zhore Deception

The Refugee Ruse

STANDALONE TITLES

Hearts on Fire (Paranormal Romance)

Taking Dictation (Contemporary Romance)

Golden Heart (Gaslamp Fantasy Romance)

Night Music: A Modern Reimagining of The Phantom of the Opera (Contemporary Romance)

Ghost Dance: A Sequel to Gaston Leroux's The Phantom of the Opera (Historical Mystery/Romance)

Flight Before Christmas (Fantasy Romance)

* Indicates a completed series

About the Author

USA Today bestselling author Christine Pope has been writing stories ever since she commandeered her family's Smith-Corona typewriter back in grade school. Her work includes paranormal romance, fantasy romance, and science fiction/space opera romance. She makes her home in Arizona's beautiful Verde Valley.

Christine Pope on the Web:
www.christinepope.com

facebook.com/ChristinePopeAuthor
youtube.com/@ChristinePopeAuthor
pinterest.com/ChristineJPope

www.ingramcontent.com/pod-product-compliance
Lightning Source LLC
La Vergne TN
LVHW041102080826
845145LV00007B/1663

* 9 7 8 1 9 4 6 4 3 5 9 3 4 *